The Sinister Trophy

John Kiriamiti

Spear Books

Nairobi • Kampala • Dar es Salaam • Kigali • Lusaka • Lilongwe

Published by
East African Educational Publishers Ltd.
Kijabe Street, Nairobi
P.O. Box 45314, Nairobi – 00100, KENYA
Tel: +254 20 2324760
Mobile: +254 722 205661 / 722 207216 / 733 677716 / 734 652012
Email: eaep@eastafricanpublishers.com
Website: www.eastafricanpublishers.com

East African Educational Publishers also has offices or is represented
in the following countries: Uganda, Tanzania, Rwanda, Malawi,
Zambia, Botswana and South Sudan.

First published 1999

Reprinted 2000, 2003

This impression 2008
Reprinted 2010, 2011, 2012, 2016, 2017

ISBN 978-9966-46-683-9

Acknowledgements

I owe special thanks to Mr. & Mrs. Jack Kioriah, who kept encouraging me, and my typist Rosemary Wambui (Mrs.), who knew exactly when I needed to have a break, especially when I overworked my mind towards the end of the book.

Preface

When I wrote *Son of Fate,* I didn't know it would open a new chapter in my life. It served to bring me closer to my beloved fans some of whom wrote to me, while others found their way to that remote place called Thuita where I was born. A good number reached me through my friends, while still others got in touch through my publishers.

Apart from wishing me success and wanting to know what became of me after I put the gun down, they beseeched me to write a sequel to *Son of Fate.* The book also prompted a reviewer in the *Daily Nation* to comment how unfair the ending was to certain characters, 'as if the author was in a hurry to put the pen down.' This sentiment was shared by another reviewer in *The People.*

It is for these reasons that I went underground and came up with this one which I have titled *The Sinister Trophy.* I have done my best to touch on all the characters my fans wanted to know more about, and it is my hope all who will read it will be satisfied.

Spear Books

1. *Sugar Daddy's Lover* Rosemarie Owino
2. *Lover in the Sky* Sam Kahiga
3. *A Girl Cannot Go on Laughing All the Time* Magaga Alot
4. *The Love Root* Mwangi Ruheni
5. *Mystery Smugglers* Mwangi Ruheni
6. *The Ivory Merchant* Mwangi Gicheru
7. *A Brief Assignment* Ayub Ndii
8. *Colour of Carnations* Ayub Ndii
9. *A Taste of Business* Aubrey Kalitera
10. *No Strings Attached* Yusuf K Dawood
11. *Queen of Gems* Laban Erapu
12. *A Prisoner's Letter* Aubrey Kalitera
13. *A Woman Reborn* Koigi wa Wamwere
14. *The Bhang Syndicate* Frank Saisi
15. *My Life in Crime* John Kiriamiti
16. *Son of Fate* John Kiriamiti
17. *The Sinister Trophy* John Kiriamiti
18. *My Life in Prison* John Kiriamiti
19. *My Life with a Criminal: Milly's Story* John Kiriamiti
20. *Homing In* Marjorie Oludhe Macgoye
21. *Nice People* Wamugunda Geteria
22. *Ben Kamba 009 in Operation DXT* David Maillu
23. *The Ayah* David Maillu
24. *Son of Woman* Charles Mangua
25. *A Tail in the Mouth* Charles Mangua
26. *Son of Woman in Mombasa* Charles Mangua
27. *Kenyatta's Jiggers* Charles Mangua
28. *A Worm in the Head* Charles K Githae
29. *Comrade Inmate* Charles K Githae
30. *Twilight Woman* Thomas Akare
31. *Life and Times of a Bank Robber* John Kiggia Kimani
32. *Prison is not a Holiday Camp* John Kiggia Kimani
33. *The Operator* Chris Mwangi
34. *Three Days on the Cross* Wahome Mutahi
35. *Birds of Kamiti* Benjamin Bundeh
36. *Times Beyond* Omondi Mak'Oloo
37. *Lady in Chains* Genga-Idowu
38. *Mayor in Prison* Karuga Wandai
39. *Confession of an AIDS Victim* Carolyne Adalla
40. *The American Standard* Sam DeSanto
41. *From Home Guard to Mau Mau* Elisha Mbabu
42. *The Girl was Mine* David Karanja
43. *Links of a Chain* Monica Genya
44. *The Wrong Kind of Girl* Monica Genya
45. *The Other Side of Love* Monica Genya
46. *Unmarried Wife* Sitwala Imenda
47. *Dar es Salaam By Night* Ben Mtobwa
48. *A Place of No Return* Mervill Powell
49. *The Verdict of Death* Onduko bw'Atebe
50. *The Spurt of Flames* Okelo Nyandong
51. *The Unbroken Spirit* Wanjiru Waithaka
52. *Tower of Terror* Macharia Magu
53. *The Nest of my Heart* Florence Mbaya
54. *Nairobi Heat* Mūkoma wa Ngūgī
55. *City Murders* Ndūcū wa Ngūgī
56. *Rafiki Man Guitar* Meja Mwangi
57. *The Gold Rush* Samuel Wachira
58. *Seasons of Love and Despair* Tee Ngūgī
59. *The Fall of Saints* Wanjikū wa Ngūgī
60. *Saranya* Ndūcū wa Ngūgī

Prologue

I had just picked the young lady from where she lay, about to die in the hands of a triple murderer, when the door was smashed open and armed police officers stormed in. The guns were all trained on me.

The leader came forward and roared at me: "Put your dirty paws off that young girl and hold them behind your head!" I hesitated. Would they arrest me? I hadn't done anything untoward; I had just tried to save a life. This must be a mistake! But it wasn't; it was me they wanted to arrest.

The lady protested because she knew otherwise, but the cops wouldn't listen. They appeared convinced I was the murderer they were looking for.

I was roughed out of the house and bundled into the back of a Landrover which took off with a screeching jerk. Apart from the five policemen with ill-shaped boots who sat to my left and right, I was aware of lying between two bodies. The way they kept bumping into me at every corner left no doubt they were dead. A sickly apprehension swept my whole body. Would I be charged with the murder of the two? Framing the innocent was a game the police seemed to have perfected.

From this position where I lay on my back facing the sky, I could see millions of stars twinkling as the topless Landrover revved and bumped in the night. Some were bigger and brighter than the rest. Sometimes they'd move from one position to another. It looked like somebody was behind them, picking them with an invisible hand from one point to another in a game of draughts.

The brighter always seemed to swallow the dull, becoming even bigger and brighter. Who could be behind these stars, playing with them the way he pleased? Could he be their Creator, and could he be in a position to save me from this one? The Landrover hit a bump and the bodies rolled over, one coming on top of me. I shoved it off and cursed. Why did fate choose to do this to me?

At the police station there was little ceremony. Like a condemned man I was led, handcuffed, into my cell. I was already dripping blood — from the two dead bodies.

Bye Son of Fate. Will you ever learn?

Chapter One

I woke up with a start. I looked around where I lay facing the ceiling and realized I wasn't in any kind of trouble. All I had had was a bad dream that had disturbed my peaceful sleep.

I sat up. My whole body was pervaded by a feeling of tiredness. I needed one thing more than anything else at a time like this, and that was to put on my tracksuit and get out of the house for some roadwork. I immediately thought of going to the gymnasium for some sparring session with my friend Supa, or Marto as he was popularly known. Usually I'd do some shadow boxing, after which I would approach the sandbag and practise some Taekwondo kicks. After such a workout I would leave the hall feeling relaxed, but today I did not feel like doing anything. I could only hope my good moods would return.

Days and months had passed by since Eva and I, Adams Wamathina better known as Son of Fate, had found the 'Garden of Eden' which we had been looking for. I wanted Eva to be happy, to be content with what she already was ... my wife! I wanted her to forget whatever suffering she had gone through in life.

I had watched the transformation in her with a sense of pride. She was now confident of herself unlike during the earlier days of our marriage. She was becoming accustomed to a different lifestyle, that of being a married woman. She had stopped being unnecessarily jealous. She was no longer preoccupied with where I was going, provided I came back in one piece. Most things did not bother her anymore; all she was interested in was keeping me happy. And I had to admit it – she was doing it well.

As for me, there were so many things that needed my undivided attention which was proving difficult to muster, yet time was running out.

These days, whenever I left home I would get the feeling I was being followed. This invisible shadow behind me invoked more fear anything I had experienced. At times I would argue that the whole thing was psychological, that it was just because I had very dangerous documents which had been handed to me by a dying man. But the shadow had persisted, sometimes giving me scaring dreams, like the one that had just woken me up.

I am a believer in forcing the body to do what it should. In a few minutes I was in my tracksuit headed for a workout. The jogging was wonderful just as was the sparring. Infact I met this boxer friend of mine, who was better known to his fans as 'Supt', at the entrance. He was also arriving from roadwork. He gave me some good thirty minutes' sparring; by the time I was through I didn't need the bag. All I did was shadow-box for a few more minutes then jog back to my place – the Garden of Eden.

By 8.00 a.m. I was already home. I showered then took a heavy breakfast. Eva was now used to my timetable. She knew what I needed and when. By the time I left the bathroom, breakfast would be waiting. After eating I would find my clothes for the day ironed and waiting.

I left the bedroom feeling swell. I needed to do something about the case currently in my hands. I had already pocketed an advance cheque of KShs. 300,000, money I had already started spending. I hated debts and this was one for certain. It was staring at me in the eye: the money had to be earned.

I was at the sink cleaning my hands, which always preceded my leaving the house, when I heard Eva's voice break into my busy mind, "You are talking to yourself Adams," she said with a smile.

"Is that so?" I asked as I turned to face her. "I am not surprised anyway. What I think I am doing is talking my mind aloud. What did I say?"

"You mentioned a briefcase and a miss Marie, and something like '... this is a lousy business.' What is the matter, Love? Your face is so pale, which is unusual for a person who has just stepped out of a shower and enjoyed a healthy breakfast. This is very unusual of you." She went silent, which to me meant she was waiting for some explanation.

"Well," I said sotto voce, "it is this Mohammed Aslam case. It bothers me a lot. This vehicle we are still using belongs to him and I haven't done..."

"But I thought you told me you agreed that you keep the vehicle because you need it for the job! Wasn't that so?" She interjected.

"Yah, it is so up to date. But I haven't done a single thing ever since to justify keeping it and, as you know, I hate cheating."

It was a frank answer. Eva came closer, put her hand on my right shoulder and pulled me closer to her. She kissed me lightly on the cheek then faced me. "You'll earn it darling. You'll do the job when the time comes and everyone concerned will like it. Everyone will be happy about it, including you and me. Right now let us follow your constant advice to me, not to cross bridges we haven't reached. Remember?" There was that characteristic wink in her left eye. She knew she had beaten me using my own admonishments. I liked it and felt consoled. I congratulated myself for marrying Eva.

I held her, squeezed her against my body and her pointed breasts pressed against my chest. They were getting bigger with the child growing inside her. I stopped for a second to admire her unequaled beauty, then let her free. "I love you more each new day," I told her, then turned to leave. I closed the door behind me, but even as I started the car and reversed out of the gate I could feel her eyes on my back. She must be watching me from behind the curtain, just like Bakari, Mrs. Wicks' gardener, used to do. Eva however did it for a different reason: love. Bakari was being nosy.

I entered the densely populated city of Nairobi. The tenseness that Eva had detected was back with me. The feeling that I was being followed had haunted me as soon as I had driven out of the gate. But no matter how I tried, I could not identify who my tail was if at all there was one. I kept admonishing myself for panicking over this case on my mind. Or had I let my imagination get too far concerning the briefcase that was handed to me by Mohammed Aslam, who up to now was in hospital?

I swang the car towards the eastern part of the city. I decided to go and see how my two boys, Chali and Mchacho, were doing. They Were still at the industrial Area Remand awaiting sentence on a criminal case. This visit to the duo was my fifth.

I was going there earlier than usual because I didn't have a heavy schedule. I would approach the day the way it presented itself, although as usual I was ready for anything.

I was stopped by traffic lights as I was about to plunge into Uhuru Highway. A newspaper vendor came over and I asked for the three local dailies. As the vendor handed me change, a street boy approached from the offside and called. "Mdoss, nipe kobole niongezee nyingine nikale chipo ... tafadhali Mdoss ..." ["Boss , give me five shillings to add on what I have to buy chips ... please, Boss"]. Well, I would have given him right away, but something made me hesitate. Instead I opened the offside door for him and asked him to jump in. He hesitated for a moment then seemed to decide correctly that I was safe. He took the co-driver's seat and made himself comfortable.

What a familiar face, I thought. I had a liking for street boys and had met a good number. While other motorists treated them with suspicion, I saw them as just human beings.

"Sasa, Halifu?" I greeted as the traffic lights gave me way. The name by which I had addressed him was very familiar in the streets especially to the street kids; it stood for comrade.

"Fit, Halifu. Nipe hiyo kobole nikale chipo, nina ubao sana." He answered. ["Fine, comrade. Give me that five bob so I can go for chips. I am really hungry."]

"Don't mind that, friend. . .," I told him, "... I'll buy you some food soon. Let's first visit some good friends of mine in prison, then after that I'll drop you wherever you prefer and buy some food for you. That right?" He nodded and said it was okay, provided I kept my part of the bargain.

I watched him through the rear view mirror as I drove down Uhuru Highway. He had a raw knife-cut wound just above the left eyebrow which left me wondering whether he hadn't been about to lose the eye. This thought made me flinch. It was too close and looked like it had given the boy a hard time as he patiently waited for it to heal. Though he looked familiar we had not met before. I wanted to ask him whether he knew the infamous duo of Chali and Mchacho, but somehow felt I shouldn't. Instead I told him some funny stories to make him feel free with me before I could ask him about himself. I just don't know why, but whenever I met a street child and we happened to talk, I always had an urge to dig into their background. Why only Heaven knows. Perhaps it was simply because like me they were all Sons of Fate who didn't know what to expect on the morrow.

As he narrated his story, which I did not think interesting, my mind slowly drifted to my wife Eva. She was expectant and we were both very excited at the thought of having a third party in our house. I was so eager to have some kid call me Papa whenever I arrived home tired or not tired. I wanted to have a feeling that after all the struggles I had had in life, the hopelessness I had once harboured and the termites of inferiority, self-doubt, lack of self-confidence and a hell of others that lingered in my life, I had eventually healed and that all were now buried memories. There was also another major reason for my desire to have the kid. I was aware I was about to go away for days, maybe even months, to retrieve the diamond in the Aslam case. With a kid to keep Eva busy I would be assured she wasn't being lonely. I was now imagining her in a free dress and the thought made me -smile. Then I became aware the boy was still talking. He had said something which I wanted him to repeat.

"You said you came from. .."

"Murang'a. I travelled to town on foot. Here and there I would jump on slow, heavy commercial vehicles as they laboured uphill. When I got tired of holding on I would alight once the vehicle slowed down and trek till another found me at a convenient place."

What I found rather interesting was the fact that this boy had come from rural areas where one wouldn't expect to find street children as there were no streets in the first place. I never imagined the street boys I saw each day had come from further than the ghettos surrounding the city.

I pressed the button on my side to lower the window despite the cold weather. I wanted to have some fresh air as the salon was already filled with the stench of his unwashed body and the glue which he carried in a tiny bottle and which he would technically sniff when he thought I wasn't seeing. What a pity, I thought, remembering with a shudder that had fate not played my cards well at long last, I would have ended up sniffing the same stuff.

At the remand home it was surprise galore for me. The boys, all survivors of the streets, knew each other. Chali had called out, "Hey Cardinal. . .", the latter being his nickname for me. Before I could reply he saw my new friend and called, "Yes Kimesh! *Vipi?* You have grown up rapidly. *Na kweli raia ni kufit sana. Angalia vile Kimesh kamejenga na vile sisi tumeslim hapa…"*

More surprise war in store for me as we drove back to town after half an hour with Chali and Mchacho. My new friend told me that the scar on his face had been inflicted by the two boys as they forcibly took twenty shillings which a good Samaritan had given him. He had also lost a few other items he had brought all the way from home plus, what hurt him most, *'Biere.'* That was what they called the glue they sniffed.

"Why did you leave your parents in the first place, Kimesh?" I ventured to ask," You are still very…"

"I told you I do not have parents!" He interrupted. "Weren't you listening?"

I looked at him and saw the dismay on his face, as if he was regretting having given the story to a deaf person. I hated myself for not concentrating. I pleaded with him and he reluctantly repeated the story.

"I told you I took off from home when my grandmother died."

"What of your mother and father?" I asked. I realized it was a foolish question from the way he turned to look at me. He must have told me three times about this. Maybe this was the time I had Eva and a free dress on my mind.

"I am sorry, Kimesh," I corrected myself in time, not sure whether, this was the right thing to do. "You told me about your father...?"

"Not my father! I never mentioned my father because I do not know of any."

"I mean your mother..." I corrected myself.

"Yes. She ran off and left me with my grandmother. Later grandmother told me that she wasn't my mother's mother after all."

"How come?" I asked. I was eager for details.

"My mother was sent away from school for lack of fees or something to that effect. I think she decided to find a casual job so as to raise the money but couldn't make it. I think when she was overburdened by problems she decided to ditch me. She left me with grandmother and that was it. Upto her death the old lady never heard of her again. She always told me that my mother had died."

"Why did she come to that conclusion?" I asked eagerly.

The more I listened to the boy's story and he answered my questions, the more I thought I had heard his story somewhere. It didn't fit word for word with what I had heard but it sounded familiar alright. I thought of my niece who had abandoned her children at home and come to this very city to become a prostitute. I started wondering whether this too wouldn't turn out to be another bad encounter, this time with a grandson. The more I thought about it the more I desired to be proved wrong.

"What is your name, again? I didn't get it the first time." I was eager to find out whether he had any connection with my family which I had run away from.

"Everyone calls me Kimesh. If you asked for me by any other name you wouldn't get me."

"But Kimesh isn't your real name. It can't be..."

"Yes, it is short for Kimenyi. My name is Kimenyi. That's all I know."

I got the picture. The story became clear. I guessed I knew who the boy was. I looked at him more closely. I was comparing him with someone I knew. The features were there alright. It wasn't familiarity but resemblance — and close too. This parking boy resembled the closest person in my life. But I had to ask a few more questions lest I jumped to the wrong conclusion. I fastened my shock-obsorbers, then asked, "What did you say is the name of the village from where you came?" I held my breath, secretly praying that the answer would be 'I don't know.'

But he did. "Do you know that popular girls' secondary school called Kahuhia Girls —?" That was partly the answer and I had no desire to hear further. There was no mistaking it: this street boy was part of me. He could be son to none other than my dear wife - Eva.

Now what next, I wondered? Do I take this boy straight to his mother or do I ditch him? Some time back I would have done the latter without a second thought because I happened to hate burdens as this one was turning out to be, but not now. Not after the changes I had had in life. I decided I would take him home.

I stopped outside a 'Men Only' shop and was lucky to find a parking bay just a few metres away. I had made up my mind - I was to buy new clothes for Kimesh, have him well shaved, then take him home. It would give Eva the surprise of the year.

As I unlocked the door to get out, the boy talked to me. *"Si basi ukamishe hiyo kobole ninunue chipo kwa ile cafe."* ["Give me the five bob so that I may buy chips from that cafe"]. But I was already absent-minded. All I wanted to do was buy him clothes and take him to his mother who would do better than feed him on chips. She would take care of him till death did them part.

"Just a minute Kimesh," I said, getting out of the vehicle and opening the door on his side. "Come with me to the shop. I want to buy you something."

I entered the shop with a feeling that. Kimesh was right behind me. As the Asian came to serve me, I turned to talk to 'my son' since I wanted him to make his own selection. He was nowhere. I concluded that he might have decided to wait near the vehicle not knowing that I had locked the doors with a remote gadget. The sales assistant was nagging me to tell him what I wanted, so I went ahead to select a few fittings for my Kimesh.

At least the thought that the boy was so security-conscious and the fact that he was so patient made me admire him. I selected four long trousers, five shirts, two handkerchiefs, two jackets, four pairs of socks and underwear. I would buy him two pairs of shoes in the next shop in his presence, I thought as I approached the counter next to the entrance where I was required to pay.

I paid for the items and the Indian wrapped the parcel very carefully then put it in a paper bag. As I waited for the change I heard a loud scream outside. I peeped out and saw a woman tearing at her hair as she screamed her head off. This being a common sight in the city's streets, I got back to the counter dismissing it as such. I picked my change and went out, all my mind on Kimesh. He wasn't anywhere near the car. I thought he had joined others who had gone to console the screaming woman. I went closer to look for him. As I looked around, I could not help hearing the sad story the woman was giving. A 'chokora', as she termed him, had snatched her purse and fled. In it was over twelve thousand shillings in Kenyan currency and five hundred and fifty dollars. I did a quick mental sum: the woman had lost about forty-five thousand shillings in total. I pitied her but there was no help I could offer her. My mind turned to Kimesh. Where are you, my dear son? Just then I realized he wasn't around. The gathering was becoming bigger by the second. Then the thought struck that the snatcher, the 'chokora' could be the same Kimenyi I was looking for. *'Christ!'* I thought. 'What a shocking thing to encounter on a day I wanted to have a good rest!'

I shook my head and smiled faintly as I threw the wrapping on the back seat. I drove home straight, not knowing what to do next. Eva hugged me as usual and helped me with the parcel which I had carried from the car with an absent mind. I went straight to the sitting room, kicked off my shoes and dropped myself on a seat. I took out a cigarette which I lit and lay on the seat facing the ceiling. I let out rings of smoke which I lazily watched vanish somewhere in mid-air. Eva brought me some coffee to counter the cold.

"What's the matter, dear?" She commented as she set the coffee stool. "You look like a sick man and I don't think you should be smoking in that state."

"Who is sick?" I feigned. "I am surprised that you think so. I am just a bit tired." I tried to force a smile which didn't get me anywhere.

"Could be you are not although you don't sound very convincing. Maybe you could explain why you look like you have swallowed a bee." I broke into a ridiculous laughter which she found herself joining. "Could it be this Aslam thing, the tigress probably?"

I eyed her for a second. Should I tell her the truth?

"I haven't heard from either of the two, dear. Nothing to do with this Aslam issue." It was an honest answer and I was somehow relieved to see that it had made her relax. As I reached for the mug of coffee she had already stirred, I saw her take and unwrap the parcel containing the clothes I had just bought for her lost son. Up to now I had not made up my mind whether to tell her about the encounter with Kimesh or not. What would she think in the first place when she heard of the name? What would be her reaction to the whole thing? Would she be shocked to the extent of having a miscarriage? This worried me most and kept me from breaking the news.

Eva took out the clothes one at a time. From the corners of my eyes I could see her admiring them. She looked so excited, like she knew for whom I had bought the clothes. I pitied her all the more.

She put them back then faced me, flashing that smile which had attracted me the very first day we met. She looked so beautiful that the memory alone made me smile back. "Your parking boys are coming out soon, isn't it?" I was surprised that she knew about it yet I hadn't told her.

"Yes, how did you know that?"

"Well, who else would you buy these clothes for? It's just a matter of common sense." She smiled again.

It touched me to see her make such an erroneous guess. So I decided to tell her the truth ... the whole truth.

"Eva dear, I hate telling you a lie. But you were right about my two boys. Yes, they'll be coming out early next month. But as for the clothes, I had bought them for someone else..."

"For who?"

"Someone else. But before I tell you who, we have to agree on something. You must promise to take everything with a very strong heart. Do you promise that? I always trust you."

For an answer she sat down and pulled up closer to me. "Adams," she called confidently, "the only news which could kill me is you being in trouble. If it has nothing to do with that I am ready for it." She touched my forehead with the tips of her lips which told me something else – that cinemas and books are the best teachers. Previously my dear Eva never knew such gestures but of late, I mean since she started reading the likes of Sheldon, she had become so educated in the finer nuances of body language. Somehow, she seemed to know that whatever I had in mind had nothing to do with me and she was ready to listen.

"Those clothes are not meant for Chali and his friend Mchacho. They were meant for your son ..." I stopped to look at her face. What a stupid way to begin a story, I thought. She was no longer smiling and I didn't like it.

"What do you mean by 'your son'?" Again I corrected my mistake.

"Well, I met him in town today. We went together to see my two friends in prison. We also went together to the place I bought these clothes for him, although by the time I was through he was gone."

Eva listened without once interrupting till I was through. It wasn't a long story but I prolonged it a bit just to lighten her heart. I tried to make her feel that this wasn't the most strange thing that had ever happened. In between the narration I mentioned about my brother's daughter whom I had met in a bar and how she had behaved before she became a prostitute. I was aware this was not what she had expected when she promised to be courageous. The surprise and the pain it caused were written all over the body.

After a short while I heard her release a sigh of relief. I turned to face her as she pulled even closer in search of support. She lay her head on my chest then looked up at me.

"SOF, I had a very bad dream last night about that boy and it kept me worried. I wish you knew how relieved I feel now just to know he is alive. What a great shame it is! I could not even imagine my son, my own son, being in the streets. I am convinced he is the one you saw. I should be proud of the resemblance you quoted but I am not. Instead I feel hatred towards myself. You know, I have always wondered where street boys came from. I did not know until today, until now, that it is from people like me ... I mean irresponsible mothers like me.

"I should have gone to check on my son long ago. All the time I was in Mrs. Wicks' place I should have asked for permission and visited him and the old lady. But I didn't. I was not brave enough. I wanted to forget that part of my life completely. When I met you, I imagined that the past was gone. I conjured a future with great happiness that buried and sealed the whole past. I became selfish, so selfish that I didn't have time to think about my own son. A son I so much suffered for a good nine months. I did not know how wrong I was in assuming one could bury reality."

She took out a handkerchief from her blouse pocket and wiped the tears which had already gathered in her eyes. I didn't interrupt her; she needed to get it all off her chest.

"Addy, I want my son," she resumed. "I want that boy more than anything else. I presumed him dead long ago because I left him in the hands of a merciless woman, but now I realise I am worse than her ... the one I used to call a beast. I realise I am more beastly."

"No! Don't talk, don't say anything till I am through ..." She cut me short as I tried to interrupt. "... I know you want to soothe me, Wamathina; to tell me that I am the best thing you've ever had, that I am the most gorgeous you've met in your life. Please don't do that because you'll be telling a lie and you don't like lying. If I were as good as you'd like to tell me, I would have gone back to thank the old woman for the help she extended when I badly needed it. I would have gone home to see my son and relieve the old woman of the burden. I should really have taken care of her till she passed away. Instead, what did I do? I spent my time hating street-boys, thinking that something should be done to rid streets of the filthy, rude and notorious boys. Yes, there is even a time I blamed you for taking too much of your time worrying about your two boys whom I figured were beyond rehabilitation. But I appreciate now how wonderful you are. You care about people who mean nothing to your life, I mean who have no connection at all with you. This one is a lesson I have learnt and I think many should learn ..." She went on and on and I let her do it. I was aware that would be the only way she'd later get back to her normal self. At long last she asked me, "Addy, do you promise to bring me my son? I'll take care of him. I want to take him to school and also want to take care of your two friends if you don't mind. I'll do it without the slightest pressure. Will you do that for me?"

Like a child, Eva believed I could achieve anything I attempted. To find a street boy who had snatched such a fat purse wasn't going to be easy. All the same, I promised I would. What I wasn't about to do was bring Chali and Mchacho to this house, not unless I wanted it to turn into a battle field, a fact Eva didn't know. She didn't know how correct she was to say the two boys were beyond repair. Bringing them here would spoil the entire party for everyone. Chali and Mchacho were just impossible. From my inner knowledge of the effects of streetlife, even her own son, if found and brought home, would affect the peace she had known. He wasn't any better, but that she had better find out for herself.

CHAPTER TWO

Ever heard of a crazy day? Wednesday, 20th June was one for me.

First, I woke up late. I always consider it late when I wake up at 7.05 am., by which time I should be almost through with my morning roadwork.

I hope by now you remember me well enough. If you don't, here is a short reminder. I am Son of Fate, alias Adams Wamathina, who has been a journalist, a prisoner, a shoe shiner, a 'mitumba' seller and a cart-pusher in the streets and city estates. That was before I became 'wanted' for embezzling money from the Welfare Association of Shoe Polishers, in short WASP. I went on the run and ended up becoming a watchman at a rich Indian's residence, from where the cops fished me out. Well, I knew a game or two which the cops didn't. As a result I slipped through their fingers to a place I had nicknamed 'heaven', where I became a chauffeur to a millionaire tigress called Mrs. Wicks.

Jogging to me was like breakfast to you if you take it seriously. I would rather miss anything else. We had slept late the previous night which wasn't normal. We had been preparing for bed when someone rang the bell to our apartment at 10.15 pm. When my wife answered she found her friend Rose Odera who was accompanied by her husband. Mrs. Odera was having labour pains and they were begging that we rush her to hospital.

Eva had come back into the room panting, "Adams, hurry . . . the car please. Rose is right at the door in a terrible condition. Let me get ready while you prepare yourself." She had rushed to the bathroom and in the second minute had been out of the bedroom, ready to go. I just put on my shoes and picked the keys.

We had reached Nairobi Hospital in twenty minutes. We had taken seats at the waiting-room while the nurses took over from us. The husband, whom I hadn't known before this night, had been called to fill in some forms. Ten minutes later he had come back to tell us some deposit was required and that he needed a boost of five thousand shillings. I had assisted and he had gone back to the accounts office.

A picture at the wall had attracted my attention. In it a group of women were seated on a form waiting for their turn to go and see the doctor. Between three and four expectant mothers sat a young school girl in uniform, expectant as well. The eyes of the rest were all on her, and there was a big question mark in all their minds: 'Is she ready to ...'

I had found myself thinking about the picture and the message it bore. 'Why should a thing like this happen? What was going on in our society? Had we become sadists who could not change? Or could it be the youth to blame?' These thoughts had carried me away until they were cut short by a strange voice that sounded astounded.

"Oh my! I can't believe it's you!" I had turned to see what was going on as the lady who had shouted the words headed straight beside me, where my wife was seated.

They had embraced each other wildly, hugging and kissing as they talked what was nonsense to my ears. My whole attention had been drawn to them. I am a curious person and immediately my mind was busy again, poking my nose where it had no business. 'Who could this lady be? How could she know Eva while she hadn't been going out for a long time? Why was she so overjoyed at meeting Eva, and why hadn't Eva ever told me about her?' Again I was interrupted by Eva who, all of a sudden, seemed to realise she had forgotten her most important treasure — Wamathina.

"Oh, come and meet my husband. This will turn out to be the greatest day in my life." I smiled foolishly as I shook hands with the lady.

She had still seemed not willing to let go of my wife. Well, if you are the type that is interested in the other side of women, this one was a woman of "class." I personally don't know what "class" is supposed to mean but since it is the jargon I hear, I thought it would help you get the picture. The lady didn't have a handbag hanging on her shoulder; she was holding a glittering keyholder that had a few keys. Two of the keys were indicators that she was driving. The third item simply told you that whatever vehicle she was driving had an alarm, while the rest told you she had more than one vehicle. From looking at her posture, the way she had groomed herself, the hairstyle and the clothes she had put on, you were left without doubt about the "class". But my ignorant Eva didn't seem to recognise it, talking to the lady as she would any other woman. I was eager to know her. I had waited for the introduction which seemed to take ages.

"Addy ..." Eva had called, "... I want to test your memory, and for God's sake do not fail me." I had brightened up, which had seemed to boost her confidence in my memory. "Remember the greatest friend I told you I have ever had in life?"

I had tried to flash back to all the stories Eva had narrated to me but found none to fit the description of this lady standing in front of me. I had thought for a while that Eva was trying to make fun, or probably trying to pump the lady into thinking she had had her in mind all through, but I immediately ruled that one out. Eva wouldn't do a thing like that. She must have mentioned this one to me. Now when was this? She hadn't made any friends lately, so I had guessed it should be in her school days.

"The classmate who used to feed you with lesson notes when you dropped out of school?" I had asked suddenly. The guffaws of laughter which had followed shook the waiting room and had eyes turned in our direction. They had hugged each other once again and exchanged knowing smiles.

"You got it, Addy." Eva had said. "This is that Susan Kabugi I told you about."

"Susan Ndung'u for the past three years," the lady had added.

"Sussy, this is my husband, Adams Wamathina." We had again shaken hands.

"What's your business here? You don't look like you need this wing in a hurry," Susan had added. They had laughed at the joke. I had smiled to encourage them. "You look so young and beautiful, Eva, I envy you."

"Thanks ..." Eva had replied, obviously flattered, "... you too don't look much different from those days, only that you seem to have eaten a good deal. To answer your question, we brought a friend of mine, who has just been admitted."

They had dismissed me and drifted into petty talk about their past. My ears had remained active.

"By the way, have you seen King'ori? Leah Wambui Kingo'ri, our friend in Four B?" Eva had asked.

"I haven't seen her since we left school. What happened to her? Don't tell me she took to her father's..."

"She did! She is a doctor here, a gynaecologist. She is the one I have come to pick. She called to say her car had broken down."

"And what happened to you, if I may ask? I guess you pursued . . ."

"No, not anything you would guess. I did law. Quite opposite of what you may have assumed. I am a magistrate, based here." If Eva was surprised, she hadn't shown it. But I was. What a gap! Classmates meeting after several years. A doctor, lawyer and a housegirl, a maid, though right now a very decent housewife of an ex-jailbird. Talk of fate and how it handles people differently!

Our friend Odera had emerged just as I got tired of eavesdropping. My attention had gone to him as he outlined his wife's condition. But the ladies had recaptured our attention when the third classmate arrived. Laughter of excitement had again rent the air. I had turned to see what this newcomer looked like and I had liked what I saw. More introductions had followed. Then there had arisen an argument which I think would not have ended had we not interfered. Each of the three had wanted the others to go and celebrate the meeting at their places. I chose a neutral ground and won. That was where we had stayed till very late which, as I told you, was the cause of my waking up late. Are we together?

Now about this crazy day. I had very many things I wanted to look into. One, I wanted to rescue Mrs. Wicks who I suspected was still in police custody since her arrest. I did not hold much grudge against her as I now realized she had just been a victim of love. It was her craving for me that had forced her to try and get rid of her only rival who also happened to be her househelp.

Two, I needed to talk to Marie, my employer's daughter. I hadn't been in touch for some time, which was wrong. My employer's vehicle was still in my possession while he languished in hospital where I had taken him after snatching him from the jaws of a python.

Three, there was a briefcase held up in a city hotel which I was supposed to pick and whose contents were of vital importance to my employer and to me as well. Without them I wouldn't be able to accomplish the job which was so well-paying and without which I wouldn't live the way I was. I mean, I would soon find myself in the streets looking for an ordinary driving job, which would in turn mean leaving this comfortable house in Buru Buru and searching for an alternative, probably in Mathare. I hated the thought.

Four, because of this case I was almost certain I would go out of the country. As such I wanted to make arrangements with my bank so that my wife could continue withdrawing money from my account. There were other things as well, but those would come later.

I had just turned the tap to have a shower when I heard the telephone ring. The previous occupier to this house had transferred the number to me and I had given it to my lawyer. Up to now no one had ever called me on the line. Those who called mostly wanted to talk to Mr or Mrs Kibet, the previous occupiers.

As I heard my wife pick the phone, I expected her to give the normal answer, *"I am sorry so and so left this residence, try number…"* Instead she hurried to the bathroom and called me.

I wrapped a towel around my groin and got to the phone. It was my lawyer,

"Hello, Adams. I've been expecting to hear from you. How's this cruel world treating you?"

"Treacheously," I replied. "No chaos, no drama . . . nothing. If there's anything wrong, then its eating me from within like AIDS." I heard him laugh, but that didn't help to comfort me. The moment I heard his voice, I knew right away there was trouble, and most probably emanating from Mrs. Wicks. I knew she was very bitter with me and I expected her to try her best to see that I landed in trouble. I kept remembering what she told me once: that money could buy anything. I now tended to believe her. I knew she could spend lots of money in pursuit of her goals. What could she have come up with? I waited patiently for Muita to come out with it.

"What prompts your call?" I asked, feigning confidence. "I hope trouble hasn't started brewing from your side."

"No bad news from this side, or let me say I am not aware of any. There's this lady from the coast, Miss Aslam. I have just talked with her and she needs you very urgently... that's the way she put it. Call her before anything else. She didn't tell me if there was trouble, and I hope there isn't." His light touch didn't help me feel better either. That message meant there was trouble of some kind- Could my friend have detected my unrest and decided not to blow the whistle? What could it be?

"Please let me have her number, I'll call her right away."

"The code is 011, the number 485831. What else do we have from your quarter?" He asked just to keep me on the line.

"Nothing, man. Just total silence, which to me is worse than chaos. It's silence that bites, but it sounds like action has just started."

I looked at the wall clock and saw it was past 8.30 am. I cut the lawyer's line and called Marie. Eva came to the table carrying breakfast just as Marie picked the other end.

"Hello. Aslam's residence. Good morning?"

"Good morning, Marie. It's me Adams Wamathina. How have you been?"

"I am overjoyed to hear your voice, Adams. I didn't believe I'd get you soon. How have you been?" Her voice was as clear as if she was calling from the next room. She was soft-spoken and pronounced her words so well that the first thing you did on hearing her was to admire the pronunciation. A feeling that I have been missing something here all along momentarily gripped me.

"I have been OK, dear. *Pole Sana!* I guess you are mad with me, but take it or leave it, I was going to call you today. Since the time we parted it is today that I got a break and I had you on my list, second in fact."

'It's OK, dear; I believe you," she assured me. I was lucky in that all my friends trusted my word and I never had to convince them that what I was saying was the truth. At least I had this to remember my grandpa for. He had advised me to make sure I always told the truth because it saved a lot in future. I endeavoured to follow his advice where lying wasn't crucial.

"Well, thank you. It was good of you to bother getting in touch. What do we have from your side?"

"How soon would you be available, Addy?" she asked in reply, "I'd like you here any second from now." Now I sensed danger. My instincts hadn't deceived me: there was something terribly wrong. My silence prompted her to talk again.

"Adams, somebody shot my dad." She talked *sotto voce,* that I almost didn't hear. I had anticipated trouble alright but not of this magnitude.

"Is he dead?" It was the only question that came first to my mind.

"No, he isn't," came Marie's reply, and it revived my spirits. "But in ICU at the same hospital. He had just been discharged."

"Then take heart. Dad will live alright. He survived a worse situation. Do you think we could get a lead on whoever did that?"

"There is a possibility, but it requires a person like you to decide. That's why I needed you."

"Are the police on it already? I can guess that."

"Yes, but as far as I am concerned they are worse than the would-be killer. They want to dig so much from me, asking about things I cannot possibly know. They don't appear to be the normal police to me."

"I can guess that too, but they are the police alright. The 'Hawks' squad. They are bad news, especially when they want to know something and they suspect that you are the only person with the information. They act like criminals, but worse because they are law enforcers. I'll come right over dear, don't worry."

I was about to hung up when she called, "Excuse . . . hallo." I listened. "Please do not come by road; you may never arrive. I'll pay for the air ticket... please don't argue." I stopped arguing, said thank you, then hung up. Now I turned to Eva who was eagerly waiting for an explanation.

"It's the coast girl, Marie. Her father has been shot." I told her.

"Christ! Is he dead?" The tone betrayed her consternation.

"He is not dead, but in ICU. I want to rush there and see what I can do. That man is my present boss. That call has shattered all my day's dreams."

I left home at 9.30 a.m. and headed straight for my office at Wicks and Wayne Detective Agency. If I was going to be of any help to the Aslams, I would need to do it hiding behind this agency which had licensed me to carry a gun and given me identification papers for a private cop. This authority had come from the Commissioner of Police whose signature was quite clear. Who else in the force would stop or interfere with me? The only person I feared was the woman who had employed me, the proprietor of the agency who was none other than Mrs. Wicks. Right now I knew she considered me enemy number one. After leaving the office I would try to settle scores with her, just as I had planned before receiving Marie's phone call. I would visit her in custody and ask her what she would like me to do for her. I was ready to help even if it meant changing or denying the statement I had written to the police, provided she kept off Eva.

I arrived at the office just as another car was reversing out of a parking. The one ahead of me stopped and signalled that the driver wanted to occupy the bay. Well, I wouldn't allow him. I was in a hurry and, secondly, I was aware there were no other empty parkings around. Furthermore, this parking the driver in front of me wanted to take was very convenient for me. I therefore decided to ignore a few written and unwritten traffic laws. I overtook the driver on the wrong side and as the first driver cleared from the parking I plunged into it. Both drivers hooted in protest but that didn't bother me. I was now a detective at work and the dicks were always in a hurry.

I stepped out in the same hurry and was in time to apologize to the aggrieved driver: "Sorry sir, I am in a terrible hurry and I'll be out in under three minutes, if you don't mind waiting." I ran off without waiting for his answer. This rowdiness on my part somehow reminded me of Chali and Mchacho, and I wondered whether they would be of any use in this mission which required plenty of guts, free-wheeling' and plenty of other dare-devil acts where discipline would have no place.

'WICKS & WAYNE DETECTIVE AGENCY,' read the signboard on door number 601. There was no point of knocking as I was the boss. I went for the handle. As I touched it I saw it go down, an indication that somebody from within was getting out. As a matter of courtesy I let whoever it was have right of way.

When the door swang open we stared at each other like we were strangers who had met at a point where none of us expected life, as if wondering whether if we talked we would possibly talk the same language. But we weren't strangers at all. We knew each other well enough. We even liked each other somehow, but this meeting was the least expected. We didn't seem to trust each other; I for one had no trust left in me and I was almost certain she had the same feelings.

I looked at her in the face. Mrs. Wicks, alias Janet Wanjiru, alias Mrs. Adams Wamathina. She was lastly the latter, or at least that was the name under which she had booked a suite at the Diani Beach, when we had gone together to the Coast for a 'business trip' before we fell out.

"Hello Janet, I am glad to see you." I wasn't sure she would talk to me just as she must have been. I extended my hand which she took. Reluctantly? I wondered then thought this was psychological. Just because I had all along thought she was bitter with me, something that I couldn't prove. She had changed a little, but that was to be expected of a rich lady who finds herself in a police cell where even common items like water were a miracle. For an answer she turned and led me inside. At the reception I saluted my secretary-to-be and followed Mrs. Wicks who led right into the director's office. I closed the door behind me.

She didn't take the director's chair. Instead she pulled an armchair meant for visitors and sat down. I decided to take the one right opposite her instead of going for the swing chair meant for the MD, who up to now was supposed to be me. I had the feeling I was to be sacked.

" Are we still friends?" I got the guts to ask.

"Not after what you did to me. You threw me into prison and fled with my house girl. Who on earth can forgive that?" She too had guts. I could not expect her to say a thing like that after what she had done. I would have expected guilt and remorse, that she would look for a more convincing excuse than accuse me of eloping with her househelp. I was used to greater surprises in life and this was one of them.

I didn't say anything at first though I felt a great urge to do so. I looked at her closely. She had changed alright and not to a negligible extent as I had assumed at first glance. She even had some pimples on her face, no doubt from mosquito bites. Her beauty hadn't completely gone but one could clearly see the face needed a retouch to look like it used to – that of a young millionairess.

"Are you serious, Janet ...?" I asked after a while. "Let's be serious for once and settle the slight difference between us. It is only the two of us who know the truth of the whole matter. Accusing me of running off with your housegirl won't help because you know what you had done. Infact you should ..."

"There's nothing to talk about," she cut in rather rudely. "I have myself to blame for involving myself with a criminal. Sooner or later I was to face the consequences. I would be a fool to fall into that kind of trap again. I'd have to be stinking crazy to swallow a bait twice, just hand over what you owe me and we are quits."

This was another surprise. That Janet had all of a sudden realised I was a criminal! And this is after I had thwarted her own criminal plan! I looked at her straight in the face and saw signs of confused hatred. What a lover this one was! Between ourselves we knew what it really was – jealousy trying to evolve into hatred. And it was taking its time. But right now I knew she could do anything to have me punished. I had a feeling that she would love, more than anything else, to see me in a position where I would go down on my knees and plead for help from her. I wasn't even sure that she hadn't initiated the plan. I had to tread carefully.

"Janet, you offend me by saying I ran off with your ..."

"Don't waste your breath! What you have done cannot be forgiven. With or without your help, I am getting out of this jam. If you have a good memory, I once told you that money can buy anything. I am now out on bond but by the time I go for the hearing of the case, that is if I'll ever go, I'll have sprayed it with money such that it will be invisible ..., inconsequential. Anyway you needn't know that. The only thing between us now is one item only, the gun ..."

"Okay, Mrs. Wicks. Let's be … let's call a spade a spade. Are we really through?" I was asking for the sake of it because that was obvious. I hadn't any need to be friends with her anyway, but somehow I wanted her help. I wanted to keep the gun and the job for the time being because of the case I was handling. To have my license to carry a gun cancelled at this stage would take me too far backward, even probably render me helpless, and force me to give up the chase for the diamond that promised to change my life. What would then happen to Eva and me?

"Adams, I thought you were cute but how wrong I was! You are just like the rest of them. I thought in you I had found a real man, one who would add two and two to make four. I was deceived by your sharp observation, your expertise in driving and the way you threw kicks at your opponents in the ring. I thought you a real man. I should have changed my mind the moment I realised you were eyeing my house-girl. What a shame you've been!

"Yes, you are so naive that I pity you. Why, for instance, do you think I gave you the job after hearing about your filthy record? Why do you think I spent my money to clear your criminal record file from the Crime Record Office, CRO, to have you in my possession? Well, I could give you good marks for the way you started the job. You impressed me. I was watching you from the moment you hit my house, your body-guard prowess and daredevil antics, like inviting my house-girl to a place you damn well knew I would be. Then there was your frankness and honesty. You made me feel like I was safe or secure from disaster I could not define. That was how you won my heart. Later I decided to let you into my feelings. That is why I reopened this office and organized that trip to the coast. I was hoping we would get enough time together so that I may spill the beans. With you beside me, I was certain of success in the race …"

"Just a minute!" I interrupted. Something had crossed my mind as my invisible adviser urged me to be all ears. "On the way to the coast I began pre-empting your plans, didn't I? I rescued a man you would have preferred dead. You knew Aslam would be on his way to Mombasa and you had your boys behind him. That's why you didn't want me to stop around that area. When I did, you had no option but to follow me. This was why you handed me the gun. You were not sure of the security around the area. I doubt whether you'd have let me know you had a gun on you had you been. This reminds me of something that has kept bothering me since it happened. The person who impersonated me at the hospital: how had he got the name . . . my name? From you Janet? Tell me I am lying."

"Those are called speculations which no one could prove even in a court of law. Adams, I am not what you think I am. I wish you took time to study me, the kind of woman I am. All women are not the same, Adams. Some of us are smarter than the smartest of the human race and the sooner you people appreciate this the better for you . . ."

"What are you driving at, Janet? From my knowledge, you only tell what you consider top secret to an enemy when you are certain he won't live to tell the story. From what I have gathered you already consider me a person who cannot be trusted. I am an enemy already in other words, yet here you are telling me everything. The next thing you are to tell me is that you murdered Wicks and probably Wayne, if they ever existed, so as to inherit their wealth. Go ahead and do it, then for God's sake tell me what will follow because I cannot stay here listening to you all day. Now that you are out of prison, the time I had set aside for you might as well go to something else. I have not the slightest doubt as to who you are now, a rich most dangerous criminal considering your wealth and high education . . ."

"Go on talking, I am enjoying myself as you struggle to prove a point. I didn't say you are an outright fool or that you are without intelligence. All I said was that you should have taken time to study what kind of a woman I am . . ."

"I don't need to, Mrs. Wicks," I interrupted. "What good will it do me to know you better than I do? All it will remind me is to be wary of you, and that I have been ever since you put Eva into trouble. You put an innocent young girl into prison, instead of paying her handsomely for the services she had rendered and ordering her to clear off your premises. Now you do not even seem moved by that inhuman act. You do not feel ashamed that I have the true knowledge about the whole thing. What else do I need to know about you? The most ruthless criminals I have met in life have that soft spot that spares children and the very old. You don't have a conscience and that's all I need to know about you.

"Let me tell you something, Mrs. Wicks. Although we didn't meet in this office to brag about ourselves, you cannot scare me, if that is what you think. You also know almost nothing about me . . . almost nothing. Maybe you think because you have a number of assassins hanging around all you need to do is point a finger at me and they'll fall on me as the rain does. That won't do. They can't touch me! If anything it's me who would maul them if I chose to. But I am not interested because none of them has stood in my way. Secondly, I am not interested in the dark side of you and I don't have any intentions to, I no longer care about the crime you committed against Eva or others in your life. As I hinted, I had come here to rescue you. I wasn't going to let you suffer after the happy moments we shared . . . the joy and the pleasures we have known together. You rescued me once and I was going to even the score, but I took too long.

"That, anyway, is not the issue right now. What I want you to tell me very clearly is: now that we do not seem to be friends any more, do I quit managing this office?"

We stared at each other for about a minute, seemingly trying to study one another. On her face I read several things. There was a degree of hatred, a portion of what I thought to be fading love and a good amount of confusion. The face was pale yet determined, the body erect, and in her I saw an embodiment of a dedicated criminal. She opened her mouth as if to talk then seemed to change her mind. I continued to stare, not knowing whether to talk or keep silent. Then it dawned on me that she was making a crucial personal decision which needed minimal disturbance. It was as if she was deciding on whether I should live or die. I gave her the time to make up her mind.

All of a sudden she seemed to come back to the surface from some deep waters. She looked at me straight in the eyes.

"Adams, will you help me?" she pleaded. "Will you join me in this thing, work with me side by side, and let us bury the past?" It was my turn to stare in confusion. When I saw her eyes were still on me seconds later, I talked. "On what thing? I do not even know of anything you are working on. If it is about this office you have not so far sacked me and I'd love to continue." But even as I said this, I was aware it wasn't the office she had in mind.

"Adams, let's stop playing games with each other. You know what I mean and you have the key to it. Will you help me? Shall we work together? I'll give you whatever funds you need."

I had already guessed what she was driving at.

"Okay; now I get it. But could you begin by telling me who shot Mohammed Aslam last night?"

I got the answer even before she opened her mouth to tell me she didn't know. If she did she would have passed for the greatest actress in the universe.

"I know you wouldn't believe me but that is news to me. I wouldn't do that anyway, because I am aware he handed everything over to you. There are so many people chasing this same thing, Adams, as you will soon find out. You wouldn't know who among them did that."

I believed her. Even criminals didn't lie throughout their lives; they only did so – when cornered.

"Second question. Did you send that person to impersonate me at the hospital so as to learn why Aslam insisted on seeing me? I want to clear my conscience on this thing."

"Yes I did, but he never got there. I mean he didn't get the chance to get to Aslam. He arrived just when you were hot on the heels of another impersonator. It was a coincidence that shocked us more than it did you. You were also wrong about the accident Aslam got on the way. I needed him alive just like many others. It was through the accident that I learned there were other groups ready to do anything to get to the goal."

It sounded funny and unbelievable perhaps, but it bore that undeniable ring of truth.

"What's the secret about this thing if you don't mind telling me?" I asked after a while.

"Adams, we have been in this thing for a long time. It didn't start today, or that day you rescued Mohammed, but no one will tell you why they are taking the risk; the few who know won't tell you. This is a dark thing, but one which will one day turn very bright. . . for the right person, that is."

I wasn't in any good mood but what Janet told me made me almost break into laughter, I have had mysteries before my eyes but nothing like this. Which people were these ready to kill each other without knowing what for? Just to keep her talking, I asked another question.

"Where is your Adams? Maybe he could help me trace the other Adams. I'd love to lay my paws on that one before anything else."

"Our Adams is dead; he committed suicide. We don't accept failures."

That was an answer which contradicted itself and it gave me something to think about later. Right now I wanted to know what she meant by, 'we.' The Kenyan Mafia? That would scare me! I would rather have the whole lot of cops on my trail than this nefarious group that never missed the target. I wanted to live, to keep on living till my star shone, after which I would find a nice lonely place where I would take my family and forget the world and its cruelty. Here I would rest in peace, going out only when my family needed it. But before that I had to run for the star. Would it ever shine? "Who are 'we'?" I got the guts to ask.

I watched as Mrs. Wicks stood up from where she was seated and made for the door. I expected her to open and probably talk to the secretary and ask for something which probably carried the answer to my question, but she didn't even touch it. She turned and paced back towards the window instead. She looked outside for a while. Again I thought she wanted to signal somebody probably waiting for her downstairs. She proved me wrong again when she turned without incident. This time she stared at a vase on top of a well polished wooden stand placed against the wall. She seemed to be surprised to find it there, and this was when I got what was on her mind. She wanted to tell me something, to answer my question, but here again, I realised, was time to take another decision. It required all her courage to tell the secret which I so longed to hear. I wanted to know as much as I could lay my hands on. I tried to soften my face. I forced some smile so that when she turned to me she'd meet a nice innocent face, which I thought would help make a positive decision. As she turned slowly I told myself: *"well, here we go my dear Jenny, just come off it."*

"Adams dear, do you seriously want to know?" Her voice seemed to come from very far away, sounding quite unlike the Mrs. Wicks I knew. It seemed too strangle her, as if it came from a person who had cried herself dry. And then she seemed to realize the smile I had put on was fake.

'WARY SONNY BOY; BE WARY.' My usual companion whispered an inner warning, 'LOOK AT THOSE EYES AND READ THEM. DO YOU READ DEATH IN THEM? THAT IS IT! THIS IS NOT THE JANET WANJ1RU ADAMS YOU KNOW. THIS ONE IS THE DEVIL'S MISTRESS! JUST KEEP ON REMINDING YOURSELF THAT. THE TIGRESS AT HER WORST.'

That was the comforter I have always had inside my head giving me the warning, making me change the answer on the tip of my lips from a strong "Yes, I seriously do" to, "Well, I really don't know ..." To my surprise I sounded very weak; I think she had scared me.

"I think it is not a must that I know. But if you think you want to tell me, I guess I wouldn't mind. This is entirely for you to decide."

She seemed confused. My answer wasn't that clear and the way my voice dropped seemed to betray my fear. She was an intelligent lady and she quickly sensed it and came closer to me, with the same hard eyes still on me.

"Adams, I want you to know, I really do. I might not like you right now but that doesn't mean we cannot work together. You have your interests, I have mine. This is why I am sure we can work together and achieve our diverse interests."

With an absent mind I nodded in agreement. What she had said was partly true. She turned and reached for her handbag which was on the executive desk on which my left elbow lay.

She opened it and took out a small compact which she proceeded to open. It was beautiful, with edges that appeared golden, and glittered with reflection of the light from the bulb that was still on. It was my first time to see that kind of thing and Janet, seeming to realise it, let me admire it. Inside it was covered with maroon velvet material. It was so finely finished that the edges of the material vanished somewhere inside the golden rim.

There were a number of pins lying in the compact which too glittered as they interacted with the light. She picked one of them and put the compact down.

"Okay Adams," she ordered," bring your right mid-finger. It is time for us to be one from now on."

"Whatever for?" I asked in surprise.

"Adams, let's face facts. We already don't trust each other and in order to do so we have to take an oath. I'll then be in a position to answer whatever questions you may have. I'll introduce you to personalities that matter, some so senior you will find it hard to believe. And you'll have all the riches you long for, Adams. All I'll do to your finger is prick it, like this ..."

She pricked her finger with the pin and a globule of blood started to ooze. 'What group is that blood?' I found myself wondering as she took out a snow-white soft pad from the compact and wiped the blood. The red spot showed very clearly on the pad.

"When I have pricked yours, Adams," she explained, "I'll rub it on this same spot. The blood will merge and join us into one. From then on the curtain will be drawn back for you to watch the movie. You'll like it Adams, I promise you that."

I stood up, my mind swirling. I needed money badly, to be a millionaire if possible. I wanted my star to shine like my grandmother had predicted. But if this money involved the devil, if that was the only way my star would shine, then I was willing to have it stay dark for ever. If this was for the same reason they wanted to slaughter Aslam, I was determined to be on his side at whatever cost. Right then, the picture of Marie Aslam waiting for me came into my mind. I wanted to leave. To the tigress I said, "I am so sorry Mrs. Wicks. I'd love to be rich and you know it. But I am not ready to go that far. My grandpa whose guidance and advice have seen me through numerous hurdles adviced me never to take oaths.

"Mrs. Wicks, you have been kind to me and I was very much willing to do anything to show my gratitude. But it appears there is little I can do now. All I can do is wish you good luck in whatever you do. I am very sincere about this."

I did not want to talk about it further or learn any secrets. I felt it was safer to know as little as possible. After all, I had the introduction letter from Aslam and, if I managed to get it into the right hands, there was a bright future for me. So why not move right over?

I stood up. I wanted to shake her hand and wish her luck but it was clear she wasn't ready for that. I therefore turned my back on her and went for the door.

Clink . . . Clank . . . Clonk . . .

I stood where I was, facing the door like I was electrocuted. The sound I had heard was peculiar, but very familiar to my ears. It always announced danger, sometimes sure death, so I stood where I was to await orders that were sure to follow.

"Good, that's why I admire you at times." There was that icy edge in her voice that would shake the uninitiated. "I admire people with guts and skill, and you look like you'd make one. You just hear a sound and you know right away what's on your back. Now turn round slowly with your hands on the back of your head."

I did that. The gun was pointed right at the centre of my chest. If she pulled the trigger the bullet would find its way through my heart. The beautiful lady was smiling just like she would while placing a mug of steaming coffee before you and welcoming you to it. Her dimples, which I loved the very first day I saw her smile, showed very clearly. They looked inviting and my thoughts flashed to the day I first kissed them with the tip of my tongue. What an enigmatic woman!

"Does this change your mind, Adams Wamathina?" The deceptive smile was still on her lips.

"No, Mrs. Wicks. It annoys me all the more, and you need to be careful."

"Let me give you another chance to think for old-days' sake. Will you change your mind? For your information Adams, no one ever sees this compact and what it contains and lives to tell the story, not unless he goes by its demands. Now the last chance. Will you take the oath?"

She looked like she would pull the trigger the moment I said no, but I was not about to give in.

"NO!" I found myself shouting. "Pull the trigger and let's get done with it. I am bored of life."

I had a feeling she wouldn't. Somehow I knew she needed the briefcase Aslam had given me and with me dead she knew she wouldn't get near it. What she was likely to do was hold me prisoner and use her henchmen to persuade me by whatever means to hand the documents over to them.

'THERE'S ALWAYS A LOOSE END, SONNYBOY, SO DON'T PANIC.' My comforter told me.

'Thank you, sir!' I told my colleague in the head, my hands still where I was told to keep them.

Mrs. Wicks buzzed the secretary then took the mouthpiece. I heard her give a series of orders, "Go and wait for me in my office. Use your key to lock the outer door ... and no one should be told I am in this office till I say so." She put the phone down and looked at me. From the way she was handling the gun I could tell she was used to it and must have used it on several people before me. I have met tough women before but none looked anything near what Mrs. Wicks looked right now.

I heard the door close two minutes later and the key was turned in. Janet turned to face me. "Come two steps inside," she ordered. "Let your hands remain there, right at the back of your head. You know, Adams, one sometimes is forced to like you. Let me be frank – one easily falls in love with you. But you are so disappointing when you mean to. Why, for instance, don't you make it easy for the two of us and let us team up? Do you mean to tell me that you gave up on the assignment given you by Mohammed? You have what hundreds of others are after, and take it from me they will not let you go the easy way. I wanted you to be at the forefront while I protected you from the back. I am capable of it. I am sure this is the only way the two of us will succeed in finding this thing. The information I have is that no one will retrieve it on his own. even you, Adams!"

The gun was still trained on me. When I didn't comment, she looked annoyed and turned to the phone. She picked the mouthpiece and placed it against her left ear. She then raised her left shoulder a bit to hold it while she used the same hand to dial a number. It didn't prove easy, what with the right hand holding the gun still trained me. Then she appeared to resolve to do one thing at a time. She put the phone down. All her attention was focused on me and I could notice some determination this time. She became erect and the gun in her hand now looked more deadly.

"Hand over the gun you have to me. Now that we are not together, I don't see why you should keep it. Do it fast please, I do not want to waste any more time on you." I knew right away that this was a test. She wanted to confirm whether I had the gun.

"I don't have it. If you do not believe that I left it at your place, you go ahead and search me." I tried to sound serious so as to convince her. I had the gun right where I stood and I was going to do anything to keep it.

When she didn't seem convinced, I tried again: "Janet, though we do not seem to be friends any longer, this shouldn't make you disregard what you know about me. I like standing by my words. When I tell you the gun is at your place you certainly know I am telling the truth. Why should I lie, anyway?" I did not want her to search me at all because I was afraid she'd find the gun in which case I would have to go out looking for another, which wasn't appropriate at the moment.

''Where in particular did you put the gun?" She asked after a moments' reflection.

"I dumped it in the right upper drawer of the wall unit."

"But that one is locked. I keep those drawers locked." She seemed not sure of that and this gave me the courage to argue further.

"I didn't say it wasn't locked. It is there even now if you haven't touched it. The keys are still hanging where I found them." She seemed to believe me but, as I have told you, Janet was intelligent. She knew it wouldn't cost her anything to search me and so she went ahead and did it.

"Turn round, Son of Fate. I do not doubt you. You might have left the gun there alright, but that doesn't mean you cannot secure another one. You forget I had your crime record file in my hands and I am not likely to forget what it says about you. I have to search you. Just be cooperative for the sake of the two of us."

I turned round quietly. Her tone had left no doubt that she wouldn't hesitate pulling the trigger if I tried to be a hero. I uttered a silent prayer for the first time in my life as I felt her soft hands frisk my pockets and explore the region of my private parts. As I inwardly said amen, I heard her sigh with relief. She seemed to have reached the conclusion that I indeed didn't have the gun.

"Thank you, our Heavenly Father, for blinding this wild woman who has no value for your children and all your creation. Now I pray that you deliver me from this evil ..." At least I felt indebted to the Creator for letting me get away with the search. The gun was right where I had put it, perpendicular to my spinal-cord where the underwear held it pressed against the body. If she hadn't asked me to turn round so that my back was facing her she would have found it, but she couldn't have expected it to be so close to her.

"That's good, dear and it leaves me a little more comfortable. Now be good. Sit over there and enjoy yourself." She pointed with her gun at the farthest corner where there was a sofa set.

I did as instructed but I was very alert. For once in a long time I found myself caressing the talisman my grandmother had given me upon her death. As I continued doing so I got a feeling that all was well, that this wasn't going to be the end. It left me wondering whether my grandmum had been that certain about the protective power of the talisman. Had it some concealed power, after all?

Janet went to the phone and, putting the gun down, picked the mouthpiece. She went ahead and dialled a number, but her eyes were still keenly on me.

Second after another ticked by as I wondered what would follow. I was getting late for other things including my boss who was, for the time being, Marie Aslam. My accomplice in the subconscious had come to me and was busy keeping me vigil. Whoever or whatever he was, because I didn't know up to now, wanted me to capture every move taken by Janet or, if you like, Mrs. Wicks. He wanted me to spring into action the moment the slightest chance availed itself. But there appeared no chance of Mrs. Wicks getting careless, which made me admire and hate her at the same time.

After several attempts, which to me seemed to take ages, she got through to where she was calling.

"Hello, give me Stranger immediately ... What kept you that long? I almost thought something had gone wrong ... Okay, hurry up." She waited, her eyes still on me. What a wary young fox!

"Hello, Stranger. You took your time but it's good to hear you at last ... Where? How? ... What time was that? ..." I could see her face change complexion as she got the story from whoever she had called. She asked short questions in quick succession. There was no doubt something was wrong somewhere and it was worrying her. My heartbeats now started accelerating as I noticed she was now and then facing away from me. *'Go on Stranger,'* I thought, *'... tell her every bit of it ... break her heart.'* I touched the talisman with the hope that it would control my heartbeats and let me concentrate with uninterrupted attention. I smiled at the thought that I was becoming superstitious. I remembered that when my grandmother gave me this talisman I would have thrown it away if it hadn't been for her insistence that I keep it. What would I be turning to in moments like this?

I kept on praying as she continued getting agitated by whatever the man she called Stranger was telling her. Her questions were now almost rude: "Who sent him? ... Why? ... What for? ... Oh my God, ... I ... I ... Didn't I say you . . . Oh my .,."

'SON OF FATE!', my accomplice roared at me, 'WHAT ARE YOU WAITING FOR? GET HER! JUMP!'

'Oh no dear, I argued, 'I missed my roadwork today and I feel so weak. She'll get me halfway, I am so ...'

'NOW ... GO.' HOP, STEP AND . . .'

Janet turned as I was preparing to spring and saw what was happening. She went for the gun, but my eyes were on her hand. I went for it. In the process we both hit the gun and it dropped to the other side of the executive desk. She let out a loud cry of horror. She kicked out wildly with surprising strength. This reminded me I was dealing with no ordinary woman but a tigress. She tried to lash out with her strong nails but I was too swift for her. I wasn't going to let my face get scarred. I pulled her away from the desk we were both leaning against. We went hard on the floor with the heavy carpet giving us some cushion. From where we were, I could hear Stranger's voice calling, 'Hello, hello . . . hello, as the mouthpiece hang from the desk. As we struggled to get the better of each other, I could not help wondering about this lady I once nicknamed tigress. I remembered the time she 'fainted' in my hands while we were jogging. I remembered too, her motherly concern while I gave her the story of my past at a coast hotel. I compared all that with what she was now, a wild beast that was trying its best to beat me in the game and probably get rid of me. This realisation made me kick out like a wounded lion. I managed to get both her hands where I was struggling to have them — behind her back. I forced her to lie on them. I didn't want to hurt her which is why the wrestling took that long. I had had several chances of bashing her teeth inside her mouth in the course of the tussle. I would have let her go had she agreed that we part peacefully. But she seemed not ready for that.

On the other hand, I was aware she could be buying time because Stranger, the person she had called, could very well be one of the Kenya Mafioso, assassins on hire, who must be working for her. He would no doubt come to her rescue as he must know this office. He must have heard her scream of horror and there was no way he would wait around while his boss needed assistance. I knew wherever Stranger had been talking from, by now he was on his way here.

From the position I had forced her into we stared at each other. This wasn't the first time I had been on top of her; it had happened so many times before. But in other times it had been under very pleasant circumstances, where our eyes and faces had smiled at each other, our lips making emotional contact. Now everything was different: she felt like a snake under my body, the hands that used to caress her were now strangling her in an effort to immobilize her. Our eyes told of the hatred each felt towards the other.

"Janet ..." I called at last, "you know I am too good for you. I do not want to hurt you. Please relax and let me go. Do not forget that I cannot wait till Stranger comes. I can do anything to you to secure my freedom, including leaving you here unconscious if I have to. Make no mistake about that. There's no way I am going to wait for Stranger or whoever else it might be. You'll decide right now: you either flex or break!"

For an answer she held her breath, and in the next second I was thrown off balance. This annoyed me and my next blow got the better of her. She lay on the floor unconscious.

I stood and watched the limp body with a sense of remorse. I felt guilty from within and bent down to straighten her body. I then knelt beside her and gave her a slight kiss on the left cheek, then another on the lips. As I turned her head to do the same to the right cheek while I muttered that I was sorry for doing this to her, my accomplice called.

'SON OF FATE ...'

'Yes, sir!' I called back as loudly as I had heard the voice.

'YOU HAVE TWO MINUTES IN WHICH TO CLEAR OUT OF THIS OFFICE. YOU HOLD THE FOUR ACES BUT FOR A VERY SHORT TIME. THIS IS A MATTER OF LIFE AND DEATH. SNAP OUT OF IT!'

'Yes, sir!' I answered, and from then on I acted like lightning. I picked her gun from where it had fallen and packed it on me. I then went for her handbag and searched for the office keys which I found without trouble. I proceeded to the mirror pinned on the wall and straightened myself up. I rubbed off the dust I had picked while wrestling and, once satisfied, I went for the door. In the second minute I was waiting for the lift.

The door opened and I sighed with relief. I stared at the faces of the people waiting for the lift to go up. Could Stranger and his henchmen be among them, I wondered? There was no time to try and find out. Most killers and hardened criminals looked very innocent. They physically looked more innocent than those who really were innocent. All the men in front of me had innocent-looking there was no way of telling who was who. I went out of the building as naturally as I could. I took my car, or to be precise Marie's, and drove off like a bat out of hell. Whoever Stranger was, I didn't want to meet him in a hurry. I had a feeling that he was the trigger-happy type that considered money more valuable than human life.

As I reversed the Merc out of the parking all my mind was on Marie. She must be eagerly waiting for me at the Mombasa Airport. She had assured me she'd only leave when I had arrived. I was aware that if I booked a plane at Wilson Airport it would take me under two hours to get there. But there was something else disturbing my mind as much as Marie – Eva. She had requested me not to leave before I got her her 'parking-boy' son. Like a child, she believed that I was in a position to reach anything any time I needed to. She didn't seem to realise that tracing her son was next to impossible, especially now when he had some money on him. But there was no way I was going to tell her that. There was no need of putting ulcers in her stomach because she would sooner or later transfer the same to me. I loved her, and to see her suffering would eat me up like AIDS.

I had to do something before I left for Mombasa. After all, I had a feeling that the moment I arrived there and listened to Marie's story, and probably decided taking action of whatever magnitude, I wasn't likely to have a break. I had started believing what Janet had told me about this 'thing' - this Aslam case which didn't have a suitable name as no one seemed to really know what it was. Aslam had told me it was a piece of diamond that was worth more than Kshs. 80,000,000, but I didn't believe him any more than I did Janet who told me that no one knew what it really was. In the first place, I didn't see the reason why several Governments were secretly chasing the same 'thing' – if all it was worth was only eighty million shillings. Aslam personally had more than that amount in his accounts and I didn't see why he'd take the risk of getting killed for more money. Janet wasn't a poor one either, and yet she too was dying to go for it. Why?

As I drove on, I was driven into thought deeper than I have ever been. Whatever this sinister parcel was, it was certainly going to take my total concentration. Already my eyesight had dimmed with the very idea. This had also carried away part of my senses because I now realised that all oncoming drivers were flashing headlights at me. On checking I found I had my full lights and hazard winkers on. I must have been driving carelessly. I slowed down, put off the headlamps and the winkers, then forced thoughts of the 'thing' out of my mind. Why cross bridges I haven't reached? I had better trace Kimesh first.

There's this priest who has featured prominently in my life, both when I am at my lowest and when I occasionally get up in life, like now. Sometimes I think Father Grol is part of my life. When Eva insisted that I find her son, the first person who had come into my mind was Fr. Grol, the reason being that he had founded an organization called Undugu Society which dealt with street children. I had seen him time and again right in the midst of the children, and there are times I thought he was made for them.

Now that I was about to get busy on tracing the sinister trophy, I decided I should, before anything else, attend to Eva's request. That I knew was the only time she would gladly let me out of her hands.

Fr. Grol wasn't there when I got to the office, but I found his personal assistant, a thick-set man who was introduced to me as Peter Foro. In the same office I met a Mr. Jones, a Mr. Macharia and another thickset they called Muiruri. If you wanted to know when there was a parking-boy and where, all you needed to do was contact these guys. I gave them my story, but not before they had taken me round showing me the street children they were trying to rehabilitate and those already rehabilitated. They of course hadn't failed to note that I had got out of a Merc250 SE. I wasn't sure that they didn't think I had gone there with the intention of boosting the kitty for caring for the over fourty children who were housed there, some who had found their way even to the university. When I gave them my story, they certainly were surprised. Some, like this thickset called Foro, looked at me with an eye that seemed to accuse me of fathering a good number of the 'parking-boys' as they referred to them. They seemed to change their minds when I cunningly mentioned I was a friend to the founder of this project and that if they thought it was out of their line of duty I could talk to him. This activated them. They weren't bad boys after all. In the next two minutes they had found, among those they hosted, four boys who knew Kimesh. One of the boys even knew Kimesh had snatched a fat pouch 'just the other day.'

"I think you are satisfied, sir, that we'll get him?" said Foro.

"Yes, I am," I said. Inwardly I wondered whether they expected *kitu kidogo. "You should as well forget it because I don't bribe,"* I thought to myself. However, they seemed to like their work.

I stood up and looked around the walls of the office in which we were as I prepared to leave. All over were cuttings from local and foreign newspapers which had written on the project. There were pictures of boys and girls sniffing glue, others of social workers talking with the street children, while others showed the founder of the project in the midst of dancing urchins. Reading from their faces, the others expected me to comment but all I did was smile, not because I liked what I saw or because I thought they were doing a nice job, but because of the secret I carried in me. They wouldn't know, but my childhood had been no better than the parking-boys'. The Son of Fate they were seeing was Son of Troubles, and driving a Benz now didn't mean he couldn't go back to the same streets later. Fate was full of surprises and you never knew when he was likely to strike.

"Well gentlemen," I said as I headed for the door," I am grateful for your offering to help. Please contact that lady immediately you get news of any kind." I looked at all their faces one at a time; I wanted them to register well in case we ever met again. They stared back at me with faces that looked hard for social workers. I attributed this to the fact that they were used to a hardened human race that was trying to learn how to become humane, and part of its hardness had rubbed off onto them. I left them staring as I entered the car, reversed and took off. When I waved a few metres away, they and their wards waved excitedly. They were good boys after all... and if there was anybody who could trace Kimesh, it was this team.

CHAPTER THREE

I found Marie waiting for me at the airport in Mombasa. She had a vehicle waiting outside and when we got to it, I was reminded of her father Mohammed Aslam bin Aslam. This was the same vehicle he had been driving when he got an accident that had landed him in a python's mouth from where I had rescued him. The vehicle had been straightened and resprayed and it looked like it had just left the show room.

As if we had discussed about it, I went straight to the wheel just as she produced the keys to request me to drive her. Whatever she had encountered had shocked her and she looked beaten. Even if you didn't know her before, a glance at her would have told you that something was amiss.

We drove in silence for a couple of minutes before she opened up.

"You took too long," she said. "I thought something had gone wrong soon after I called you."

"Well, something did go wrong,' I said. "But at least for now I guess all is well back there." I wasn't very sure about that because the way I had left things, there was plenty I'd have loved to know as well.

"What was it? Do you mind telling me?"

"No, I don't; but I'd rather we talked about it later. Right now I think it best that we go some place and get comfortable. Then we can discuss all that we have in detail. How's Papa, by the way? Have you ..."

"Dad is OK. I went to see him soon after I called you. The doctor told me we have nothing to worry about. He says dad might be in a position to talk this evening, though his advice is that we wait till tomorrow to give him adequate rest."

I didn't comment on that but I felt the doctor had said that to avoid killing two souls. You don't get admitted to the ICU and be in a position to talk that soon.

"You look bothered, Adams," she said after another stretch of silence "... could it be anything to do with what I called you for?"

I involuntarily looked in her direction. She was right, but what was bothering me most was an incident I was trying to connect with the whole thing.

The more I thought about it, the more I believed there was some connection. While at the Wilson Airport I had decided to call Eva to let her know the time I'd take off. There were two coin booths but only one was functioning. The gentleman inside had made a call, talked for close to five minutes, cut the line and then dialled another number. I had gone closer, intending to let him know that respect could only be given to those who gave it to others. I was aware he felt disturbed by my closeness, which is exactly what I had wanted. As he dialled the number once again, it had vaguely appeared to me that the number was familiar. If I hadn't missed one digit, I guess I'd have guessed exactly where he was calling, I had then argued I was being bothered by irrelevances and dismissed the issue from my mind.

He had talked very briefly. It had been simple introduction, like he was reminding someone on the other end that he had called again. "Have you changed your mind?" he had asked, then stopped to face me rudely, as if he wanted to tell me to keep my distance. I had ignored him and turned to look at a light aircraft which was about to land. But I couldn't help hearing and noting that he was talking with some authority, trying to scare whoever was listening to him. It however hadn't meant anything to me then, my argument being that the caller was one of those guys who liked their presence being felt just because they happened to be in authority. He had hung up by banging the mouthpiece like it had annoyed him and left the booth smiling to himself. I think it was for this reason that I had taken a second glance at him.

"Did you talk to me? I am sorry the question doesn't seem to have registered in my mind." My remark took Marie by surprise.

"I think you need some rest, Wamathina." She said and went silent. I drove on deep in thought. It was when we reached a point where I needed her advice that I spoke.

"Are we going home straight?"

"Yes. Now that I have company, I'll feel peaceful for the first time." She forced a smile.

"What is that supposed to mean?" I asked.

"I had sworn not to go back to that place. I've been receiving threatening calls from anonymous callers since last night. They make me feel like I am getting crazy. Christ! I wish Dad gave up the whole thing. It is going to kill him."

"What do the callers want? What are they asking you to do?"

"They all sound crazy to me. One is offering me five million shillings or death."

"In exchange for what?" I asked.

"Papers, letters, maps. He doesn't seem to be certain of what he wants. He tells me to persuade Dad to give them up. If he cannot I should steal them or do anything I can to posses them. If I do not succeed I am promised death for me and my dad. I am terribly scared, Wamathina!"

That was a real shocker, as it certainly was dangerous, especially coming from a person who'd do anything without second thought. This had already been demonstrated by the shooting of Aslam. Marie had all the reasons to fear for both her life and her father's. Whom did this caller in particular represent?

"Is it the same person calling everytime or are there more than one, and do they come from the same group?"

"No!" She screamed at me like I had offended her. "There are others. Even female voices have called twice. But I feel I could recognize their voices anywhere. They are so disturbing that they have become engraved in my psyche."

"What other offers or threats have come?" We were now driving uphill on a private road that led to the Aslam residence.

"One of them told me to beg my father to give up the chase and hand over the documents to them, or he gets killed. That caller shot him the following day."

I stole a sideways glance at her. Something in her tone had betrayed her; she was on the verge of weeping.

Well, this 'thing' was fear-inspiring but the sight of Marie's pale face, and the tears welling up in her eyes, made me feel brave and eager to do something. 'What 'thing' was this and what 'something' could I do?' I found myself wondering as I stepped on the brake pedal. We were home already. As I put off the engine I remember telling her, "He couldn't have shot your dad. That has to be someone else." I was then talking my mind aloud.

"How do you know that?" She asked in a strangled voice, seemingly surprised that I should say that.

"Simple logic, Marie dear. Because shooting him would not give the killer or the gunman what he wants. The killer just knows something others do not know and wants your father's mouth shut … I do not really believe what I think, but my instincts tell me crazy things which I do not even want to talk about, I badly need time to work out how we can get out of this thing once and for all. It tires me to death whenever I think about it. That is ever since that key landed in my hands."

The telephone started ringing as we entered the big, beautifully-furnished sitting room. I saw Marie's face turn even paler. She looked at me, seemingly telling me to pick the phone if I wanted to hear the caller because she wasn't going to. I could guess why; the phone had turned into a nightmare in her life. I pushed her aside and went to pick it.

I listened without talking. The caller took time at first, then decided to break the silence which is exactly what I wanted.

"I know it's you. You are scared to talk. I am now with you. Very close to you. I just want you to tell me, Yes or No. Did you change your mind? Will you get me the documents?" It was a man's voice. I didn't talk, all I did was to bang the phone. I was aware he'd call again and I wanted to tell Marie what to do in case he did so.

"Who was it, Adams? The same people?" Marie asked me, fear written on her face. I didn't answer her. My hand was still cupped on the mouthpiece on its cradle where I had banged it. My mind had taken a flight from this vast sitting room which was filled with everything you could dream of, plenty of beauty that distantly reminded me of Mrs. Wicks' 'Heaven'. My instincts were telling me a very strange thing. Had I heard that voice before today? I was staring at a picture on the wall but all I could register was the framework. Marie was talking to me but I wasn't getting a thing. An image was forming in my mind and all my senses were concentrated there. Did I know the caller? Had I seen him somewhere, sometime? The image was forming into a picture of a person. My mind went back to the voice I had just heard. It had been deep although the caller was trying to disguise it. *A man of about 35, dark complexion. A sharp nose that looks good on a face that is round with slightly big eyebrows and thick eyelashes. Dressed in a grey suit of light material, a red-stripped white shirt and a simple neck tie.* As I concentrated on the image, the picture of a man so dressed formed in my mind. He had been about five feet nine inches tall. He had put on a smile which to me had betrayed his pretensions of honesty.

'Who was this man?' I asked myself aloud, without knowing I was doing so. Marie came closer and touched my shoulder.

"Adams, what's it? Who was the caller? Do you know him?"

"Yes, it's him. He is the one. I … I … I know him!" I heard myself stammer. By now the picture was becoming clear.

"Wamathina, please come with me. I beg you not to argue." She pulled me by the left hand and I followed her, like a man in a trance, upstairs. I noticed the stairs were carpeted; our footsteps were swallowed up so that you couldn't detect a sound. Once upstairs Marie led me into a huge bedroom which at a glance told me was hers. There was a double-bed covered with an expensive-looking bedcover, with two pillows covered by two similar pillow cases. To me this was wonderland. You shouldn't forget that I was only a chauffeur who happened to land on a rich woman's territory which had led to all this. Up to now, the star which my grandmum had told me would once shine opening up a new world of heavenly life hadn't yet shone, and I was up to now on my heels chasing it. The bed was so close to the heavily-carpeted floor that even if you fell from it you would strain no muscle. No doubt Marie too was living like the tigress millionaire who, just this very morning, had held a gun on me.

"This is your room, Marie. And it's smart. Why am I here if I may ask?" I said, just to try to stop looking like a fool and out of place. For an answer she pushed me toward the bed and told me that she had lived longer in the house and I shouldn't pretend to know who lived where.

"Just make yourself comfortable, Wamathina. Have some good rest while I prepare something for you to eat. Maybe after this you'll have got used to the place. Your mind will be cleared and you'll be in a position to judge good from bad, which is what I want us to discuss!"

The sight of the bed and the mention of something to eat worked wonders. I needed both badly. I felt so tired and so worked up. In the following ten minutes I was well away in dreamland.

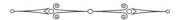

I do not know how long I had slept, but when I woke up I felt some relief, like a person who had just put down a heavy load from his shoulders. The ticking of a wall clock that came clearly to my ears made me turn to the wall behind me. It was getting to 3.55 p.m. Considering all what I had done since I left home that morning at 9.30 a.m., and the time taken by the chartered plane to get to Mombasa, I figured that I had had a good hour's rest.

I stretched from side to side, feeling the muscles and giving the body some relaxation. I knew I had missed something very important to my body but there was no time for it right now. I turned and stepped out of the bed. Then I noticed a piece of paper lying right under my nose, I got a feeling it was meant for me. I picked it and read with a smile.

A.W.

Well done! Now be good once again and walk into the bathroom right opposite you and do the necessary. When you are through and dressed up, don't bother finding your way down, just press the red button on the head of the bed.

Thanks, M.A.

As I put the note down to prepare myself, I saw some movement that almost made me run out of my skin. 'The gun, man!' my instinct told me and I went for it. It wasn't there. This was happening by reflex and it took under one second. By the time I faced the 'enemy', I realised it was nothing but my reflection in a mirror at the foot of the bed. The image that I saw behind the mirror didn't look relaxed. It looked frightened and probably afraid, and fearful to look at. Am I in a haunted house for God's sake, I found myself wondering? I started to realize that this 'thing' Aslam had handed me was nothing more than trouble. He had hinted that to me but I had not taken him seriously. There was no way I could have believed or listened to the fact with a cheque of Kshs. 300,000.00 in my hands and a beautiful daughter under my undivided care. Like a fool, I hadn't stopped to consider why Aslam was willing to part with such a big amount of money and offer a good commission for the sale of the trophy that I was supposed to retrieve from a neighbouring country. There were so many things that came into my mind now which I should have considered before I accepted to have anything to do with the whole affair. It was too late now, especially because I already had spent part of the money I was supposed to use while on the job. How would I pay back the money except by doing the job?

I stepped out of the bedroom fifteen minutes later. I was fully dressed because I had found, inside the large bathroom, some light clothes Marie had selected for me and placed on a specially-constructed stone table. I didn't press the button as instructed by the note. Instead I opened the door leading to the verandah, through which I saw the stairs leading to the living room. I stepped out and went down the stairs.

The first thing I noticed was that Marie had disconnected the telephone. She had simply picked the mouth piece and put it beside its cradle, which meant that whoever called would find it engaged throughout. This was the only way available to her to put off the anonymous callers.

"Good morning, madam!" I joked when she appeared from the kitchen. She looked startled but immediately composed herself. With a smile she came to where I was seated.

"Hello . . . it's afternoon. You look yourself now. How are you feeling?"

"Swell. And you? If you asked me, I'd surprise you by telling you that I am now looking at the real Marie Aslam. I almost didn't recognize you at the airfield." She laughed in what I thought was agreement.

"I wish you knew what your presence here in this room means to me. I feel like I've been released from some kind of prison. Two more days here alone and I'd have been nutters."

"I do understand and I am very sorry about it. The whole affair is very scaring," I admitted to her surprise.

"Wamathina, I want us to discuss this thing very seriously. This is the principal reason why I called you. We may find ourselves regretting things too late and this would leave us blaming ourselves throughout our lives. Dad's life is more important to me than the whole of heaven and earth combined. I wouldn't give away his life for anything. And I have a very strong feeling that unless we are careful, this is going to happen. I have been receiving those threatening calls and I happen to know how bad they can be. You listened to only one before you went to rest and your reaction was that of a confused person. You even thought you knew the caller. Just imagine the feeling you would have after a dozen such calls."

Well, she had a point. While in the bathroom some minutes back, I had thought back to the whole day's events up to the time I took the phone in this residence. The picture of the man forming in my memory had become clear. It was the man in the booth at Wilson Airport. The man I had thought of as being curt and rude for calling two consecutive numbers while ignoring my presence. He had called a number which I had thought was familiar in my memory. Now I had no doubt about it: it was Marie's number he had called.

In the living room after a heavy lunch, which was taken around 4.15 p.m., I gave Marie the whole story. I was glad that she understood why I had looked like I was sleep-walking when she led me upstairs. Understanding though didn't help bring her worrying to an end.

She was not interested in anything more than convincing me to give up everything for the sake of her father's life. She wanted the two of us to overrule the old man's decision and give the briefcase to the callers. But which callers, I asked myself? From the little I had learned from Mrs. Wicks, this chase had been going on for some time and there were several groups involved. Even from Aslam's own mouth we had gathered as much. But Marie wouldn't listen to that kind of argument.

"I am sure, Adams, that the moment we hand over the documents to any group involved the others will get to know and they'll now go after each other. Let us not argue about this, Wamathina. It is a matter of life and death – my father's death. Do you realize that I have no other living relative I know apart from my dad? If that one has to go, I'd rather go with him. Adams, you have been very good ever since you rescued my dad. You have even gone a step further and identified two suspects, Mrs. Wicks and this other man. But where does that get us? Can you say that if you put the two out of the way Dad will not be in trouble?"

I shook my head without talking and listened.

"Well, at least it's good that we agree on that fact," she resumed.

"Let me ask you another question, Adams, and please do not feel insulted. I have given the whole thing enough thought and consideration. Do you see anybody, even the toughest security officers, standing between my dad and a bullet? Even if they are promised the whole world, none can dare do that. No one can give his life for another. Or do you know of one who could do that?" Again, I shook my head in agreement. My argument that I had spent part of the money I was given by her father so as to do the job and that I couldn't pay back didn't make her change her mind at all.

"That's peanuts to my father, Wamathina. Dad is a multi-millionaire and it beats me why he's risking his life for a few more millions. This is why I sometimes think this sinister thing is not what Dad told us it was — a piece of diamond worth eighty million shillings. That one is a pure lie. I am sure my father cannot risk his life for that kind of money ..."

"What do you think it is, Marie?" I cut her short. "The rich want to get richer every day. It must be something strange though. Those others I know to be running after the same thing are millionaires too. Again, according to your father, there are several governments that are interested. Why? Yet from what he told us, he is the rightful owner of the trophy or treasure or whatever you want call it. He has the documents to prove this. It has the code name MABA, which translates into your father's and grandfather's full names, Mohammed Aslam bin Aslam. Why? And you want us to overrule your father and give up the documents! If we did that, it might be the end of him and whatever wealth he has. He does not look like a person who does not know what to touch and what not to. You know, Marie, you are putting me in a very awkward position. In the first place, I do not want to see you suffering. The way you are reacting to this thing might easily give you a nervous breakdown. Then there's your father who trusted me with this thing, including you too, for he is up to now afraid for your life. He believes you are likely to get into trouble, being his only child, which has proved true, so he asks me to take care of you as well. And here you are now, Marie, convincing me to disregard all your father asked me to do and instead give away the documents. Do you see the position ... my position? Put yourself in my boots. I am certain, Marie, that even if we gave up those documents your father would still be in trouble. It is my belief that if most of those who are after the documents knew that they were no longer in your father's hands, he'd have been in a grave by now."

"Why?" she asked. I could see my argument was convincing her bit by bit, but at the same time she appeared to be getting more afraid.

"If you can remember, I told you this afternoon that whoever shot at your dad must have known that he no longer has the documents." She nodded her head and appeared very attentive. "... they say that dead men tell no tales. With your father out of the way, his mouth is sealed for good and the secret he knows remains secret. Even without the documents, your father still knows too much about the whole thing to be considered safe by the guys at the top. Most of those running after this thing and those making anonymous calls to you, are watchdogs, like I am to your father. We are what you hear referred to as *'Watu Wa Mkono'* in Kiswahili - WWM. That is, people to be used by those with the money All the WWMs have been instructed by their masters to use whatever means possible to get the documents from your father, one Mohammed Aslam." I was surprised to see lines of laughter draw on Marie's lips. Perhaps it had something to do with my admission about being among the WWMs.

"In this case Marie, it is unthinkable for a *Mtu Wa Mkono* to go shooting your Dad unless he has acquired the documents, which we both are certain they haven't. We are also aware that one of those after the 'trophy' knows the documents have been handed over to me, and you can as well guess who that is. What I do not know for certain is whether the latter is working on her own or she is but a powerful MWM. She is a very rich lady and has her own WWMs, but I seem to think she's acting for more powerful persons. Fortunately for me, the lady loves me and wants me to work with her on this thing. I am therefore certain she wouldn't let loose the secret that the documents are in my possession. She could do anything to protect that, including assassinating your father. So far I know, I have her guarantee of security although I cannot let her know I know it. She believes I am good and that I could possibly do a nice job, but she is also certain that I cannot do without some kind of backup. The problem is she is aware I can never work with those criminals of hers. She knows I am a freewheeler who sticks to my beliefs and convictions. So she has to give her backup secretly."

Marie nodded. I was happy she was now following the meaning of whatever I was saying.

"... So Marie, what we should be discussing here now is what we are going to do about this chase and not how we should do away with it. Once we are on the run, the whole world behind this will come after us, and the faster we do it, the better the chances for your dad. Throwing the documents to the wolves is throwing your dad to the wolves as well ..."

"What if we gave him back the key and you told him that through your investigation you have found out that this case cannot ...?"

"You want to know my frank answer to that? I guess you want me to tell him I have failed or something close to that." She nodded and said 'yes' sotto voce. "What he'd likely do is close his eyes, never to open them again. Take it from me, Marie, that whichever way we look at this thing, it stinks and it is dangerous. This is one of those 'devil's alternative' kind of thing. The safety of your father – and he seemed to know it – will only come when this deal is over. By then this evil-looking secret will have been so blown up by the press that there'll be no more need for fear. It will by then be simply top public talk. That will also be the time all WWMs will know what they were killing for, me and you included." That one amused her and I was glad to see her smile in agreement.

"Are we together now or do I need to continue?" For an answer she let out a sigh of relief, stretched her body to flex her muscles and faced me.

"I was convinced that the only way out was to give up everything, but now I can see things from your point of view. Let me say that you have convinced me, but how do we go about it? Where do we start and when?"

"Marie dear, I do not know," I said frankly. Then it crossed my mind that I knew. In the first place I had everything that counted in the case. Secondly, our aim was not to go hunting for those who wanted Aslam dead or to bring them to book, but to go for the trophy and hand it over to Aslam. My answer was wrong and Marie needed to be told the truth. I turned to her.

"I am sorry, Marie. It has just come to my mind that I know from where and when to start." I paused to light a cigarette for the first time since I left Nairobi. I let out rings of smoke and watched it find its way out of the living room. "I do not want to put you into this but I have to go with you to get the briefcase from the hotel. After that I want to find you a nice place where I'll leave you while I take off. A place where the anonymous callers won't reach you. I'll keep in touch and advice you when I need any help. As to where and when to start, the first step will be to get the introduction letter. Immediately the lot is in my hands, I will take off for Tanzania. I want you to make arrangements for this place. Find a person you can trust and hand over everything to whoever he or she is. Take only what you think necessary during the period you'll be away. During that period, which should last about two weeks, you'll be visiting your father from Nairobi. When you cannot make it you'll only need to call the hospital and you'll be furnished with whatever you want to know. Are we together?"

"Yes. I already have a person to take care of this place. We have a good number of family friends who are always willing to help, so that is no problem. The only thing I feel you have not decided wisely is about leaving me behind. I can be of great assistance to you, Adams. If I cannot do much, at least I can give you company. And I am a good driver, for your information." I inhaled again and looked her in the eyes. She appeared quite serious about it. I wouldn't have minded her company. Indeed it would have been a great idea, but I had a feeling that going with her would double my work. I had reasons to believe my opponents were ruthless people who'd go as far as kidnapping her and asking for a ransom, which I was sure would be the introduction letter which I wasn't about to part with. What would follow after this was inestimable.

"Marie, your father is right now in hospital with bullet wounds. We cannot leave him without the person he loves most, you. If he happened to hear that you were out and had accompanied me, he'd worry himself to death- He knows too well how dangerous this mission is. And do you realize that if those enemies wanted to get the letter from me the easiest way to do it would be to kidnap you and demand it as ransom?"

I watched as her face became ashen with the prospect. Then my attention shifted to what needed to be done before leaving for the mission. I had only two days.

CHAPTER FOUR

June 23th, 1997. It was, I remember very clearly, a Saturday. The Pajero glided on the road at high speed, like an aircraft on a runway getting set to take off. Behind the wheel was Miss Marie Aslam. She drove like she intended to prove a point. She was indeed a very good driver.

The engine was humming almost noiselessly even at those high speeds. The inside of the vehicle was very cool despite all the windows being closed. I looked at the speedometer and saw that Marie was doing 145 to 150 KPH very comfortably. I felt relaxed enough to break the long silence that had built up after a long discussion.

"I admire the way you drive. In most cases I feel very uncomfortable when being driven, somehow thinking I am the only careful driver. Do you ever feel that way?"

She laughed a bit and cast me a sideways glance. She was in a jolly mood which made the journey to Nairobi an easy and enjoyable one.

"Well, you can now guess why I volunteered to drive. It wasn't to prove I could do it; I just wanted to feel safe. If there are two people who get uneasy while being driven I am one of them. Unfortunately fatigue is catching up with my muscles. I'll be forced to like your driving, like you've been forced to like mine."

"I am serious, Marie ..."

"I'm also serious, Wamathina," she quipped and chuckled a little.

"Who said I'll drive, anyway? I am about to have a nap," I told her, as I shifted a bit to get more comfortable, then closed my eyes. I adjusted the seat and pushed it a little backwards.

"You can't be serious, Adams. That'd be punishing me and I'd soon ditch the vehicle. May I ask you a question?"

"Most welcome. Go ahead," I said, my eyes still closed.

"I want to see your eyes when you answer. Sit up please. P-l-e-s-e!" I readjusted the seat and opened my eyes wide.

"Thanks, you are very obedient. I like you for that."

"It's not a matter of obedience, Marie, but curiosity. Have you not learnt that I am a very curious chap who will once face the same fate as the cat?"

She had to step on the brake pedal slightly to kill the speed so as to gain road control as she burst out laughing. I smiled knowingly. Women liked hearing about their menfolk's weaknesses so as to capitalize on them. It was great to have a light moment after what she had gone through, so I didn't mind looking like Bogi Benda or Juha Kalulu, the popular cartoon strip characters, for the time being.

"I think I already know that," Marie countered amid peals of laughter, "that's why it sounded so funny to me to hear you admit it. Do you know that you make one want to know more about you? I think you appear strange even to those who know you." That reminded me of Mrs. Wicks whom I did not want to think about at this stage. The tigress had managed to instil some kind of inexplicable fear in me, which I had had to fight with plenty of willpower. She was a very dangerous woman who would stop at nothing to get whatever she needed. In my estimation, the possibility of her being a Mafia Godfather or Godmother or whatever other titles existed for crime grandmasters was very high.

There was nothing as dreadful as a person who could pull the trigger without second thoughts and that was the type of boys Mrs. Wicks hired. They did not need to know why your life should be terminated as long as their master or mistress said it should. That knowledge and fear was however not going to stop me from pursuing my star. I didn't know whether my grandma meant that I should go after it through such risks or whether it would still shine even if I stayed at home. But I had a feeling that if it was really going to shine, it wasn't likely to find me asleep. What had surprised me as days passed by was that whenever I thought of my grandmother and her words about my star, I found myself caressing the talisman she had put around my neck. Like this very moment on our way to Nairobi, which action attracted Marie's attention.

"I have always wanted to ask you, Adams: what is this thing you hang round your neck? I have seen you on several occasions touching it lovingly. You are a strange man ..."

"Is that why you made me wake up, I wonder? If that is why, then you are. . ."

"No please, I am sorry. You seem very eager to have your nap, but I am not going to allow that under any cost. My question was ..." she hesitated. "I think it's a little personal. Do you mind?"

"I don't," I said. "I have nothing to hide my dear girl."

"Thanks. Is it true that you were that lady's driver? Were you the personal driver or were you ...?" I had not expected that kind of question, but since I had promised her I'd answer, I went ahead.

"Well, yes. I was her personal driver. What of it?"

"There wasn't anything more than that? I mean, you do not look like you ..."

"There's something you are driving at, Marie, but it looks to me like you'll go round and round before you come to it. What makes you doubt that fact?"

"The address you left at the hospital, and then when I came to the hotel. You remember how it was booked, I mean under whose names?"

"Yes, under Mr. and Mrs. Adams Wamathina," I said curtly. "Ask me *why*."

"No, that's simple. It could be for hundreds of reasons. But tell me, were you living together?"

"Yes, and not only that. We were also sharing the same bed. I think that takes care of everything. Only don't ask me what was happening at night because I wouldn't talk about it."

This time Marie had to stop and park at the roadside to laugh herself dry, which gave me time to answer a call of nature.

"Give me a hand, please," she told me when I was back. "I've done over two hundred kilometres non-stop. I promise not to pry into your private life again."

"I don't have a private life, Marie. That one is now a thing of the past," I told her, then wondered why I felt I should let her know.

"You are a funny chap, Adams. You always don't seem to agree with others ..."

"Not really. Have I ever told you of my past? I think I have not. You may be taking me for one great hero just because I happen to carry a gun which is not normal in our society, or because you think I am a good driver who normally drives big cars. But it has never occurred to you that I get nothing out of all that. What is there to gain out of having a license to carry a gun? Or out of driving a Pajero like this one, or your father's Benz which up to now is at my residence, or being chauffeur to a millionaire lady who turns out to be some kind of a criminal? Just tell me, where's my life leading to? I am only a tool, just like a hammer or a chisel or a comb. It's great to have a beautiful lady like you beside me, a most beautiful rich lady who is free with me, and ... well ...so loving. But where does that get me?

"Let's imagine something, Marie. Suppose your dad decides to give up this whole affair, takes the key from me and flings it into the ocean. Do you imagine what would happen after that? There would be total darkness for me. Assume even that he doesn't ask me to give back the cheque whose money is already half spent. That'd be great, but I'd have lost my job on which all my hopes in life are based. Two, he'd expect me to hand over the Merc which I am already used to and which my wife and I treat as ours. That would be a great setback since I cannot afford to buy even a secondhand Volkswagen. I'd be forced to get back to the criminal lady whom I now treat as a danger to my life. Out of want, I would be forced to accept some of her black deals that would inevitably lead to trouble if they backfired. I hate trouble."

"Do you get what I mean? *Private life!* When trouble strikes, private life ceases to exist. You are thrown into prison where there's no privacy, where what you call private life is extinct. I know you have never given it a thought, but imagine you are in a place where you are forced to strip naked in front of over five hundred people. You do not have a single thing on you. You are forced to jump up with your hands above your head and between every three jumps, you bend and touch the floor with your arms straight and legs astride. Then, when you get out of the cage, you emerge to face poverty. You come to meet the suspicious eyes of society. You are forced to socialize only with your type, for every other person who doesn't fit into your category tends to be an enemy, very unfriendly and completely uninterested in whatever you might be worth.

"Have you ever wound up the windows of your car when you saw a poor person come towards you? Give me a frank answer."

"Yes, every driver does that. I mean you don't wait. . ."

"Don't explain. There's no better reason than that you are avoiding him. You don't treat him like a normal human being created by the same God who created you, or born of a woman like you and your relatives. In most cases the person is just crossing the road because a chance to do so has availed itself. In most cases he doesn't even notice you because his mind is on his safety. If he happens to glance at you he may only be admiring your luck, but to you its pure hatred and lack of understanding.

"Have you ever stopped to think that such people notice your actions, the hatred and the demeaning of their values as human beings? What do you think such a person feels and concludes about people like you?

"This is why, Marie, whenever there's any little misunderstanding in the city, such people gang up and become one – to react aggressively towards the rich. That is normally the only time they get a chance to express themselves, sending a message to you of the upper class that if you wish them to be cooperative and friendly you should accept them the way they are."

"Just tell me," Marie asked, her tone rather accusing, "what would you do if you saw a person like that approaching and you didn't know who he was, what he had in mind and what he'd do to you in case . . ."

I had to smile because I wasn't in a mood to laugh. *How ignorant you are, Marie!* "I thought."

"Marie, you may believe me or not. But whenever I see such a person, if my window is closed, I open it and salute him. The response is normally so good that you feel happy and are grateful that you saluted them. When you say you do not know who he is, what he' has in mind and what he'd do to you and the like, don't you see that you have really given yourself the answer?"

"How? What answer?"

"I'll pose another question, and please give a frank answer, as it will answer your questions. If the same person were putting on a very expensive suit, a nice necktie, a nice pair of shoes, he was clean-shaven and looked very neat, would you bother closing the window?"

She thought for about ten seconds then spoke.

"I think I wouldn't ..."

"Well, there's your answer. Does being well-dressed tell you who the person is, what he has in mind and what he'd do to you? And do not forget that this is the same person. You are not afraid of him just because he happens to be smart. So, simply, what you do not like is the poverty of the poor man and not his person. A poor man of course cannot afford good and expensive clothes. Your reaction to him is the same as you'd get on seeing a dog or a beast coming your way. Just fancy that."

"The gap between the poor and the rich is brought about by the rich, by the way they behave towards the poor. If the rich would be kind to the poor, not by giving them what they have but by simply showing them sympathy, you'd be looking at and living in a most wonderful world … exactly what its Creator had in mind."

I drove on in silence for a long stretch. Marie seemed to be wandering far away from the co-driver's seat. I decided to interrupt her again,

"Well Marie. I guess you now see very clearly where your hero belongs. I was fished out of that very lonely class of people by the millionairess so as to serve her, and from the way things are moving, it appears I am soon getting back there. Don't pity me, because I am used to it. I haven't enjoyed this kind of life for one year. I guess you have also noticed that I haven't got used to it. I hesitate stepping on a carpet, and it is with great courage that I do not kick off my shoes. I am even at times ashamed of using these basin toilets in millionaire-class residences. I belong to that class where we refer to ourselves as 'standing corpses' – corpses that are waiting for just a slight shove to fall on the ground where we belong. Worse still..."

"STOP!!" Marie suddenly screamed. By reflex, I stepped on the emergency brakes and pulled the vehicle to the side. Before I pushed the gear into neutral, I had a gun in hand.

"What's it! Where is it?" I asked in a strained and tense voice.

Marie sat back and gave out a long sigh of relief. Her eyes were on me and the gun in my hand.

"Oh my God!" She cried out sotto voce, looking like a defeated person who had lost a game she was so sure to win. "I am sorry, Adams. I did not intend to make you stop the vehicle. It was the story. I have heard enough of the sad part of it. I got a feeling you were about to unfold the saddest part of it and I am not strong enough to stomach that much. You know you make me feel guilty … it's like you have me in mind".

"I am sorry too …" I said to her, "… I did not have you in mind at all. Remember I began with your kindness and love. I am sorry."

"Adams. Please, do not regard yourself as such. You are ..."

"Let's forget about it Marie. You like me, that's all there is to it.

But that wouldn't change the truth. I have accepted this risky job because I want to kick poverty out of my environment, out of my system ... and this is why I am determined to win, because if I lose, I'll have lost myself. Did you note the speed with which I drew the gun?" I asked.

"I find it difficult to believe it wasn't in your hand in the first place. I was badly shaken, you know I am not used to ..."

"Never mind that, dear girl. That's the speed of a hungry chameleon. It has to flash out its tongue like lightning if it is to catch a fly. Note: the chameleon is known for its slowness and the fly for its swiftness. The chameleon has to counter those facts if it is to survive. So have I. Before my grandma died, she prophesied ..."

"You have told me that before, Adams. It is about your star, I guess."

"Yes, I am sorry,"

Marie put her right hand on my left thigh to console me. I drove on silently, deep in thought.

CHAPTER FIVE

Friday 29 June.

I kissed Eva goodbye, took my safari bag and got out of the house. I was all set to get out of the country. Fortunately for me, the East African states had just cemented their unity and I was as such assured of an easy pass to Tanzania.

"I wish you success, darling," Eva started as she hugged me for a goodbye, "be in peace wherever you go. I'll pray for you ..."

"Same mistake a second time, dear. Have I ever told you the story of the squirrel?"

"No. What has it to do with me or your going?" Eva asked.

"Let me tell it to you because it might help you in future. It is a story of the squirrel and the farmer. It always happens when planting time comes. The farmer plants maize and calls it a day. Immediately he leaves his farm the squirrel comes and digs up the maize and eats one after the other in a line. He does this during the day because he goes to sleep at night. So the farmer gets wise and after replanting he decides to hang around till darkness closes in. The squirrel, sensing no movements, gets out and heads for the first seed. From his hiding place the farmer throws a weapon which misses the swift squirrel, which runs away to its hiding place. Just two minutes later, the squirrel thinks, 'Well, the farmer thinks he is smart! I am now sure he is tired of waiting; he cannot be there since yesterday.' He gets out, only to be surprised that the farmer has not even sat down. He runs off again, but another minute later he is back in the field. Get me? Exactly like you!"

"Where do I come in for God's sake?" She asked, surprised.

"Well, it has to do with the squirrel's poor memory. Can't you see that? It forgets what it has seen and heard in two minutes. When I came looking for a job at Mrs. Wicks' place you intended to pray for me to get one. What did I tell you?" She remembered, and as she burst out laughing, I closed the door behind me. I could feel her eyes on my back as I drove out of the gate.

'PRAYERS WOULDN'T CHANGE THINGS, DON'T YOU THINK SO SON OF FATE?'

'I do,' I answered not sure who had asked me the question.

Marie was waiting for me at the Panafric Hotel where she had been staying since Tuesday. She had just finished her breakfast and was now busy perusing a local newspaper.

"How is Son of Fate?" She saluted, standing up to shake my hand.

"Beautiful. . ." I said as our hands locked excitedly "... and how are you? Eight hours only and I was already missing you, knowing that you were only a fifteen-minutes drive from me. Eva said Hi."

"Thanks. She's such a nice lady. You are a lucky boy, Adams and so is Eva. I envy her."

She appeared serious alright. I didn't know what to say after that. I wasn't used to flattery if that was what her statement was meant to be.

"Am I keeping you waiting?" She asked after a while. Five minutes later we left.

Marie wasn't giving me an easy time. Not that she was demanding … no. She was, like Mrs. Wicks, a rich lady who had everything she could dream of. But you couldn't compare her with Mrs. Wicks on anything else other than that. Marie was born with a golden spoon in her mouth, unlike Mrs. Wicks who had been adopted after probably having had a hard time. Marie had self-discipline and self-respect which became clear upon looking at her. She was not the least proud of what she was – a daughter of a multi-millionaire who could drive herself to school at the age of sixteen and who had had sleek cars at her disposal ever since.

Her hair was naturally beautiful, the type which needed no chemicals to look good. It was long and black and was easily styled the way she pleased. Like her father Aslam, she had a soft-looking body with the browness of an Arab and no signs of pimples or sunburn on the skin. Her height, slightly above five and a half feet, went along beautifully with her body which carried a slightly thin waist that produced the most beautiful back you ever saw. Looking at her made me wonder why she never thought of contesting for the Miss Kenya or probably Miss Africa title. I didn't know much of what they looked for in such contests though. I remember meeting a Miss Fatuma who was then Miss Africa, but she wasn't anywhere near Marie's beauty. To my eyes, here was Princess Cleopatra.

I was getting the impression that Marie was in love with me. Yes, though she was trying not to be open, at times she'd forget and betray her feelings. This was giving me a hard time because everytime it happened, my thoughts would find their way to Eva. But I didn't have the courage to put her off. She had met Eva on several occasions and the two had adored each other. I hoped she'd bear this in mind and make it easier for me. She was admirable and the more I stayed with her, the closer and freer with each other we became. However, the prospect of the relationship turning emotional was scaring.

After parking right opposite the Norfolk Hotel where we found an empty space, Marie waited for me at the roadside so that we could cross the road to the hotel together. A few metres away was the main campus of the University of Nairobi. Three ladies carrying some files passed by and as they did so, they all eyed me after one of them spoke to the rest. I thought I vaguely heard my name mentioned. I wondered how any of them would know me, especially by name, since I didn't have any genuine friends or relatives after the death of my beloved grandmother. I concluded it could be just another Mumbi – the puffadder I had met in a certain bar who turned out to be my niece – and immediately dismissed them. I did not want anything to do with anybody who could remind me of family relationships after my own brothers disowned me when I left prison. I wanted to lead a lonely life without being lonely. I had Eva who, to me, was everything.

Marie was at her best. I never saw a lady so beautifully dressed like she was today. She also seemed to be in a very jovial mood this particular morning and she cracked jokes every other minute. She seemed to have noticed the exchange between the three ladies as they passed by. She grabbed my hand and pulled me closer to her.

"I wont let go of this hand, man. I feel afraid you might be robbed from me by those beauties who are eyeing you. I don't trust them just as I don't trust you. You are a womanizer, you know that? You deny it! You are a real hit with women, which makes you a very dangerous man. You would make me die of jealously were you in my purse." *What a thing to say,* I thought as we crossed the road.

"Well, well," I said with a short laugh, "I have never heard that before today and I didn't know I was a womanizer. What a shame! I'll have to apply myself before I lose all. But..." I said after a pause, "I have a feeling you do not know me well enough. Unless maybe, I have the wrong interpretation of the word womanizer. You know what it means?"

Her answer came without hesitation: "Simple ... a man who attracts women, or a man who makes women fall in love on sight."

"Wrong! You are wrong, Marie. A womanizer is a man who runs after women, or who pursues women for casual sex. Get that. I am very far from being that!"

That revelation almost made her good mood run aground. "I am sorry, Adams. Christ! What a thing to say of you!" She gripped my arm harder, apologetically. "Please do forgive me. I am so sorry, I didn't know how to put it. I thought ..."

I had to interrupt her: "Take it easy. Your interpretation of the word was intended to flatter me. We are not English to know every vocabulary in the dictionary!" I squeezed her hand, and with much effort, restrained myself from kissing her. It was in my mind to do so because apart from liking and admiring her, that was the thing most likely to console her. She seemed to read that in my eyes which must have given me away. With a blush she told me.

"It's okay, I understand. You are so good to me, Adams. I am quite okay with you ... please know that and keep it in mind. Okay?"

"Okay ... and thanks. You are also good to me."

We were now inside the five-star hotel. I entered the manager's office with Marie close behind me. I felt proud to have her beside me. Love of beauty of whatever kind is a common weakness in the human race and I am no exception.

I noticed that the manager, though he welcomed me warmly and gave me a hearty grip during hand shakes, eventually landed his eyes on Marie after giving me a lengthy glance.

"You are most welcome. I am Collins Baraza," said the heavily built man who looked every inch a manager. He looked the type that managed with an iron grip which could be the reason why this hotel, which happened to be one of the oldest in this capital city, had not lost its glory. His demeanor however didn't mean much to me. He wasn't my boss and I was certain there would be no time I would fall under his wrath, or his dragonic fire, if that was what he exhaled.

"She's Marie Aslam ..." I began by introducing her because up to now his eyes were on her. To put him off her I added a simple lie, "... my fianceé. I am Adams Wamathina."

The trick did it. His eyes relaxed and he invited us to take seats.

"It's a pleasure meeting you. What can I do for you?" Now he seemed to be in a hurry, maybe after realizing that Marie was not an open case.

For an answer I took out the introduction note Aslam had given me and handed it over to him. After reading it he looked up with a smile. Turning to Marie he said, "Your father is my friend. How is he doing?"

Marie gave me a quick glance which was enough to read my face. I did not want her to give the true state of her father and she seemed to understand.

"Dad is okay. He asked me to convey his warmest regards. He has been away for some weeks." I didn't know she was that good at telling a lie, but that was exactly what I'd have loved her to say.

"Thank you. No wonder he has been so quiet. Well, give me a minute." From a drawer in the executive desk he took a key and left the room for an inner one. About five minutes later he re-emerged with a brief case in his hand.

I'd have thanked him, grabbed the briefcase and left to study the documents and whatever else was inside from the safety of Marie's room at the Panafric Hotel, but I remembered in time some advice my grandfather had given me. He was long dead, but his words have lingered in my memory ever since. He had cautioned me never to carry a parcel of whatever kind without knowing with certainty what I was carrying. "Fools carry explosives on their backs just because they do not stop to think. If you were asked what you were carrying inside a bag in your hands and you cannot answer, or when you do answer you say you do not know, why shouldn't you get arrested? People, my son, have turned beasts, They use others to make their ends meet. When you are caught in the act the master doesn't know you any longer. Let anything you are to do remain suspicious until you prove yourself wrong. During the Man Mau struggle for freedom we used to smuggle ammunition from towns to the forest using ignorant messengers. Women would be given baskets containing what they thought was packed food. But right at the centre of the packets was ammunition. We'd use different methods with the men. Be wise, son. A little curiosity is not dangerous, but helpful".

I therefore took out the key from where I had hid it and, disregarding his gestures of a person with plenty to do, opened the briefcase. The code Aslam had given me was very clear in my mind. Marie came closer as I took out a long and wide sheet of paper which carried the map of where in particular the trophy could be found. It indicated the shortest way from all directions, through the border to the point marked with black ink – an oval-shaped large spot with lines running downwards. I remember having a quick glance at the route from Kenya and mentally marked the border post. On the sketch, it didn't seem like a long journey. I was about to fold it and put it back when Marie took it from my hands. She appeared more interested than I was.

I next took out an envelope that was addressed to a Mr. Assanad Karim bin Saiga. That, I thought, was the introduction letter. So I put it back, telling myself I'd read it later. A second envelope, which I tore off, carried a small card, cut diagonally. It had a message that I couldn't read even were the other half available. To me this was a coded message. I pushed it over to Marie and commented that it was a 'gorilla script,' which made her laugh. My attention then shifted to another document which had interested me but, like with the card, I did not understand a single thing in it. I put it back. There would be plenty of time to study them, I thought.

We left the office ten minutes later. The manager didn't bother showing us out, which aroused my curiosity. Outside I commented on his behaviour.

"Well, my dear fianceé, you surely met a typical womanizer behind that door. It was all in his eyes. Did you feel it?"

"I wish you were in my boots to know how embarrassed I felt. How could he show it that openly? I am your fianceé." She chuckled a little then added, "... I wish that were so."

This comment took me off guard. How could she say that? Was she serious? Funny enough, deep inside I found myself thinking along the same lines, a thing that had never happened since I married Eva.

"Are you aware we are carrying a bombshell with us?" I asked Marie as we approached the outer gate, heading for our parking.

"In form of?" She asked, apparently not understanding what I meant.

"Well, the briefcase. This is what is killing your dear dad. I hope it won't kill us. Do you realize now that the mission is on?"

"You are talking in riddles, Adams," she said

"I am talking about the chase. It is on. There's no turning back now."

Her face told me that she still didn't understand. I was forced to explain because it just then occurred to me that after getting possession of the briefcase, like she had commented, I had changed from talking openly to something close to using Jesus' parables.

The weather outside was fine. There was a coolness that touched your body, opening up the nostrils to fresh air in gulps, which made the blood feel relaxed. That was the feeling shared by Marie and I as we stepped out of Norfolk. It was still early and we had plenty to do together before we parted. I intended to send her to 'my' office, WICKS & WAYNE, to spy on what might be going on there. I wanted to know whether Mrs. Wicks was still around and to find out how whoever would be in the office would behave if one asked to see the M.D., who was supposed to be me upto this moment.

"I still insist we go together, Adams," Marie told me as we waited to cross the road "... imagine that long journey all alone. You'll be very lonely and you will leave me lonely. Going to stay with your wife will not solve the problem between us. We can go out to pass time, visit all the parks and wherever else there is fun, but the problem is both our minds will all be on you."

I seemed to notice some unusual movement around the hotel. Rather, I thought it was not usual because I had not been to this hotel before to know what was usual and what was not. Whatever it was, my instincts told me something was wrong somewhere. It was funny that although Marie was right beside me and still talking, I didn't catch a single word of what she said. My eyes were moving around suspiciously. I was trying to make up the shadow that used to haunt me and which I suspected had to be Stranger, Janet's senior MWM. I noticed two ladies crossing the road from the opposite side, right in front of us. My interest wasn't in them, but rather some gentlemen deep in discussion just a few steps away. What surprised me was that when we stepped out of the hotel just under a minute ago they had not been there. Maybe they were not up to anything as they didn't appear interested in us, but appearing not interested didn't mean they were not.

Marie went a step ahead to cross immediately a vehicle which was a few metres from us passed. The driver let the two ladies cross to our side. The next thing I knew one of the ladies was wrestling with my left hand which held the briefcase. The second gave me a push and with this, the briefcase was gone.

I reacted immediately I regained balance.

I gave chase but just three steps ahead I bumped into the chest of a heavy gentleman who seemed to have just grown from the ground right in front of my path. "Sorry, sir. It's those ladies ..." I apologized. But he didn't let me finish what I was saying. Instead he grabbed me by the collar and started calling me names. I did not mind it because all my life was riveted on the two ladies who were about to enter the very vehicle which had stood in our way as we had been about to cross.

'SONNY BOY - REACT!'

It was my comforter who always came whenever I was in a black spot. I never once argued with him; I reacted. The size of my opponent didn't matter. My martial arts instructor had always reminded me that the bigger they are, the harder they fall. After all, this hulk of a man holding me didn't know what to expect from a person so small in comparison. I had to hit hard if I was to expect good results. With my two hands I gave the bulldozer two double chops on both sides of his tummy, which made him jump off the ground in pain and disbelief. The moment he touched ground I gave him a jab and finished it off with a snap kick, to the surprise of the crowd that had gathered in a matter of seconds.

By then the two girls were about to enter the opened doors of the Nissan Sunny twenty metres away. There was no option. I drew my gun, already cocked, and aimed at the lady with the brief case. I was about to pull the trigger when I was grabbed from behind by a screaming lady. The bullet went off but missed the target. When I turned I saw it was Marie who had held me. I almost slapped her but I held back with much strain. She realised this and immediately started crying. This touched me and I had to hold her. She rested her head on my chest while I held her back with my right hand still holding the gun which was still smoking.

The man I had hit had woken up, dusted himself and vanished into the big crowd. A minute later the police arrived from Central Police Station which was only a few metres away. I took out my private cop's badge which a police chief inspector grabbed and looked at. He ordered his subordinates who had guns trained on me to relax. Giving me back my badge, he requested me to accompany him to the station for a statement.

We took close to thirty minutes at the police station. The Chief Inspector had good enough respect for what I was, but he was very suspicious. It was with much effort that I managed to convince him that there was nothing of importance that was robbed.

"You know, Mr. Adams, I have been in the crime office for over twenty years and I have never had a story where ladies robbed a man. In most cases they go for conning. From what I gather it is apparent they were waiting for you. It is like they expected you to come out of the hotel carrying the briefcase. Then, what makes it even more curious is the fact that you are a private investigator with a licence to carry a gun and to use it just like me or any other police officer."

"I do not know why you private investigators do not trust the police, though I would understand the pressure comes from your clients who may not want to involve the police."

"But ... eh, eh ... I think that we should understand that whenever there is an investigation to be done by whatever party, there is most likely a crime committed or one about; to be committed, and this is why I strongly feel we people should work hand in hand."

"Like this man who blocked you ... he must have been a member of the gang, otherwise he shouldn't have vanished into thin air after what took place. Then there is this car which blocks you and gives way to the two ladies who go ahead and rob you, then enter the same car ... The whole thing stinks, but since you have your client here ..." He smiled as he gestured towards Marie. He was right of course, but I was not going to give him the whole story. In any case, he wasn't likely to be of any assistance because the only thing I would have liked was to get back the documents, and that wasn't likely to happen.

I was mad about the whole thing and all I wanted right now was to go to sonic place and rest, rest as much as I could before I took the next step which up to this moment was unknown to me.

We drove straight to Panafric Hotel where I followed Marie to her room. I hadn't opened my mouth throughout the ten minutes it took us to get to this place. I was so worked up and I wasn't happy with Marie, and she seemed to have realized this. She ordered soft drinks which were brought immediately. I lit a cigarette, lay on my back on the sofa and immediately got lost in a strange new world ... a world that seemed not to make any meaningful sense. Marie gave me plenty of time to get lost in my dreams. Then she came to where I was. She touched me on the face, then stroked my hair with her left hand, while saying something which I heard vaguely.

"I am sorry, Adams, I am really sorry. I now see what you meant." It was as if she was talking from a distance, although she had never been so close to me before. She was seated on the same sofa on which I lay facing upward. Her body was against mine from the waist upwards but I didn't feel her presence. She spoke again and this time I heard her very clearly.

"Adams, tell me please: would you have shot that lady?"

I looked at her without answering. I was so annoyed that for the second time I felt like slapping her, but again the inner part of me restrained me.

"Yes. I would have done it!" I answered, almost screaming at her, "I would have shot her without caring where the bullet got her. Do you realize what this means to me? Those two idiots have brought my life to an end. . . a dead end. All my hopes in life have gone down the drain this morning and you've contributed to it. . ."

"And you wanted to slap me ... isn't it? Would you have . . .?"

"Yes, Marie, I would have and I am sorry that I didn't. If you had listened to me in the first place, we'd be seated right here in very different circumstances. We'd be reading the map and trying to decode the messages contained in the letters. We'd be revisiting our strategies, trying to look at everything critically before embarking on the practicals. Now we have nothing to talk about but to console each other, which is as good as useless."

"I am finished, Marie. All my hopes were on your father. I was sure to get him the good results for which he had promised to pay me millions of shillings. You remember him promising me part of the millions we would fetch from what he called MABA?"

For an answer she lay her head on my chest and started sobbing loudly. My frank answers had shocked her and she didn't seem to want to believe the mess she'd caused. Between sobs, she tried to cool me down.

"He will still give you the money, Adams ... I'll make sure he does it, that he pays you for the work you have ..."

"What work?" I interrupted her, mercilessly. "What have I done to be paid for? All I have done is put him in darkness. I do not deserve any single penny from him but rather, punishment. I've lost a game I was so sure to win, Marie. Now I have no option but to go back to the woman who had given me... Well, what I mean is I'll have to go back to my office, sit tight, and make arrangements for you to get back all I owe ..."

I found I had nothing more to say. I had talked all I had for the time being and all I needed now was time to rest and think. I put one hand on Marie's back and with the other crushed the butt of the cigarette I had just finished and then started caressing the talisman my grandmother had given me. Like with a child, consolation and great hope started to permeate me. Marie was silently lying where she was without stirring. I sensed she had changed her breathing and her body had turned limp. She was in dreamland. I pushed myself back to get enough space for her on the wide seat, then pulled her up gently and lay her body comfortably on the seat with her head still on my chest and her hands round my neck. From this position I enjoyed the breath that came smoothly from her, giving me plenty of warmth which I needed right then. Minutes later I joined her in dreamland.

Some stretch later I woke up with a start, my heart thumping fast and loud. But I did not want to open my eyes. I was afraid to encounter the wild beast that was waiting for me to stir so that it would go ahead and attack me. I felt the animal's fur brush against my face once again, its claws pressed around my neck. I felt them caressing me, trying to determine whether I was alive or dead. Its chest pressed hard on mine, making sure that even if I stirred and realized I was trapped, I wouldn't have much left to do to save myself. Oh, my God! What a dreadful way to die, with so many debts unsettled! What would happen to my wife Eva and the kid who would come five months from now? What a pity that after all my struggles I wouldn't see my own seed and look after it! *Christ! Don't let me die!*

The dream came to an end when Marie sat up and shook me gently.

"Adams, what's it? You were trying to scream but the scream wouldn't come. And you were breathing so heavily that you woke me up. You pressed me against your body and almost crushed my head."

That explained everything. Marie had been the beast in my dream. It was her hair that had caused the dream when she turned her head and it massed all over my face. The realization that there was nothing to the dream consoled my mind. I sat up.

"Thank you, Marie." I said.

"What are you thanking me for?"

"For waking me up. Such dreams kill the dreamer. People have been found lying comfortably in bed – dead. No signs of strangulation or evidence of murder. From then on you waste plenty of time and money looking for a murderer who does not exist. In this world we so much love to stay, there is no rest. Not even for the richest or the most honoured. It appears God was very serious when he cursed man."

"What do you mean, Adams? God never cursed man. He created the Earth for man to inherit and to rule over everything in it. He gave him power over all the beasts and ..."

"That wasn't the argument, Marie. I never talk of anything that I haven't thought of. The earth you are talking about was cursed because of man. In His annoyance, God also cursed man. Listen to this: *"In toil you shall eat of it all the days of your life."* Do you know what toil means?"

She nodded.

"Then there you are. If you remember this, you would stop getting angry at whatever comes to block you from getting what you want or are pursuing. In my case I feel I shouldn't get angry any more at what happened to the briefcase. Instead I should be thinking of the best way to retrieve it. I think this is God's doing. He doesn't want me to get the millions your father promised me that simply. He wants me to toil! He told man that the ground would bring forth thorns and thistles. Why? So that he should labour, cutting the thorns and thistles, to make fields where he would plant food for subsistence. Those two ladies: one was a thorn and the other a thistle, and I have to cut them somehow so that I may plant and eventually harvest. Meanwhile, they are also toiling, going through their part of the curse. Risking getting shot by ..."

"Are you telling me you are not angry anymore?" Marie asked suddenly. "Not even with me?"

"My God, no! I am not angry any more. You don't get tens of millions of shillings by just driving across the border with an introduction letter, getting the trophy or whatever it is and driving back to the country and handing it over to your boss. I knew it wouldn't be that easy, just as did your father. But that does not mean I cannot get angry again. We have to get angry in life now and again, and when that happens, one cannot foretell the kind of action one might be forced to take. It was out of anger that God cursed his own image – man.

"So, let us forget whatever happened and think of toil, plan our next step. If there's any time that the idea of going with you ever made sense, it's now."

I was surprised to see Marie jump out of the seat like a child and clap her hands. She turned to face me, all her beauty coming to life. She was now staring at me with a smile that made me stand up and go to her. I opened my arms wide to take the whole of her. She came to meet me and we hugged each other. I just stopped short of kissing her.

"Thank you so much, Adams," Marie said. "I've been praying for that. I might turn out helpful in one way or another." She had her arms around my neck, looking at my eyes with her head held up. For the second time I enjoyed the breath that came out of her. I turned her head a bit and touched her left cheek with my lips.

"You are most welcome. But I'll have to coach you before we leave. You know what we should do right now?"

She shook her head. "I don't want to make the wrong guess."

"Well, I'll drive ahead while you follow close behind. We will leave your car with my wife while we explain to her the change of plan."

The shock that hit Eva on hearing that the letter of introduction, along with the entire documents, had been robbed warned me to tread carefully in future when breaking news to her.

She opened her mouth wide, covered it with her right hand which had just dropped a china cup to the floor breaking it into tiny pieces, and remained like that without a single word coming out of her mouth for almost twenty seconds. I had to rush in and hold her.

I realized immediately that like me, all her hopes of a better future were hinged on what would come out of a successful resolution of this case. I now realized it had been a terrible mistake to let her into the secret. For a long time I had learnt the hard way that whoever depended on man was a loser, in fact a total loser, because man was not predictable. Yet this time I had made the mistake of making my family depend on one man, Aslam; a man whose future was now hanging on a shoe string and who depended on God to defeat his foes. Like a fool I had had the guts to pray for him to stay alive so as to be there when I brought him MABA after which, I was certain, I'd get well paid. I had never stopped to pray for myself!

"What will you do now? Give up everything ...?" Eva asked in a beaten voice, a voice devoid of hope.

"No, Eva. Why should I? Haven't you learnt that I never hope against hope like you are doing? I get a strong kick out of unfavourable situations like this one. I now feel I want to go for the gold more than ever before. What brought us here is a slight change in the plans"

I knew I had to comfort her. I wouldn't stop until I saw her smile. When she did I knew all was over that her hopes had again been rekindled. This time they were hinged on fate rather than man.

I kissed her good-bye for a second time this hectic day, wondering whether there would be anything else to force me to come back home yet again. I watched the two ladies hug each other lovingly as they wished each other well. How reassuring this was! Here were my two greatest friends and lovers who never wasted their energies being jealous or suspicious. I was a lucky man indeed.

CHAPTER SIX

"We have a tail, Marie." I announced as we turned right to take Juja road from Outer Ring road. I heard Marie laugh a little and I wondered why she should do that.

"Where is it?" She asked jokingly.

"Two cars behind us," I said. She chuckled again and touched my left shoulder, a gesture supposed to tell me to stop making jokes where I should be serious. Suddenly I realised she did not understand what I meant.

"I am sorry, Marie .." I explained "by a tail I mean we have somebody following us. Two cars behind us. One of them is a Trooper with two occupants in the front seat. I want you to help me find out how many occupants it has in total. Stop looking behind! Use the side and the rear-view mirrors if you wish ... and don't get so worried. You were laughing just a second ago!" It was my turn to chuckle like a fool.

It turned out to be a vehicle belonging to the Undugu Society. Immediately she told me this, I pulled up and parked alongside the road. I knew the driver had recognized me and was hurrying up to catch up with me.

"Hallo! How are you doing, boys?" I saluted as I got out of the vehicle. We shook hands.

"We are doing well, sir. We were heading to the office to call your home when we saw you take the roundabout. We've been chasing you, hoping we'd ..."

"Yeah, I spotted your car following me but I couldn't make out who you were. Well, meet my friend, Marie. She's from Mombasa. I know you visit there regularly.

"Marie, these energetic boys are Foro and Muiruri from Undugu Society. I gave them some job some time back and I guess they have something for me." I turned to them. "How is the going?"

For some seconds they looked at each other. Then Muiruri spoke.

"Well, we found the PB ... He is doing very well. You know these boys are funny and they love each other very much. You remember he had snatched some money? You heard the boys from our centre mention that." I nodded in agreement. I didn't want to mention that I was around when he did it and that I even had a rough idea of the total amount he had got away with.

"... He constructed a shanty in Mathare." Again they looked at each other and chuckled a little, which told me that I was about to listen to an interesting story. Marie was very attentive and I could see her curiosity rising. Maybe she was thinking that whatever we were listening to was connected with the sinister trophy which had previously occupied all our attention.

"Don't tell me he is a landlord now," I said. I was eager to hear the story.

"He is, but a landlord for PBs only. That is the funny part. The shanty is the smartest in the area, properly roofed with old but good corrugated iron sheets, so unlike most shanties. The site is another interesting place. It is on a rocky ground, which is why the space was empty. Somehow he drilled the flat part of the rock and erected strong posts. He put up a neat and strong twenty foot square shanty without comparison. Being on such a rock, its floor is naturally plastered." Here we all laughed at the boy's ingenuity.

"Another funny thing," continued Muiruri, "he has built a shade outside which serves as a kitchen. He has two aides who cook, and the food is sold to PBs only. He also sells glue and cigarettes to the same boys. Everything that he sells is controlled by the fact that he is selling it to needy comrades. The food goes for five shillings, same for a tiny bottle of glue. Those who want to shelter from the rain or cold at night pay five shillings. This means that for fifteen shillings a PB will eat food, sniff some glue and have shelter overnight. We visited there last night and found over a dozen of them. Even two of the boys who ran away from our centre are holed there.

"To be frank, we didn't know how to approach this PB in connection with your request. We therefore thought it advisable that you accompany us there. Maybe when we get there we shall know how to go about it"

That was it. The whole thing was now in my hands, just as the case of Aslam whose daughter was up to this minute standing right beside me, seemingly thinking and believing that Son of Fate could bring the whole world under her feet.

I hated the kind of trust Marie had in me and her refusal or reluctance to believe the truth, that I was nothing more than an ordinary person who had been forced by fate to acquire endurance, strong and stony guts and daredevil courage which at times turned out to be my own enemy. She didn't seem to understand that had I been born under the same circumstances she was, I would probably have been so soft she'd be afraid of touching me lest I crumbled. But life had been hard on me, forcing me to harden so as to cope. When the world becomes your teacher you have to become wise, intelligent, witty, and most of all, slippery. You need to know and judge what to take on and what not to touch. Like this moment, I wasn't going to involve myself with this PB who happened to be the son of my wife. I was sensing danger and my instincts never failed me. I wanted Eva to make her own decision. She had insisted on having her son whom she didn't know and whom I suspected was an unrepentant criminal. Now that he had been found it was up to her to decide, and approach him. I loved her so much and I was ready to do anything for her, but there are times when personal decisions are of vital importance, like now. I turned to face the two gentlemen who had given me time to make up my mind.

"Thanks a lot my friends. I had full trust that you'd trace that boy. If there's anybody who'll be overjoyed it is my wife. Do me a favour, please. Just drive up to my place, speak to my wife, explain everything to her, then assist her in whatever way she requests you. You know how to approach your boys; just do it your way." I reached for my jacket's inner pocket and fished out some money.

Unfortunately for me, my hands fell on a one-thousand shilling note and had to hand it over to them. For the first time I saw what their smiles looked like. As they turned to get into their vehicle, I was certain the job would be well done. *'Money can buy anything,'* I remembered Mrs. Wicks telling me. For the first time I got what she really meant.

Just before Foro and Muiruri turned to go to their car, I remembered that they didn't know where my house was. I quickly gave them directions and watched them swagger off with a new spring to their gait.

"I am still waiting and for God's sake stop being so mean," Marie announced as the traffic lights along Ronald Ngala Street turned red. I knew what she meant and I didn't pretend not to.

"That story has nothing to do with our case," I told her. She wouldn't know that all the time I had been quiet, I had been battling with the question whether to put her into the picture of what you'd call my 'private life' or not. For Eva's sake I opted not to, and as such I twisted the story. "I have mentioned two parking boys to you sometimes, have I not?" I asked her, knowing that I never had. She shook her head.

"Oh, I am sorry then. I have two street friends who almost landed me in trouble. My wife knows one of them and it is him we were discussing. She wants to rehabilitate him ..." That took care of that. I didn't want to mix the present case with anything else and I meant it. Time was running out and so much depended on it – Time!

We drove back to the Panafric where we were to do our final touches before we left. I had noted in my memory that the town marked on the map with a star in black was called Mgambo, and that was our destination. From this town a short thin mark in red indicated a farm or ranch or whatever else it was meant to be, where the boss - one Assanad Karim bin Saiga - was to be found.

Apart from this I barely knew anything else, not even how to get there. I was surprised to learn from Marie that to get to Mgambo we had to drive back to Mombasa and cross the border via the South Coast. I listened to her intently, liking her good memory and eagerness to help.

"We'll cross the border at Lungalunga or Vanga on the South Coast. From there I noted a town called Mtandikeni. Also marked were Tanga and Korogwe, then our destination Mgambo ..."

As she explained, the map that I had been robbed of came back to my mind. Everything in it seemed to tally with what Marie was saying. Her memory must be photographic, I thought to myself.

"Now tell me, do you prefer Lungalunga or Vanga?" I asked.

"I have gone as far as Lungalunga with my dad and I would therefore prefer it. He was going to visit a friend who picked him from there and I had to drive back. It's not very far from Mombasa."

"Thank you, Marie, I see you have taken this thing seriously and this is exactly what is needed. We will take off today spend the night in Mombasa, then leave very early in the morning. I'd like us to be in Tanga early in the day But you'll need a few lessons before we leave."

I took out the two guns I had unloaded and put one of them on the table.

"Look at this one. It is a .38 Police Special. At least that is what they call it. It is a light gun, that carries eight rounds of ammunition." I demonstrated everything as I showed her how to cock it, how to release the safety catch and how to pull the trigger. She repeated everything I showed her about five times before I put that one down and produced the Browning. This, I explained, was heavier but more accurate when used by experts. Again I instructed her on how to use it. I was aware she wouldn't be of much use with a gun, but I knew that when worse came to worst, every human being was equipped with a sixth sense which came in handy and enabled actions one would have thought impossible.

After all it was necessary that she knows how to use what she was about to carry in her purse. I didn't want to have the two guns on me for one or two reasons.

I took the phone and called the receptionist. "Give me a line, please," I said when she answered.

"Go ahead, sir. Press number six, then dial your number."

"Thank you." That's how good they are in these five-star hotels, unlike what we are used to next to the slums. 'How comfortably the rich and powerful live,' I thought as I followed the instructions.

The phone was picked on the second ring.

"Wicks and Wayne, can I help you?" A female voice said.

"Yes, may I talk to the MD please?" I said, trying to disguise my voice a little, incase Mrs. Wicks took the phone.

"I am afraid he hasn't been in for some time. Would you like to leave a message?'

"You are expecting him then?" I asked

"Yes, sir. Any day, any time. Any message please?"

"None. Probably I could talk to Mrs. Wicks herself. Could she be around?" I asked, with my heart beats sounding louder than normal.

"I am afraid she too is away. If you could ..."

"Okay, don't bother. I'll call later if I do not get in touch with them before lunch hour. Thanks a lot."

"Most welcome," the lady said and hang up. I had learnt at least two things. One, which was most important to me, was that I was up to now regarded the MD of Wicks and Wayne Detective Agency. Secondly, I got to know that Mrs. Wicks was not around and that she did not hold much grudge against me, otherwise she'd have given instructions that I should not get into that office or be contacted by anyone on phone. So far, all was well. At least it was good that she fought her battles silently and secretly, even though such coolness was quite dangerous.

"Am I entitled to know who this MD we were calling is?" I turned to see Marie wearing her best smile.

I liked it.

"Well, he is supposed to be me. Do you remember calling me a spy when we went to see your dad in hospital?"

"Oh, I get it now. You have a way of reminding people of things they've forgotten. Well, what next?"

"Put one gun in your purse, whichever you prefer. Secondly, call the receptionist and book out. We have no more time, to waste. I want to have this vehicle serviced right away. Then we get the hell out of this city where I am suspicious of whoever approaches my path. If I could get hold of that thorn or thistle ..." I stopped short and joined Marie in the laughter that followed. You have to force yourself to like whatever you are doing in order to do it well.

The vehicle took slightly over one hour at the D.T. Dobie workshop. In the next hour we were on our way to Mombasa. We stopped shortly at Voi where we took light meals. Two hours from then, we were relaxing in different rooms at the Nyali Beach Hotel where Marie preferred to stay.

In the evening I took the phone and called Marie's room, informing her that I intended to go out to relax my mind. She opted to join me and requested me to give her some thirty minutes to get ready. I didn't mind her company and I told her I'd wait. I relaxed on the double bed facing the ceiling, a cigarette dangling from my mouth, deep in thought.

Suddenly I had a feeling that someone was opening the door. It was over twenty minutes since I talked to Marie, so absent-mindedly I concluded it must be her. But when it opened, I found myself facing the barrel of a gun.

"Stay still! Don't even touch that cigarette you are trying to. Just lie still until instructed otherwise!"

The voice alone would have sent a snake running back into its hole. It was a hard voice that announced danger, a voice that was fearful to listen to. The man entered, his right hand holding the gun that was pointed at the spot between my eyes. Behind him entered two other gentleman, if you may call them so. The second had a gun too but the third, who looked a little relaxed but more lethal, didn't have any weapon. I guessed he was the boss, which turned out to be right. He came closer, but making sure that he didn't get anywhere between me and the two gunmen.

The three were smartly dressed in light clothes that matched well from head to toe. The first was clean shaven and the other had the popular 'box' haircut. I estimated their ages to be between twenty-seven and thirty. The one who entered first was shorter than the second by close to two inches. He stood at about five feet eight inches with a physical build that fitted the height perfectly. From my judgement, I had no doubt that the two were fighters. The boss was no doubt getting to fourty years of age of thereabout. He was slightly shorter than the others but heavier. He didn't seem to care much about his hair but it looked good all the same. They had one feature in common, a light complexion which left you in no doubt as to their ancestry. The boss then took over the proceedings.

"You are Adams Wamathina, isn't that so?" He asked me.

I was so annoyed, more so by my carelessness, that I couldn't give a straight-forward answer. After all, what did it matter now? Being soft wasn't going to help me any more than being rude.

"Supposing I told you I wasn't?" I posed, in a tone slightly rude. This seemed to activate them. The thickset came to me and forced me out of the bed. He searched me first thing my legs touched the floor. He didn't have to look for the gun in two places. He touched it the first time and disarmed me promptly. 'What an expert,' I thought. Who could these guys be, I wondered? Cops or criminals? I was certain about one thing, though – they were after the trophy because outside this I had not made any enemies. Fear gripped me. Under two hours since I entered Mombasa and already in the hands of the enemy!

"Where's the other gun?" The 'boss' asked me menacingly.

"Which other gun? Why would I need two? I have a license to carry one only," I said. Just then something got into my mind. I waited for it to develop before I concluded my suspicions.

"We have information you have two guns. Will you produce it willingly or do we make you do it?" The boss said threateningly. I was right about my suspicions. Who else knew I had two guns on this earth but one Janet Wanjiru, alias Mrs. Wicks?

For an answer I said, "You must be Stranger. I was wondering when I'd meet you!" That appeared to shock him.

Well, he might have been tough, ruthless and a super fighter, but he lacked the most important quality that a real man should have – intelligence! He couldn't figure how I had got his name. He should have had an inkling that I and his boss had a relationship of some kind and that she might have mentioned his name to me.

With surprise written all over his face he asked me whether we had met before, to which I nodded. He couldn't even add two and two to make four, and remember I had cut his conversation with Mrs. Wicks in the office when I disarmed her and went away with the second gun. Or was Mrs. Wicks playing the same silent and secret games even with her most trusted hitman?

"Answer the question, don't keep us waiting!" The first man with his remarkable hard voice told me.

"Go ahead," I said. I wasn't worried any more. They weren't here to kill but to capture me; of that I had no doubt. All I prayed now was that Marie didn't turn up before they took me away.

After my answer they looked at each other. The two younger men seemed intelligent and I was afraid they'd figure out I had an accomplice. But my fear wasn't realized as they seemed to be in a hurry. It was nearing the hour when the hotel would be packed and they wanted to avoid that. They searched the bed in a hurry because that was all I had in the room apart from the clothes I had on. Then darkness fell on me. Stranger might not be intelligent but he was smart. Pretending not to be satisfied that the second gun wasn't really on me, he turned me round to give me another search. I fell for the trap because this was normal. You could search a person as many times as you wished just to make sure he didn't shoot you the moment you turned your back. I was still with that thought when I felt a heavy bang on the back of my head. I felt a stinging pain that went from that point down to the last toe on my foot. Then darkness relieved me of the pain as I became unconscious.

I don't know how long I lay so, nor where I was. The sharp pain that had rendered me unconscious came again. I tried to figure out what it could be as I slipped in and out of consciousness, but the strain I gave my mind sent me back to darkness once again. This time I was aware I was losing grip of the Aslam case and it hurt me even more. The sharp pain came once again, but now I was ready for it. I wasn't going to strain myself again lest I went back to the world of darkness and loneliness. I let my body relax, and as I did so I felt the pain easing. I loved that.

The realisation that I wasn't dreaming hit home. It was becoming obvious that I was in a strange place and that my body was not free. The first thing I realized was that my hands were tied from behind and that I was lying on them. The picture of what must have happened started coming vaguely. Again I let my mind relax. 'It will come slowly, you have all the time in the world,' I comforted myself.

Stranger! Yes, it was Stranger I had met last. It was Stranger who had done all this to me! I listened again to this distant voice which was giving me names. It wasn't the same that always came to me; this was cool while the latter always talked to me with authority.

I felt jitters crawl all over my body. I realised I was in the hands of an enemy or enemies, the same people who had kidnapped me.

Again I heard the distant voice. I was even able to make out that the voice was feminine. I was turned a little bit. Whoever was doing it wanted me to be comfortable as she seemed to realize I was getting a hard time lying on my tied hands.

"Oh, my God, this is bad. Come on dear, why don't you come to? You are a strong man who can stand more than ... oh, it looks bad." My body relaxed a bit after my comforter relieved some of the weight from my hands. I was even able to breathe more comfortably. I stayed still, my eyes still closed but my ears ready to trap any sound that was made around. There was no movement at all. If there was any other soul in this place apart from the lady who had talked and turned me over, then they were dead silent.

"... they shouldn't have done this to you ..." The distant, very soft voice continued. There followed a feeling of a soft light touch on my lips which awakened me fully, but I made sure I didn't open my eyes nor stir. I wanted to hear whatever this tigress was saying. She kissed my lips once again and continued with her dream.

"... Stranger is a bad boy. Why hit this beauty of a man so hard? Why him, of all people! Those weren't my instructions. All I had wanted him to do was bring you to me ... alive. But ... yes, I had warned him that you aren't a soft one either, that you are a good fighter because I know how you do it. You are not soft, Adams, and you must have resisted being kidnapped. All the same, I hate to see blood oozing from any part of your body, let alone the side of your head.! I still love you, Adams... Oh yes, I do! Do you remember how we met ... I will never forget that day. You are not the forgetting type either, so you must remember that you personally presented yourself at my residence, seeking for a driving job. I did give you the job straight away, didn't I? I had to because you were so wonderful... irresistible. You attracted me the very first minute I saw you lying in the garden, enjoying yourself just as you would in your own home. You called me a tigress when you wanted to know how bad Mrs. Wicks was just before you found out that you already had met her. Yet even after realizing I was the woman to give or deny you the job, it didn't bother you. You simply smiled. I can clearly see that smile as I give you this first aid.

A lovely smile it was, coming from a man who had realised he'd made a terrible mistake that could have cost him the job he was so in need of. And as Dolly Parton would put it, 'You were the one to sleep with me at night.' just as she would ask, 'Why did you have to do this to me?' Son of Fate, did you really have to leave me for my poor housegirl.

"*According to your story which I remember very clearly and which I believe, I was the first woman in your life after fifteen years of sexual starvation. I relieved you of all that misery - and enjoyed it too. You loaded me with all the love you had carried for over fifteen years and I didn't mind it. I needed you too, just as I do now. I needed you more than you could imagine because no other man ever dared approach me. Could be after all you were right to brand me a tigress . . . sometimes I think I am close to being one. But my dear yellow rose, did you have to leave me for Eva? That's the only part in your life I hate you for.*

"*Do you know how it feels to be left for another... especially in my case where the 'other' was my househelp. . . a house maid ... my own servant? But I cannot hate you, no matter how I try to. I badly need you SoF:, I want to have you always. I once swore you were all mine. I was very serious, just as I am now. I won't let you go away from me again, no matter what it'll cost me. But I swear one thing – I'll not hold a gun on you again, even though I'll have to be very careful how I handle you because you are so slippery. I have tried all I could to hate you, but I just can't. You finished me when you unleashed your love on me at this very place, the place where you were to abandon me to go for that junk. I was Mrs. Adams then, Mrs. Adams Wamathina ... Oh my, I think I am getting crazy!*"

You couldn't have imagined I was listening to all this. At this point I felt some wet substance fall on my face. I didn't have to open my eyes to know that it was drops of tears. With my experience I knew Janet was still much in love with me. But could she be trusted?

Her hands felt so soft and experienced as she washed the wound on the side of my head. She would sometimes turn me a bit and brush her lips against mine and mutter love words. After about ten minutes, her caressing and lullabies sent me back to dreamland. But before I went out I was certain of something happening – she was expertly loosening the nylon strings Stranger and his henchmen had used to tie my hands behind my back.

"... you left me unconscious in my office, dear, but I cannot do the same. I cannot stand seeing you tied like a criminal while all you have done is deny me just a little love. Still you told me you were coming to rescue me that same day... thank you for that Adams, I believe you..."

When I at last woke up I felt completely relaxed. The coolness of the room and the fresh air I inhaled, plus the comfort of where I lay, contributed to my quick recovery. I already knew I was a captive of Mrs. Wicks. I was also aware that she would do her best to make sure that I did not get hurt again, that is if I complied with her demands. I didn't want to have Stranger or his henchmen anywhere near me again. But I swore if I ever did that by some chance at some open ground, we were certainly going to know who between us could hit harder than the other. As for Mrs. Wicks, I didn't know what to think of her. It was wrong of her to have me kidnapped, but I also felt I had wronged her too when I hit her and left her unconscious. To make the matter worse I had stolen her gun. That wasn't fair and I should have anticipated her retaliation.

What I found amusing and somehow disturbing was that she was still in love with me. More so I didn't hold the slightest grudge against her after what she had done to Eva. Right inside me I felt I wouldn't mind sharing the same suite with her just like the first time. She was, after all, a good and clean-hearted lady whose love, kindness, self confidence and intelligence one could not afford to ignore.

I sensed there wasn't anybody else in the room and I opened my eyes. One look around me and I knew where I was – the same suite which some time back had been booked for Mr. and Mrs. Adams Wamathina. I jumped out of the bed and the first thing I realised was that I had a white Tee-shirt on. I went to the mirror to see what I looked like. I wasn't such a wreck and I wondered why in the first place I had felt like I was breaking up. I was able to see the small wound on the left side of my head close to the back. I might have bled much but that was not the type of wound to put me out of action for a long time. What I think had done me in was the impact as the cosh used on me crashed against my skull.

I looked around for a towel, picked it and went towards the bathroom. I had undressed and hadn't bothered to cover my groin with the towel, because I was aware I was all alone, when the bathroom door opened and I found myself face to face with my former boss, Mrs. Wicks.

"Hello, dear," she greeted, "you are up at last. You don't look bad at all." It was like I was in this room out of choice.

"I am okay. You don't look bad yourself. How are you?"

"Quite fine ... Just take a shower and join me. You need something to eat?" She asked, came closer and touched me on the wound. She didn't comment but turned me around and kissed my cheek slightly. She patted me on the back and said, "Enjoy your shower."

What, for God's sake, was going on between us? We were behaving like nothing had gone wrong between us. Just like we had booked this suite together and now were planning what to do next.

My mind started flashing back to my past as the warm salty coastal water soothed my body. For the first time I felt pity towards myself. Fate hadn't given me a break yet. Just as I had earlier hinted to Marie, driving big vehicles which didn't belong to me and moving about with rich young and beautiful women who no doubt liked me did not mean that I was any better than I used to be. The only difference here was that I had moved my slavery from a lower class to an upper one. But I was still a slave. A student, I argued within me, was a student, right from form one to the university. The difference was in the knowledge already acquired.

I remembered the time I left jail to find my wife, Joy, married to another man. I was a shoe shine boy then and there were times when I was so happy. I would wake up from a shanty which was infested with bedbugs but which I was used to, go to a public bathroom, clean myself then trek to town. I would take breakfast only when I had earned enough for it. In most cases I didn't take lunch, yet I was happy and had time for light moments with my friends. We would discuss how each spent his evening and night. We also discussed our women who also hailed from the slums, some of whom had never tried to fit a pair of shoes on their feet but whom we found amusing and nice, just like I presently found the likes of Marie and Mrs. Wicks. There were hardly times when I'd feel I was playing with a fiend, as I was feeling now. Yet this was the time I was supposed to feel that I had got closer to the sweet fruits of a few million shillings in my pocket after getting Aslam's trophy. What fate was doing now was taking me for a ride. It was pushing its jokes with me a bit too far. How and why, I wondered, should I land back into the hands of the very lady I had enough reasons to believe was an unrepentant criminal and still feel I was in good hands? Was this lady fated to make my star shine, or was she fixed between me and my star so that any time it tended to shine she'd block it? Would this star my grandma had talked about ever shine, giving me a chance to control my own life without depending on rich beautiful women whose interests were quite different from mine? Right now I should have been beside my expectant Eva, trying to help her get back her lost son, consoling her each time she broke down. But now here I was, taking all the time in the world inside the bathroom, afraid of getting out to face the wrath of the rich lady who thought money was everything in life. A person who thought that the likes of Eva, who was once her servant, should never be loved. How would she take it if I told her that life in slums was sometimes so beautiful and wonderful and that there were times when I missed it? That there were hundreds of thousands who could never find happiness anywhere else but in the ghettos?

I thought I was doing myself injustice trying to get back to a past that would never come back! I decided to live for today instead of going back to yesterday, for this was the only way I would improve my situation. I gave myself time to think about Eva but I suddenly dropped it. What assistance would I give her from a bathroom in Mombasa, I wondered stupidly? Then I thought of Marie. This was another one who thought that Son of Fate was a hero while all the time fate moved about with a noose round his neck waiting for him to slip so that he tightens it and gets rid of him. Did she find out that I was kidnapped or know that right now I was in the hands of the very tigress I had told her about?

I felt like my head would burst and I dashed out of the bathroom. I was going to face life as it came, but I promised myself that whatever I did, it would be to my own good, and Eva's. Without caring whether Mrs. Wicks was watching me or not, I kissed my talisman and like on many other occasions before, I felt consoled. At least this one would keep me in touch with my grandmum. One day, when I was through with all this mad business, I would visit the place I buried my grandmum, pray beside the grave and do all that she had asked me to do before she died, including assisting Kareithi the herdsboy to move to the next stage ... I mean, graduate from a boy to a man.

"Those are not my clothes," I told Mrs. Wicks as she put a pair of trousers, a short sleeved shirt, a pair of socks and a handkerchief on the bed for me to put on.

"They are – I bought them for you,' she said, and faked a smile.

"Where are mine?"

"Well, I sent them to a laundry. Why are you insisting?"

"Because they are my clothes. Is it wrong to ask?"

"No, it is not wrong..." she said and came to me. "Please, Adams, take everything easy I want us to forget the past. Let us forgive each other because this is the only way we'd expect forgiveness from God. I have personally forgiven you for all the bad you have done me and I'll never mention it again, never, I also want you to forgive me for what I did to you. I want you to take me as you did when we first met..."

"As my boss?"

"No, no... no ... Oh, my! Adams, please understand. I have tried to hate you but I have finally given up. Love is something that one cannot overcome. It is not something that you just push aside and say you have given up. I have had enough of trying it and from now on I want to lead another life. Love is supreme in one's life and it is not shakeable ... you cannot shake it off like you would anything else you do not like. You have bothered my life since the day you left me in this very room. There's even a time that I felt I wanted to die. I wanted to commit suicide, but somehow God saved me."

"Well, I haven't led the kind of life one would envy. I have done bad things in life, but so have you and millions others. But a day arrives and one realises there has to be a stop, a point where one should say enough is enough and start living. We turn to God. If one does not do this, there then follows a time when life loses meaning. It is of no value and becomes a meaningless life ... a life that our Creator never meant us to live. You have taught me so much, Adams . . . more than anyone dead or alive ever taught me. And I guess this is why my heart refuses to let you go. I've prayed seriously and God's answer seems to indicate you are the one for me."

"Believe it or not, Adams, but I have given up so much that was awaiting me just because of you. I want you to know that I did not do this to you because I need your assistance; it is you I want and that is all. I want you in my life, I want you to stop whatever else you are doing and come to me for my sake. I'll give you everything you want that is within my ability. I want you to marry me, Adams. I believe that is what our Creator wants ..."

It was such a surprise that words failed me. She had started weeping and the tears were flowing ceaselessly, making round dots on the floor. I was touched, but all I did was go ahead and dress.

How in God's name could she propose marriage to me? Could she be serious, or was this one of her gimmicks? As I buttoned up my shirt, I talked my absent mind aloud.

"Are you born again, for God's sake?"

"I am, yes I am," she said. It brought me to the surface from the deep sea of confused thoughts.

"I beg your pardon, you are what?"

"You asked me a question, Adams, and I gave you the answer."

"Which question? I am not aware of having asked ..." Then I suddenly realized what must have happened, I was used to talking to myself or speaking my thoughts aloud whenever I was deeply troubled, Eva had caught me talking to myself several times and that was how I knew I had the problem. I must have done the same now.

Mrs. Wicks a born-again Christian? The world is full of wonders!

One thing was however certain to me. I wasn't going to marry her for anything in the world!

When I was fully dressed, I went to the mirror to see what I looked like. What I saw gave me confidence. The weariness in the body had completely vanished and the wound was not much visible after combing the hair. Satisfied, I turned to face Mrs. Wicks who was monitoring whatever I was doing.

"I am going out to see a friend," I announced. I knew I wasn't a prisoner anymore; her story had told me all I would have needed to know.

"Must you go?" The disappointment was discernible.

"Yes, I have to. And please tell Stranger to get out of my way!"

"Adams ..." she called in a pleading voice "... we agreed not to remind ourselves the wrong we've done each other."

"Where's the gun?" I asked just to change the subject.

"Do you still need it? I thought we agreed you'll give up everything and let us settle?"

"We agreed? I need the gun, I have a job to do ..."

"Open that drawer over there."

I did. It was lying there. I picked it. Now what next, I wondered? I had a feeling our dialogue wasn't over yet. I pretended to get out of the bedroom to the table room from where I'd get out. Just as I expected, Mrs. Wicks called after me.

"Adams, are you coming back?" I sensed some tenderness in her voice which had not been there seconds before. Since I got out of the bed on gaining consciousness she had been talking to me very kindly, like the very first time some months ago when we had shared this same room. She behaved then like a mother to a child who was going out into a world full of dangers. This was how I knew her, the impression I had got of her and which I had wanted to keep with me. But she had erased this when she held a gun on me and fought me like a tigress in her office. Now she was lovely again. *What a woman!*

"Mrs. Wicks ..." I called. But she didn't let me finish.

"Adams, please, I beg you for the second time to drop that title. I told you Wicks wasn't my husband but my foster father. I also explained to you why I hid myself behind that title. I am grown up now and I do not need it. Call me Wicks, Miss Wicks if you must use my father's name. But I'd prefer Janet or Wanjiru. I requested you something earlier on and you haven't answered me, and right now you are talking of going. I want an answer before you leave." The voice was not authoritative as usual, but rather full of respect and humility. Again I felt touched but decided to stick to my ground.

"Okay, Janet... I prefer that one ..." I said, then added, "I have everything we have discussed in mind. You'll have to give me time to decide. I have to think hard and right now I have plenty of things before me which I must look into. You know I like being frank with you, Mrs. W. . . sorry, Miss Wicks. This question of marriage does not come in. I mean, it is not easy for us to trust each other after what we have known of each other. Especially when I think of what you did to ..."

"Stop!" She interrupted with a voice that was like a scream. It took me by surprise and I almost shielded my face with my left hand as I was used to doing whenever some fight broke out. "I told you we must forget the past and stop talking about it. I thought you understood what I meant and if you didn't, I hope you'll understand now. I am not the Janet who held a gun on you, not the Janet who framed that young girl who served me for such a long time and was so good. I am a new Janet. I am ready to apologize to her if you could trace her for me."

"I want to tell you something you have never known about. You just don't know how much you hurt my body in this very room over three months ago. You couldn't because I braved it so well, and again because you were always under the influence of alcohol whenever you did it. With all your experience you didn't even detect that I was a virgin. . ."

She now started weeping. As I absorbed the shock, I went close to her and supported her. She was right on one point, that I didn't know until this moment that she had been a virgin when we met. Also, just as she had said, whenever I went to bed with her I had always been under or pretended to be under the influence of alcohol. I got the courage to hold her from the alcohol that enabled me to erase my inborn inferiority complex. Which shoeshiner and cart pusher wouldn't have required alcoholic guts to get anywhere near a highly educated young millionairess, let alone think of going to bed with her? Even the alcohol itself had to be concentrated to achieve such results.

More surprises were in store for me.

"... You cannot guess even now as you stand there that I am carrying your baby. Please Adams, use your brains positively for once in your life. You can't be so naive for God's sake. I love you, Adams. No other man has ever been close to me, no other has ever touched me, but you. That's why I once thought of suicide when you left me here and vanished for months ..."

Well, I was beaten and had no words left in me. I held her and caressed her beautiful hair, her head against my chest. After a minute or two, I turned her head up and kissed her lightly on the lips. That was the only way I was certain would console her.

"I'll come back. Just go ahead and take super alone. I'll take mine somewhere else with a friend, okay?"

"Thanks, I'll wait for you. I am happy now that you understand." She really looked happy, but I still didn't understand. How does one understand a situation like this? One minute this most beautiful lady is a tigress, the next she is so soft you would think she'd pass for a peace-keeper. I went out, still not knowing what to make of this enigma.

I met Marie at the lounge of the Nyali Beach Hotel where she was waiting for a porter she had sent upstairs. On seeing me she jumped out of the seat like she had just realised she was sitting on a rattle snake, prompting many curious people in the lounge to turn in our direction. We hugged a little, then she requested that we go to her room for me to brief her. We met the porter coming down the stairs and Marie took her keys.

"What happened? I was dead worried. I have ascended and descended these stairs a dozen times, wondering what might have happened." Marie had said all this as we reached her room.

"It's a long story..." I said, as I stubbed a cigarette which I felt was doing me more harm than good.

"I am ready to listen. Maybe after the story I'll get some appetite, because I've lost it."

"It was 6.15 p.m. when I called you, wasn't it?" She nodded. "Well, I had wanted to go to Mtwapa to see a friend. I think I have mentioned a Mr Cicheru to you. I had gathered he has opened a pub on his farm, and close to him is another pub called Tropicana where I had expected the person who impersonated me and managed to see your father is holed up. While I was chasing him out, he had dropped a receipt from the hotel. I had wanted Gicheru's assistance because I have a feeling this impersonator was behind the snatching of the briefcase. When you told me to give you thirty minutes to prepare yourself I agreed because I needed company. So I expected you to come by 6.45 p.m ..."

"I was late by under five minutes, surely you could have . . ."

"Well, that doesn't matter. It was even better for me that you delayed. I lit a cigarette and got lost in deep thinking. At around 6.40 p.m. I sensed there was someone trying the door knob and I automatically assumed it was you, so I didn't bother facing the door. In the next second I heard some voice giving me orders to stay still. When I turned to face the door, I saw three men enter, two training guns on me. On realising the situation I prayed that you did not come in time because they'd have kidnapped both of us. Right now I am from the hands of the kidnappers who carried me unconscious to the Diani Beach Hotel."

"How did you get away, in God's name?" Marie asked in a strangled voice. She was so angry, I'd never seen her like this. "I wish the devil who planned it drops dead!"

"Shut up! Don't ever say that again!" I wouldn't want to imagine Janet dead and I felt bad Marie had insinuated it. Marie was now staring at me with her eyes wet, tears almost ready to flow down her beautiful face. It is then I realized the mistake I had made. I went to her. I knew she had never seen me like this before, I mean in such a terrible mood. I took her, just as I had taken Janet, into my arms.

"I am sorry Marie," I lied, "… I am sure you didn't get the reason for my barking at you like that. I almost killed that lady. I was so annoyed with her, I wanted to kill her. Look, if I had someone like you encouraging me, I would not have thought twice. I'd have gone right over to her room and shot her, then trouble would have followed. Do you get what I mean?"

She nodded in agreement.

"Sorry, I hadn't seen it that way."

"I am happy you understand," I repeated Janet's words to me a few minutes ago. I was happy to see that Marie had relaxed and could smile again. Why did most women like hearing and believing lies, I wondered? You tell them the truth and they get suspicious and angry. They do not want to believe even when it is the real truth. But just make up a story and you have them nodding their heads in agreement. How would Marie have behaved if I had told her the truth, especially that the lady she had referred to as a devil was expecting my child?

I woke up with my heart thumping loudly, like someone frightened. I wondered what was happening this time. Was I unconscious again, and if so what had caused it? I then heard the distant voice of a man: *"... if he is strong enough, it happens when one is highly fatigued ..."* Then I heard Marie's voice: *"Do you think he will remember..."* The voice seemed to be getting out of the room and I didn't hear the answer. Then the door was closed and I knew the two were on their way out. I stepped out of the bed and looked around. Nothing told me anything. I decided to follow them out. As I got to the sitting room, Marie entered.

"Oh, you are up? How are you feeling?" She asked me.

"I don't know. Not anything I can explain in a word. I don't even remember going to bed. What time is it?"

"It's after midnight, ten to fifteen minutes past. Your watch is on top of that bedside locker."

"Who was your visitor?" I asked

"Oh, you heard him? He's my physician. I called him to have a look at you."

"I am surprised. Why was I supposed to be attended to?"

She smiled and said nothing, which told me she had much to tell me but wanted to do it at her own pace. But I was so curious I wouldn't give her the time.

"I am still waiting to hear the story, Marie. I am very eager, you know. The whole thing sounds like it concerns me and anything concerning me which I happen not to know makes me very curious," I said and smiled weakly. I wasn't feeling very well and I disliked it. After a while Marie took out some prescriptions from a drawer and came to me. When she was close enough I noticed some bruises on her arms.

"What happened? Looks like somebody was trying to strangle you!" I got a feeling that something had gone wrong. I was surprised to learn that it was me who had caused the bruises.

"That's why I called my physician. I do not know what got into you. One minute we were discussing in a very friendly manner and the next minute you were ... I do not know how to put it. You held my upper arms, squeezing me so hard that I had to scream. That's how I got the bruises on both arms."

"I seem to remember that, though it is not very clear. My God, what the hell got into me? Did I ask you anything?"

"Yes, whether I was going to marry you. Shortly before that you were talking things I could not understand. You were rather talking to yourself than to me..."

"Sorry, Marie. I think I have had so much stress lately. There are so many things that have been troubling my mind ever since that briefcase was snatched. I think what broke me down completely was that lady. She told me ..." I held my tongue just in time, remembering what I had told her earlier on. But I had already given myself away.

"I knew you hadn't told me everything but that doesn't matter. What makes me happy right now is that you are progressing well. The physician said that if you woke up and happened to remember what had taken place before you lost your strength and fainted, you will have recovered from the stress. But he said that needed a very strong person which he didn't think you were. He however seemed to change his mind when I hinted to him that you are a sportsman and that you do gymnastics twice a day ..."

As she gave me the story, I vaguely remembered having walked towards her and grabbed her upper arms. Then I had heard a strange voice roar: *"Are you going to marry me? Answer me: will you marry me?!"*

"No! Nooo! I won't." Marie had screamed the answer. *"You are hurting me, Adams. Please let me go."*

It was quite clear now. That's what I had done. I had then pushed her away and staggered to the bed. From then on, it appears I had lost consciousness until three hours later.

What I failed to understand was why I would all of a sudden want Marie to marry me, a thing that had never crossed my mind. But whatever had happened had warned me that Marie wasn't open for marriage. I had never dreamt of marrying or proposing to her. However I was glad that, after all that had happened between us, we were ready to bury it and move over to other things ... just as if nothing had happened.

I found Miss Wicks waiting for me. She was lying on the large sofa reading the New Testament. We talked – for hours. She didn't seem to be in a hurry to go to bed just as I wasn't. I had had so many hours of rest which I had not planned for, and what I felt I needed more than anything else was some gym workout which I sometimes did indoors. Once again, she tried to convince me to drop this mission and I found her reasoning very apt. Like me, she had observed that there were people who used others to achieve their own ends, people who used others for personal gain. Strange enough, she even talked about the likes of Stranger and his gangsters, how they were used by powerful people to commit crimes that didn't pay them but only benefitted their masters.

"... Such people are so dumb they cannot realize they are being used. I'd hate to think of you in that light. I am aware that needs make people what they are, but I believe there are limits anyone with control over his mind should not exceed, Adams. You are doing this job for payment, for money. Here I am, asking you to give it up so that we get engaged. I have enough money for us to live on. After all, unlike what I told you some time back, I have realized money isn't everything in life. Like they say, money can buy a bed but not sleep, a house but not a home. It can buy all that is in the market but cannot buy happiness and contentment which is all we need in life. These can only come from one source: living the way our creator intended us to live right from the beginning.

In other words, they can only be acquired from God, by turning to Him and doing what He wishes. I wish you knew the freedom I feel in me since I turned my interests away from spiritual hunger. This hunger is what the human race has and it is our public enemy number one. If we could. . ."

I had to interrupt her inspite of the interest I found in her preaching. What she was doing, though unaware, was to flash back to the lectures I used to give her when in a talkative mood.

"Janet, dear... you are letting yourself get eaten up by yet more termites in different shapes. Do not try to preach to me, for God's sake. Just live simply, trust yourself and your work, and be good to yourself by being good to others. We are living in a very cruel world, Janet, a world that no one but its creator would understand. Sometimes I think it has gone beyond Him ... that even He has lost control."

"Look at the very rich who want to get richer. Theirs is not hunger but lust. The richest do not know what other stage they want to get to but they have that insistent urge to aim higher. They do not appreciate that the final stage is one, a return to the dust where we are made to believe we came from. Anyway, this is not the time to discuss Utopia. As long as we are on this earth, we are going to struggle and there's not a single way we can avoid that. I do entirely agree with you on some points, Janet. Unfortunately I cannot give up this case at this stage. I realize you are not aware that I went for the briefcase. It was robbed from me within minutes of being handed over to me. All the documents are gone. As such, I have no option but to go ahead because I cannot go back to Aslam to tell him that I've lost everything. In the first place he wouldn't believe me and even if he did, I wouldn't have the guts to go to him empty handed like a child would to give him the story. Remember I have his three hundred thousand shillings for the job. I have no alternative but to do something about it. He had made it very clear to me that this would be a risky undertaking, yet I willingly accepted it."

Miss. Wicks was surprised to learn of the loss of the introduction letter and the briefcase. She was quick to point out that without them I was as useless and hopeless as the rest of the people who were on this chase. She remained silent for about two minutes, seemingly deep in thought.

"Did the hotel manager leave the room at any time while you were still waiting inside?" She asked at last.

"Yes. He left us in his office and entered an inner room from where he brought the briefcase".

"That manager is my number one suspect. He tipped somebody who must have been hanging around the hotel specifically for the day the briefcase would be retrieved. Otherwise, you must have had somebody following you all along, which I am sure you would have noticed."

"Now that you mention it, I remember he took about five minutes in that other office or whatever place it was. We spent the five minutes easily because we were excited, discussing his behaviour when we entered his office. I even think I heard his voice at one time and thought there was another person in that other office. This must have been the time he betrayed us. No wonder I became suspicious immediately I stepped out of the hotel premises. I noticed, or rather sensed, something suspicious around us. If I had suspected that beast then, he would be in a hospital bed right now if not the Lee Funeral Home. He should praise his god that it never occurred to me he was the Judas."

I could read Janet's concern from her face as she read annoyance on mine. "Just take it easy, Adams. Please don't get worked up. I cannot advice you to go back to him because that'd only worsen things and waste more of your time. I wish you'd only understand how bad the whole thing is".

"Janet, tell me honestly. What is the secret behind this thing? It looks like it keeps on pulling whoever hears about it without giving anyone a break."

I was surprised to hear Miss. Wicks laugh, not out of excitement but pity – because she understood what it was.

"Adams, the whole affair is devilish. I've never faced anything this evil in my life – and I wouldn't deny having faced a good number of sinister things. You have heard about devil worship I guess."

"I have, but don't tell me this is what the whole thing is."

"No, but that is the closest thing I can compare it with. What would you say about the people who worship the devil? Would you say they do not know who and what the devil is? That they do not know it is wrong to worship him? That they are not aware the devil's work is to destroy, to demolish whatever good he finds? Yet they ignore all this and go ahead, adoring him. They know too well that if there's anyone to be worshipped and thanked it's God. But they are – just as you had put it, which is why I laughed – they are pulled by imaginary magnetic power to the evil one. Fancy that. This is something evil that is pulling everybody who hears about it just as you put it. I am telling you that I could have done anything to anybody who tried to block me from reaching it. Luckily or fortunately, I was pulled away from it by some stronger power. There are others like me who are up to now fastly tied to it. People with enough capital to start any kind of business they could dream of. But if you asked them what they are running after they wouldn't tell you. They don't know what they are really doing."

"You asked me to be honest with you; I will be. The best answer is ..., I do not know. But I have a hint that whoever gets possession of it will most likely make millions if he doesn't get killed. Another thing which I know for certain is that there is a very strong clandestine organization which is after robbing whatever the thing is from the rightful owner. Some very powerful individuals in the cabinet have a strong hold on the clandestine group . . ." She sighed before she continued, ". . . This is the group that had me in its grip. It is the group I was working for before I was pulled out of it by the power of Jesus. Thank Jesus for this. This is why I hate seeing you running after it..."

"But I am not among the robbers! I am doing it for the rightful owner!" I protested.

"That's the only difference. The problem is, the robbers won't let you get anywhere near the trophy. You started the chase this very morning and within seconds of collecting the introduction letter and the map, they were on your neck. Whoever has the introduction letter now is the rightful owner. The person the letter is addressed to knows no one else and recognises the bearer of the letter as the rightful owner. This puts you in a very awkward position."

I nodded in agreement. I sensed the truth of the matter, but that didn't mean I was-going to give up. I would still retrieve the briefcase, somehow.

"Despite those odds," I said, trying to sound confident, "I am going to get the trophy and hand it over to my employer. That I'll do, whatever it will cost me, but I am not ready to suffer the shame of facing Aslam with the story of the loss of the brifecase."

"You have the determination of a bulldog and all I can wish you is success. I won't try to stop you again. If you wish for any kind of assistance from me, just let me know. I am ready to assist you, Adams."

"Thank you Janet, that's so encouraging. We shall be crossing the border tomorrow."

"We ?"

"Miss Aslam and I. Do you remember her?"

Janet nodded and looked suspicious. "What assistance will she give you? I guess you decided to go with her after the loss of the papers."

'Yes. Anything wrong about it?"

"I didn't say so, did I? But if you could allow me to give you some piece of advice. .."

"I am all ears, dear. Anything that could assist me or anything new in connection with this thing would be of great help to me."

"Well, I mean I was only forewarning you that going with Miss Aslam hoping to influence whoever the letter was addressed to won't help. Those of us who have been chasing this thing for a long time happen to know that even if Aslam himself, who happens to be the rightful owner, presents himself personally without the letter, he will come back empty handed."

That was news to me and I told her so.

"That's very interesting ..." I said, "... why is that so? I never thought about it."

"Because this thing is shrouded in mystery. Aslam is quite sure he cannot possibly retrieve the trophy on his own. Yet this is the time it was agreed, between those who know every detail about it, that the trophy would be released. It was not going to be released until a certain personality died. He died eight months ago and that was when the chase started. The person or persons who are supposed to hand over the trophy do not know anything other than that whoever has various documents identical to those they have at home is the rightful owner. They wouldn't even talk to anyone who goes there without the documents, and you can as well guess there's plenty of security in place. This is why the robbers cannot just walk in, hold them up and get away with the trophy. The residence is surrounded by a fifteen-foot high stone wall that is reinforced with barbed wire on top."

"Have you been there?" I asked in surprise.

"Yes, on several occasions. There's only one path, a secondary road that leads to the villa, which is surrounded by a forest. The place is a fortress, Adams."

"That's an exaggerated account, I guess . . ."

"I am giving you a picture of what kind of security to expect so that you may lay your strategies well in advance."

"What's your advice, Janet dear?" I asked

"Are you serious, Adams?"

"About?"

"Seeking my advice?"

"Certainly, I have learnt to trust your opinions, your know-how rather, if not you."

"That's not very amusing, you know."

"Janet, I am sure you have not forgotten that I prefer being honest".

"I know and I like you for that, Adams. It makes things easier. But I want you to trust me as well, not only my opinions and knowledge. I am a different person . . . Janet Wanjiru, born again. That is my advice," she said with finality.

She was silent for a stretch before switching to a different subject. "I am sorry to keep you waiting, Adams, but don't worry. It is only that I want to clear something with you before I know what kind of advice I should give ."

"Go ahead." I said

"Are you sympathetic to my situation? I mean, do you share feelings with me about my pregnancy ..."

"Janet, I am with you. I know what you are trying to tell me. You still want to know whether I'll marry you. I requested you to give me time to decide. This is not a simple matter. Janet, it is not something you decide about in a hurry or just because there happens to be an expected child who has to have a father. You just mentioned that I might get killed in the process of doing this job. If that happened, what good would it do to promise you marriage? Marriage, Janet, is not the same as friendship. It means getting tied together for the rest of our lives. We have to be ready and we cannot commit ourselves before we are sure we adore each other. Not just the simple love of sharing a bed today and tomorrow, then getting tired the following day. After all, you know our culture. When a man gets married to a rich lady there's always that feeling of inferiority on the side of the husband, while the wife feels superior because she's the bread winner. You may not agree right now but later when we disagree you may find yourself charging that you collected me from the streets and rehabilitated me, and you know too well that I cannot possibly stomach that."

"Let's put it this way, Janet... we have something between us – the child in you. For that I have unending love for you no matter what happens between us. After all, if I could give you one secret about a man, he feels proud to have a child with a virgin. That love never dies even when the two have entered marriages.

In order to avoid ill feelings in future, let us give ourselves time. Let us continue loving each other as if we were married till time tells us otherwise. By then I might have made a good life out of myself and this inferiority complex in me might be dead. I'd then proudly propose to you."

I had lied deliberately. There was Eva who up to now looked like an angel to me. My argument however won Janet's heart and she demonstrated it by weeping, caressing me wildly as she did so. I was therefore assured of good advice which, to my surprise, included being promised security back-up from Stranger and his two trigger-happy killers. I refused this. I would have nothing to do with Stranger whom I suspected and believed could most likely double deal. But I did agree with Janet that the best thing to do at this stage was to try and retrieve the introduction letter, which could only be done by going straight to the villa to waylay my robbers. It wasn't going to be an easy task, we both agreed, but it had to be done.

CHAPTER SEVEN

We went to bed late that night. By the time I got some sleep, I could mentally see the route to the villa just as clearly as the back of my hand. Janet's advice was of great assistance as far as the route and possible traps were concerned. She even gave me names of two people whom I could contact in Tanzania if I badly needed some assistance.

The telephone rang insistently. At first I thought I was dreaming so I dismissed it from my sleepy mind. But it continued and I realized it wasn't a dream. I picked the mouthpiece lazily and sleepingly put it to my ear.

"Hello, good morning, it is six am on the dot. You asked to be woken up at this time."

"Thank you, madam. Just do me a favour and call again in about five minutes just to make sure my drowsiness doesn't outdo my desire and get me back to dreamland."

The lady on the other side laughed loud enough to be heard by Janet, who turned to face me

"Who is that bursting your ear-drums with laughter?"

"Room service. I had asked them to call me six on the dot. I hope it's all on the same bill." I laughed for no reason. I guess I was feeling uneasy and was only trying to make the load on my mind lighter by laughing it off.

"Oh, I hate to see you leaving," Janet told me. She was now fully awake and already on her feet.

"Me too. I hate this temporary divorce and hope it'll take only a few days." Again I laughed for no reason, but it brightened Janet up and she came to me.

"Thank you ..." she said, sotto voce. We held each other and let our lips touch before she excused herself to take a shower, after which she promised she would pack up my suitcase.

As Janet closed the bathroom door behind her, I picked a cigarette and lit it. I was feeling uneasy. What was it that was bothering my mind so early, I wondered?

Just then the phone rang again.

"Hallo, suite three zero five," I announced. I guessed it was the lady downstairs doing what was part of her job. I was right.

"Hallo, it is five past" I could sense she was smiling.

"Thanks, I was able to conquer my bodily desires. I am up and about to get out." I said and as I was about to put the phone down I got an idea. I hadn't called Eva since I left Nairobi and I just realized this was part of what was bothering me.

"Excuse me, madam. Could you please give me a line to Nairobi?" I was put through in a very short time, which pleased me as I did not want any delays in case Miss Wicks got out of the bath.

"Hallo," Eva's voice came through," It's you, Addy dear? How good of you to call!"

"I knew you wouldn't be in bed. But don't ask me why because it is just a feeling I had. How are you?"

"Wonderful. I have some news for you." It didn't come as a surprise to me. I had already sensed some kind of excitement in her voice.

"Let me guess," I told her

"Don't. I'd hate to hear you make the wrong guess."

"Did you succeed?" I pushed on with the guess nonetheless.

"In what?"

"Convincing Kimesh to stay with you? That you are his mother?"

"I succeeded and ..."

"Just a minute, dear. Did he get convinced that the owner of the Benz who gave him a lift was his father?"

Eva burst out laughing before I was through. The laughter eased my uneasiness and I was able to think straight. As we enjoyed our hide and seek game on phone, I sensed rather than heard

Mrs. Wicks leaving the bathroom. Without turning to ascertain the feeling, I told Eva: "Just make an interesting story for me. I'll call in the next hour. Please do not argue. I love you." I blew a kiss over the mouth piece. I turned to answer the question which I was sure would be the first when Miss. Wicks opened her mouth. I was right.

"Who was that? It's you who called I am sure?"

"Yeah, you are right. I promised to wake up Miss Aslam. She told me she's a heavy sleeper," I lied.

"I guess she must have been overjoyed to listen to the last three words."

I sensed she was jealous.

"Okay. I hate her! Does that make a difference?"

"Oh, that's great. I am glad to learn that."

"What do you call that dress you are in? See through?" I asked. I wanted her attention diverted to something else.

"No. It is called *For Your Eyes Only*. And I can see you are making sense of it. You like it, don't you?"

"I think so. The designer must have been a genius and a psychologist too. You see, he makes sure the man sees everything at a glance while at the same time the wearer psychologically feels fully dressed. To me you are as good as nude, which I don't mind of course, but as far as you are concerned the dress has served its purpose. I wouldn't be surprised if you answered a knock at the door just as you are."

"You make me feel like a loose woman," she said with a blush. I took two steps forward and held her.

"Don't feel so. You are such a responsible lady and at times I feel so proud of you." That at least was true, and it made her happy.

By 9.30 a.m. we were already out of the country. We had no problem going through. We had changed money at the border

and now we carried bundles of Tanzanian shillings, although we still had some Kenyan currency and a few US dollars. I was aware that to get my way through to the very end I would be forced to corrupt some of those I'd encounter on the way. And you never knew what currency they'd prefer.

We drove in silence for a long time. I was immersed in deep thought which abhored interruption, and Marie seemed to realize it. She was the first to break the silence, though.

"Be careful, Adams. You are doing a hundred and eighty and you have touched a hundred and ninety on two occasions."

"I am aware. My whole mind is on the road. You see, there are no potholes to hold you back like we have where we come from. Secondly, just look ahead and see how straight the road is ... you can see over three kilometres ahead. This place is wonderful, can't you see? I just love it"

"Cut the speed down to 150 kph, please." She said

"No. Instead, I'll touch two hundred in the next two minutes. Do not forget we are chasing someone who is over twenty hours ahead of us. This is one of the few light risks we have to take. We have heavier and greater ones ahead. We have no option, Marie, having decided to take this job." I glanced at her to gauge her reaction. I concluded that she had made sense of what I said.

<hr />

I hadn't called Eva as promised and this was worrying me. I knew how easily she got worried or excited when I failed to do as I promised. She always thought that I had got involved in some kind of accident or was in the wrong hands. I hadn't got the time and as the Benz roared on the road, I only thought of the nearest town from where I'd call home. The next town was to be Tanga and at this point we were hundreds of kilometres away.

My thoughts wondered away again, this time to Janet Wanjiru who wanted me to marry her. Up to this moment I hadn't made up my mind or given her a serious thought to determine whether or not she had any hidden agenda. At times I thought and believed she was serious about the whole thing. There was one thing I was certain about – her love for me. There was nothing to doubt about her having been a virgin – (though I wouldn't have known had she not told me so) – nor of her being attracted to me. Eva, who was her maid, had been quick to notice this and was at one time afraid that one of us would likely lose our job with the risk weighed against her.

As it turned out months later, she was right. She not only lost her job, but her freedom as well. Janet had framed her of stealing and fled with me to Mombasa, thus killing two birds with one stone. At a lonely beach hotel Janet had unleashed all the love she had read of from romantic books and pregnancy had resulted. I had therefore no reason to doubt her love for me, and each time I thought about her, I felt myself in a different world filled with love and romance. I would see Janet and myself on an island of our own. Every time this touched my mind I would get an itching wish for history to repeat itself.

It had. I had found myself in not only the same hotel but the very suite that was once booked for Mr. and Mrs. Adams Wamathina. This time round, I didn't mind sharing the bed with her inspite of the very knowledge that I was already a married man ... married to a woman I so much loved. This was worrying me because I hated cheating and lying, and I was doing this to Eva. Was there a chance that Miss. Wicks was trying to bewitch me to leave Eva and marry her? Would she use the I had heard about, that would terrorize me till I turned all my attention from Eva to her? Fear started building up in me. I hated entertaining these kinds of thoughts because the more I did it the more I would distance myself from Miss. Wicks on account of a thing I had no proof about. With the knowledge that she was expecting my child, things were not the same again; I wouldn't hate her for anything. I'd hate to see yet another child. bearing my blood going away from me, like Githure went away with Joy. I was as good a man as any other, but not a bull!

"But," I found myself thinking, "... didn't my grandpa advice me not to marry a rich woman because she'd at long last sit on top of my head and claim leadership of the house, contrary to the teachings of the Bible? Hadn't he told me that women never grew up, that they were like those males from my community who had not passed through the traditional ritual of moving from boyhood to manhood via the knife? I remembered him telling me, *"Muici na kihii akenaga kiarua,"* which translates to, "Whoever steals in the company of the uninitiated feels secure when the uncircumsized goes through the ritual of circumcision." A man who has not undergone this rite has no secrets. For our womenfolk he had the same to say, 'He who steals with a woman feels free when she dies," meaning that women never grew up in mind. Going by my grandpa's advice, if I married this rich lady time would come, no matter long it took, when Miss. Wicks or Janet Wanjiru would look down on me. I hated to entertain the thought, imagining how bad it'd be especially for me, a jail bird. Would she always remind me of those buried memories that I hated revived?

'You are sometimes very traditional grandpa,' I thought as I drove on.

I had driven for less than a few kilometers when I felt a sudden bang inside my head. It was like an electric shock which goes through each part of the body through the blood vessels. I stepped on the brake pedal by instinct, cutting the speed tremendously. I'd have stopped, but the throb in the head went as suddenly as it had come. I let go the brake pedal and stepped slightly on the accelerator. Then I sensed something crawl into my psyche. It was something familiar – the adviser in my system who always came to my rescue.

"DON'T EVER SAY THAT AGAIN!" The voice roared at me.

"Yes, sir." I answered as usual.

"YOUR GRANDFATHER SHOULD LIVE IN YOU ..."

"Yes, sir ... I understand," I said.

"FOLLOW YOUR GRANDFATHER'S MATURE ADVICE ALWAYS, AND YOU WILL FIND YOUR WAY THROUGH THIS MAD, WIDE, WILD WORLD," said the voice.

"Yes, sir. I understand," I said. I was still doing a steady 120 kmph. I wasn't aware I was talking aloud until I turned slightly and was met by the stunned face of Marie.

"Christ," I thought, "... this has become a disease, talking my thoughts aloud. Will I ever hold my secrets long enough if this kind of thing goes on? What will Marie think of me and my dialogue with an invisible entity?" The questions flashed through me as I pondered on the best and simplest explanation. Before she could ask the question I was so sure was coming, I decided to give her a second surprise.

"This receiver is almost inaudible. I forgot to recharge it because I had forgotten all about it. I sensed rather than heard him ..."

"For God's sake, Adams! You'll drive me mad. What are you talking about and with whom!" What I saw on her face told me to answer her and do it in a hurry or she would become hysterical. She looked like she'd blow up. I smiled to make it light.

"Marie, you look like you are staring at a ghost. What's wrong with you? Or you think I've gone nutters because you cannot hear this receiver? Don't be so naive. What do you take this traditional looking necklace for? Do I look that old fashioned to put on a traditional necklace or a talisman? I've just communicated with a friend. I couldn't talk much for the fear of consuming its entire charge. I should have recharged the set before we left Nairobi."

"So that is a receiver?" She asked. "It must be very sensitive." At least she seemed to have swallowed the bait.

"You'll hear it humming when we are in a silent place. With the engine running you cannot hear a thing. At least we now know that the letter hasn't been presented. No one has gone past point A."

"How do we know that?" Again she looked confused.

"I have just talked to our informer. What's the matter with you? You just asked me whom I was talking with. Point A is the junction, and the only one that goes straight to the villa. It is about 10 miles from this point inside the forest. I wonder why this sultan had isolated himself."

"Had?" She asked. I was glad I had won her confidence now.

"Yeah, he is dead. He died eight months ago"

"You seem to have gathered much information since yesterday. That must have been late last night because I am sure you'd have told me about it in the evening."

She seemed suspicious and the feeling that I had trapped myself got me. This young and highly learned generation needed plenty of caution, among them Janet and Marie who spotted a flaw immediately one emerged. But this was okay with me provided I stayed on the alert and stopped pushing my lies too far. I never liked telling lies either but could spring up a few whenever trapped.

"Yeah, you are right. I didn't go straight to bed when we parted." I was about to explain when she interrupted. "I can guess who the source is but I am not bothered. What else do we know?"

"The place is a fortress ..." I answered, pretending not to know what she meant by *the source*. "... plenty of security from within and without. I am planning to jump over the wall." I was now carried away by the story; my whole mind absorbed by the job at hand.

"I thought we agreed the first thing we should do is get there and try to explain ourselves. Only if they refused were we to waylay those who robbed the documents from us!" She reminded me.

"My source tells me that even if your father went there personally without the letter of introduction they wouldn't talk to him. Those on the other end know no one personally. They don't know the owner of the trophy or that whatever the thing is belongs to your father. They wouldn't even point out Aslam from Onyango, Kamau, Rashid and a dozen others. All they have known for the last eight months is that one day, someone, or certain people, would get there with an introduction letter addressed to the dead sultan, and that among the documents there'd be a card supposed to be the second part of the one you held in your own hands yesterday. Whoever that is will be regarded the rightful owner of this devilish thing. As concerns the second issue, let me put it plainly: it is next to impossible to rob a robber. The robber is always on the alert, well knowing that mankind is full of evil and that man spends most of his time planning how to outsmart the other. However we shall give the two options a try for the sake of ... You never know what might come up."

"What else is there from the source, that I should know?" Marie asked with a sigh that indicated defeat or something close to resignation. I was aware she hadn't anticipated all what she was hearing now. The help she had had in mind when she offered to accompany me was pegged on the hope that she would make use of her sex appeal to get us through by convincing whoever had the documents that we were the rightful messengers. Now what she was hearing was totally different.

"There's a lot more my dear. Plenty of discouraging information," I said

"How did my father get involved in this devilish thing?" Marie wondered aloud. She now looked and sounded resigned.

"That is one thing we'll never find out, Marie. Not unless we got the guts to ask him. Personally I wouldn't dare poke my nose where I sense danger. You know Marie, it is very difficult to know how the very rich operate. You wouldn't even know how they acquired their wealth. To be honest with ourselves, it is impossible to acquire some kind of wealth from scratch as most claim. The English say that behind every great fortune there's a crime. I believe that. I also believe that the very rich are normally silent criminals. This, if you ask me, happens to be the worst category of criminals. They are silent smooth criminals. Call them SSC if you like. That's what we call them in the streets."

"In the streets?", Marie asked, looking up at me.

"Yes, in the streets. We are not in office all the time. You have your official jargon just as we have our street ones."

"Oh, I see what you mean. My God! I've never thought about what we have just said. I cannot imagine my father being an SSC. He is such a soft. . ."

"Yeah, there you are ..." I interrupted. "... a soft criminal. It amounts to the same thing, a soft smooth criminal. Marie, how in the name of honesty could you make a net profit of hundreds of millions of shillings out of a clean deal, and where the hell would you get the capital to start a business that nets such?"

"It is not possible, Adams. I agree with you," Marie's answer came after a moment's silence.

"Yes, Marie. You are being honest and that is very good of you. It pays greatly to be honest with oneself. But let's remind ourselves one thing: we are not out to investigate anyone. We are out to do a job, a well-paying job, and all we should do is concentrate on it. There goes the beep again but it is too faint. My friend is trying to reach me again, but the distance seems to pose a problem. This will be a big setback, though we were not depending on his assistance." We drove on in silence, I feeling content I had won the battle.

CHAPTER EIGHT

I called Nairobi from Tanga where we arrived shortly after 11.00 a.m. For the first time since we got married and moved into the house in Buruburu which we had christened the Garden of Eden, Eva was not in. I let the phone ring on and on hoping that she'd just enter the room from somewhere, the toilet, bath, shop or even our residential compound and pick it up, but to no avail. I reluctantly put the mouth piece down. As I left the booth I was a worried man. What bothered me even more was the realisation that Eva would remain a headache to me if I didn't do something about it. The logical thing was simply to forget her for the length of time I would be on this job that needed my undivided attention. Could I really manage that, bearing in mind my closeness to Eva?

Soon after we left Tanga and continued with our journey, we arrived at a small town called Hale some minutes after midday. From here Marie gave me a hand behind the wheel. As she drove along the smooth road, my attention was diverted to her. A jolly youngish girl who looked at life from a peculiar angle. A reasonable lady who, from my point of view, would have made a good judge or senior administrative officer because of her ability to stand to reason. She was among the first lot that went through the 8-4-4 school system and had followed it to the end. She did eight years in a coast primary school, four at Mugoiri Girls Secondary in Central Province, then joined Nairobi University. She'd have landed a nice job with a city firm but her father Aslam wanted her, his only child, to take care of his wealth. After all, you didn't do a job just because you happened to know how to do it. People got employed to earn money and she already had enough of that. All that was required of her now was to manage it and to spend wisely.

But that would not satiate her youngish blood. I had noted her eagerness to taste 'life' while she still had the time.

***

I was back at the wheel as we entered the final leg of our journey. We were now approaching our destination, the town known as Mgambo. I was on the lookout for anything that would give me a clue to the presence of whoever robbed me of the vital briefcase. Though I hadn't found it necessary to tell Marie so, I was ready to do anything to retrieve the introduction letter. Anything, including using the gun. That is why I had carried it. I wasn't going to let the robber stand between me and fortune or to block my star which I was certain would shine if I saw this thing through successfully,

"Have you ever been out of our country before today?" I asked Marie, to break the silence which was becoming uncomfortable.

"No . . . and I have never had the desire to do so."

"Why not?"

"Well, I've never thought about it. I think I hate being lonely, away from those I am used to. I like it when I wake up and find that I am safely at home where I can scream for help and have someone at hand to assist me."

"I see. And how do you feel right now?"

She turned and searched my face. The smile on her face announced satisfaction of some kind; she was happy about something known only to herself. For the first time I noticed the beauty of her eyes as they shied away from mine. She answered me after a while.

"How do I feel? ... Okay, at home"

"Why so? We are not in Kenya!" I reminded her.

"I have a Kenyan beside me. I think that's all that matters."

I glanced at her again. I noticed yet again how beautiful she was.

To my surprise I again talked my mind aloud.

"You are such a beautiful lady, Marie. I love you." She turned to face me. This time I was not able to face her, hit by some guilt that had not touched me before.

"Is that why you wanted to marry me? To take me for a second wife?" Marie asked me boldly. I was lost for words. I was already regretting having started all this.

"Adams," she called when she realized I wasn't talking.

"I am listening," I said.

"You didn't answer my question. I am waiting for an answer."

"That's what I am waiting for too, Marie. I am also eager to answer you."

"Waiting for?"

"Yeah, waiting for an answer to form in my head because up to this moment I do not understand why I asked that million dollar question. I've never wanted to have a second wife – After all, my grandpa advised me not to ..."

"Adams ..." she interrupted. "... I am tired of hearing about your grandfather. He's yours, not mine, and I do not want him to be a factor in my life. I cannot be led by a person who probably died before I was born. This is the computer age, not the stone age, for God's sake. Please stop boring me with dead men's advice."

I applied emergency braking and pulled aside. Fear had gripped me and I needed to brace for what I was sure was coming next.

"What's wrong. Why are you stopping?" Marie asked me, seeming to have sensed danger that wasn't there.

"I was waiting for a bang." I told her absent-mindedly. My thoughts were on the bang I had felt when I had talked of my grandpa being just what Marie had called him – traditional grandfather.

"What bang are you talking about, Wamathina? Sometimes I think you move away from your mind. That stress . . ."

I refused to listen by moving my mind away to something else. I didn't know what to tell her this time. But just to contain her, I made up another poor lie.

"You don't seem to be with me on the road, dear. Swear that you didn't see that antelope which I almost hit and I'll take you straight to an optician."

She didn't deny or accept seeing the antelope and that took care of the bang' debate. I drove on.

"Marie ..." I called after a while, "... you want to know what I'd call this age you are so eager to praise? The backwards age. We are going backwards. When I was a kid I used to see my dad wearing trousers with 'turn ups' and that was the fashion then. Look at my legs and see for yourself what I am putting on, over forty five years later. Worse still, this material cannot be compared with what my dad used to wear. You girls these days are putting on mini skirts which I grew up staring at and which had disappeared by the time I was a teenager. According to your father, the thing we are chasing dates to over a hundred years back, which means it is far older than him. Why doesn't he and those others interested give up the ancient junk and get back to modern business? We may have computers and computerised people like you, but where does that get us? And who told you there were no computers before this age?"

"Are you complaining just because I called your grandfather stone age?"

"Yeah, and don't ever repeat that again. Those old boys and girls had discipline and lived like angels under whatever circumstance they were. This one is an age none of them would envy – an age where girls your age are marrying their grandfathers without batting an eyelid."

"Okay, dear. I am sorry I didn't intend to hurt you that much. I just wanted to welcome you to this age, no matter what it is to you."

"Thank you, I feel welcome but I'll stay alert," I said.

That took care of that, and we were good friends again.

We arrived at Mgambo a few minutes past six. Even this late the sun was high, promising at least an hour of light before darkness closed in.

I was tired and I felt I needed plenty of rest if I wanted my mind to remain intact and make proper decisions. But inspite of this, I still decided to look around the town. I needed to become familiar with this place in case trouble broke out. I would then know where to enter through and from where to make my escape.

The town harboured more old buildings than modern ones, which told me that it was old. It had, from my judgement, a population of between fifty and eighty thousand people, most of them living on the outskirts where they grew food crops for subsistence. The residents, I noted, were a curious lot that scented an intruder the moment one showed up. A good number would stare at our vehicle until we vanished into another street. It was clear they were not used to visitors and didn't care having them around.

Unlike in our country Kenya, most of the sign-boards on buildings and streets were in Kiswahili. You hardly saw an English word. The residents appeared close-knit. In the evening you saw groups seated in circles, taking a brew they called 'Bege'. Children, their fathers and grandfathers would take it alternately. Despite their reluctance to have visitors, whoever happened to pass us greeted us with remarkable respect, and this somehow helped to erase the unease one felt as a result of their stares. We booked into Hotel Granado which happened to be one of the most recent buildings in the town. You felt like you were being robbed when asked to pay Shs. 1,500.00 per night, considering its class, but when you converted that into Kenya currency, you realised you were to pay only about Sh. 200.00 which was quite cheap for a self-contained room, plus breakfast. I took room No. 205 while Marie took No. 215, right opposite mine, with a veranda six metres wide separating us.

After bathing we met at the dining lounge where we took light drinks before I decided to take a quarter Bond 7 whisky to steel my guts. We had decided to visit the villa to see if luck was on our side. If it was, whoever was there would give us a chance to explain ourselves. This thought made me touch the talisman lovingly, my mind wandering far away into the depths of the forest that I knew surrounded the villa we were to storm on the morrow.

"Is he trying to reach us?" Marie asked all of a sudden.

"Who? What do you mean? Someone trying to reach us?" I asked, not realising what was on her mind.

"I thought that necklace has a receiver... you talked about..." My God, how could I forget the lie I had told her in such a short time? I wasn't aware I was caressing the necklace, leave alone thinking about what it was supposed to be as far as Marie was concerned.

"No!" I answered curtly, standing up. "Come on, let's get moving. We'll be there in under twenty minutes." I led her out.

We reached point 'A' from where I decided to inquire. This was the point where five roadways leading in different directions conjoined, where Mrs. Wicks had instructed that I seek advice. There was a barrier on only one of the five roads and I guessed that it could be the one we wanted. Mrs. Wick's hadn't remembered to mention this barrier which would have made it easier for us.

"Good evening, sir," the uniformed guard greeted. "Could I be of any assistance?"

"Good evening officer. We are on our way to bin Saiga's residence. Which of the five ways is it?" I asked

"Just a moment please. I'll raise the barrier for you. You are on the right road. Looks like there is a party or something. . ." "Why?" I asked, sensing he had some news. "Yours is the sixth vehicle in the last ten hours. I've not seen that number in the last six months, I mean since the sultan died."

"You mean bin Saiga? Was he a sultan? We are not aware. We are just messengers from his grandson," I explained, and wondered why I was doing it.

"That's what he was. To us he was the whole world. He was the father of our community and the founder of this town. Travel in peace and have good luck."

His prayers prompted me to give him Tshs. 1,000 and thank him for his courtesy.

The road was not tarmacked but all-weather and very smooth. On both sides were lined kilometres of trees and shrubbery which became thicker with each kilometre we covered.

"Have your gun ready," I told Marie after about seven kilometres. Mine was handy and loaded for action. I kept reminding myself that I had no ammunition to waste and that I needed to be very accurate if I decided to use it, I also needed to remind Marie not to repeat the mistake she made when the briefcase we were chasing was snatched.

"Marie ..." I called her, "I am ready to shoot to kill anybody who crosses my path. You understand? Anybody. Please just keep your distance when trouble erupts."

She didn't say anything but nodded her head. I could see she didn't like what I had said and in a voice that was markedly authoritative. We drove on, both apprehensive and my eyes alert and busy like never before. I now fully realized this mission was not simple or pleasant. The Benz rolled smoothly and silently, almost like the engine had been switched off. Only Marie's breathing reached my ears ... everything else was dead silent.

All my five senses were on high alert for trouble, and so was the 'sixth' that controlled reflex actions in me. It was through this 'special sense' that my invisible friend always reached me. At this moment I needed him more than at any other time. We drove on.

'Boom . . . boom!' The sound came from a distance, I stepped on the brake pedal, instantly cutting the speed almost to zero.

"What's it?" Marie asked me, seeming not to have heard anything. She had heard the sound alright, she admitted, but didn't know what it was.

"Well, those are bullet shots," I told her as I stopped the vehicle. "Look, I'll enter through that foot path over there. Follow me at a distance of ten metres. Do not accelerate lest the engine attracts attention. If you see anything suspicious, stop, take your gun and stay still till I come. If you think for any reason that I am heading into a trap, hoot. You understand? Take care not to panic or you'll have both of us killed."

She nodded her head to indicate she understood. I jumped out of the vehicle and disappeared into the forest.

After about thirty metres, two more shots rang out somewhere to my left. I turned in that direction and slithered deeper into the thicket, I was now as cautious as a cat timing its prey.

I detected some movement a short distance from where I was. Then I saw the figure of a man barricaded behind a wattle tree. After a few seconds, which seemed too long to me, the man ran from behind the tree to another, coming closer to where I was hidden by a thick shrub.

"Who are these rivals?' I wondered. 'Could they be fighting for the introduction letter? If so, how did the other party know that it was already stolen from me and on its way to the addressee? Or is Mrs. Wicks still part of this?"

The man jumped again to another tree and a shot rang out.

From my position I could see a great deal of the battlefield. I could see two vehicles parked a distance away from where I was. Whoever these two warriors were, they had come to the warfield driving.

The first man once again leapt from the wattle tree to take cover behind another thick tree which was close to where I was hiding, prompting fears of being caught in the crossfire in me. He didn't make it. From right opposite him came a louder and heavier sound of gunfire that echoed throughout the forest. Then suddenly everything went dead silent. The bullet had hit the man right at the centre of his Adam's apple. The impact lifted him a few feet off-ground, then he fell into a heap – dead. It had been ruthless – and fast. I had witnessed a man move from life to death and for a minute or two a wave of anger towards the gunman swept through me. It was momentary, however, and disappeared as I started wondering whether I wouldn't do the same to the killer if he came close enough to threaten my life. Anyone would be a target, as I had told Marie, if he stood between me and my fortune.

The killer gave himself about five good minutes before he showed up. I knew he wouldn't come out gun in hand like a fool and that he wouldn't be certain his victim was dead just because he had seen him go down. He had to be cautious just like any other person who engaged himself in 'black' deals. When he appeared, he first did a quick survey of the surroundings, then he approached the dead body cautiously, not aware that he was being watched from close quarters. *Where had I seen this person before?* I asked myself. He was so familiar I felt I had seen him before.

He frisked the dead man's body thoroughly from pocket to pocket and from organ to organ. There was no suggestion of being in a hurry. He might to not have known whom he had killed but he certainly knew why he had killed him, and he appeared set to take his time to find what he was after.

It was not the kind of scene you watch peacefully, especially knowing with certainty that the two were not acting in a film. The reality was that one was a murderer and the other the victim. I was all attention on whatever the killer was doing. From my position, just a few metres away, I sensed I also knew what he was looking for. It had to be the introduction letter. So he already was aware that the letter had left my hands for those of a robber who now lay dead at his feet after taking lead through his Adam's apple? The thought that this killer had known all along that I had the letter and that he had been most probably following all my movements to the day it was robbed from me made me shudder. It meant that all those following this satanic thing were professionals in the game of killing. Again I recalled what Mrs. Wicks had repeatedly told me, that there was no way I could win this battle by myself. She had therefore floated the idea of backing from Stranger, another cold-blooded killer. Now, as I lay hidden behind a shrub watching this trigger-happy killer turn his victim's pockets inside out, I sensed what my dear Janet who loved me dearly had meant. She knew I was good in boxing and karate, good in the mouth when arguing or telling necessary lies, but not a professional in the field of espionage or anything of this magnitude.

'WHAT A GREAT SHAME MY DEAR SON OF FATE! THIS APPREHENSION IS JUST REDUCING YOU, MY DEAR BOY, FROM THE MOUNTAIN YOU THOUGHT YOU WERE TO AN ANTHILL.' *It was the bastard in my head who sometimes liked ridiculing me. At times he was that harsh.*

I hated and loathed the thought that I would lose this game. 'I have to win!' I told myself, knowing too well that victory always went to the luckiest of the lucky.

Something I saw on the killer's face when he turned in my direction jolted me out of my thoughts. At the same time my friend in the head became friendly.

'THERE YOU ARE, SONNY BOY. HE'S GOT IT, THE TINY CARD CUT DIAGONALLY AND THE ENVELOPE CONTAINING THE INTRODUCTION LETTER. IT'S TIME TO ACT!'

The man was grinning as he held the items in his hands. He put his gun away and, using both hands, perused the items before putting them into an envelope he had fished out of his pocket. I got ready for action. I wasn't going to let the letter and the other items get out of my sight under whatever cost. They were robbed from me, I argued, giving myself an excuse to kill. The gun was already cocked and all I needed to was pull to the trigger... which I now did.

My God! I missed! A fraction of a second had saved him. He had just bent his head, which I had aimed at, to pick something from the body of the man he had just murdered. I fired a second shot but by then he was already off my firing line. He somersaulted into a bush then jumped behind a thick shrub a few metres away. I fired a third time and waited. Why didn't he fire back, I wondered? My initial fear had dissipated, my thoughts getting a new focus. All that mattered now was how to retrieve the introduction letter, get back to where Marie was waiting and give her a surprise. We would then move to the concluding stage of this scheme that would possibly open access to millions of shillings.

The silence that followed was more pregnant than the gun shots. I raised my head to study the situation and see if I could crawl closer to my enemy. What I saw made me smile inspite of the unfavourable situation. The gunman was negotiating a corner over forty metres from where I lay. If it wasn't for the coat and the white cap I had seen him in, I wouldn't have believed it was him.

I took another five more minutes lying low, just to make sure there was no trick to the disappearing act. Then I got up to investigate whatever had taken place.

The dead man's face was familiar. He was none other than the fellow I had observed call Marie from a telephone booth at Wilson Airport. He was lying there in a pool of blood, his Adam's apple disgustingly agape. I didn't like him, but I pitied him. He had died, like many of our type, chasing a dream that would only have benefitted bigger fish. Already, doubts were crowding my mind.

'THIS ISN'T THE MAN WHO ROBBED YOU, SON OF FATE. HE CERTAINLY CANNOT BE THE ONE WHO ORGANIZED FOR YOU TO GET ROBBED.' So, how did he get possession of the introduction documents? What happened to the person who snatched them and who is he or she? Miss. Wicks?

I hated the very thought.

As I continued wondering what might have happened, something else caught my attention. There were two guns lying on the ground. One of the two was certainly the victim's as it lay only a few inches from his right hand. The second was partly hidden in the branches of a nearby shrub. This, I immediately sensed, was the gun that had killed this man lying here in a pool of blood. I guessed what must have happened. My shot must have taken the killer by surprise. In his frantic jump for cover he must have lost grip of his gun, which explained why he hadn't fired back. Panicking, he had opted to make a run for it.

There was nothing for me to do here. Time was running out and darkness first approaching in this forest. I decided to get back to where Marie was waiting for me. It wasn't far from this point and it took me under five minutes. I didn't have to ask her to know that she had been badly shaken and that she was overjoyed to see me back all in one piece, I asked her to drive back to the road leading to the sultan's villa.

"I was worried, terribly . . .," She said, as she took off after a three point turn.

"Take it easy ..." I assured her, ". . , all is well with me."

"There was a gun fight, isn't that so? Gunshots were echoing all over."

"Yeah, but as you can see, I didn't get hurt. Turn right, we have to get to the villa immediately The killer got the introduction letter."

"Which killer?"

"Well. . . let me just tell you that I had another glimpse of the introduction letter minutes before it vanished into the forest. I'am guessing that the person who just robbed it from the one who had it might be presenting it to the villa in the next hour. I want us to be there when he does that."

Marie didn't seem to know what to say after this. She was overwhelmed by the knowledge that just a few minutes back I had been a short distance from the documents that mattered most in this case. But as she put it, she was happy that the gun fight had left me unhurt.

"Did anyone get hurt back there?" She asked after a minute's silent drive.

"Yes," I answered. I had decided not to give her the details.

"Badly?" She asked.

"Well… let me say yes."

"You don't seem eager to tell me the story," she said.

"You are right," I answered. She drove on silently for another minute.

"Wamathina …" Marie said in a changed tone that told me she was serious, "… I want you to tell me whether someone back there got badly hurt,"

"Why?" I asked curtly.

"Because we should be doing something about it than driving ahead leaving someone dying and maybe needing our help."

"Look here, Marie. The person back there doesn't need our help at all. Do you get it? Secondly, we have entirely nothing to do with him. In any case, we have only one thing before us, and I do not need to remind you what it is. Let me warn you not to repeat the same mistake you did when we lost the letter. Cut the speed to 30 KPH and make sure you do not go above that. This is a zone where we are supposed, to use our ears more than our eyes."

The villa was surrounded by a thick bush and scattered tall trees. The main gate came into view after one negotiated a sharp corner. One had to mount a bump which would throw one off-balance even at the minimal speed, then one came to the gate. We were fortunate that Mrs. Wicks had mentioned to me these security arrangements. Somehow I knew I had to drive dead slow as I reached the gate. I noticed that the bumps were not old. If they had been there since the villa was built, then they had worn out and had been recently renovated. My guess was that this had been done after the death of bin Saiga to slow down visitors to the villa for one reason or the other. That included the likes of me… dogs of war who were running after something they did not know.

I remained silent as Marie drove towards the villa. I had so much on my mind and at times I felt like my head would burst. It wasn't a comfortable experience to witness murder, to see somebody you recognized lying in a pool of blood just because the victim happened to be in possession of some documents. I couldn't help imagining myself in the dead man's boots, and that thought alone gave me the jitters. What would happen to Eva and my child? What kind of a life would they lead after my death?

Again I found myself flashing back to Eva's son. I recalled how I had met him, our ride together and the rapport we had struck, to the very minute he had snatched a lady's handbag. The boy was as bad as the rest of the parking lot I had met. I had found out he was Mchacho's and Chali's friend and these two were just horrible, unrepentant and confirmed criminals who wouldn't change even if you promised them heaven. Kimesh wouldn't change either and I wondered what his mother would do on realising this.

My mind again went back to the dead man we had left behind. Should I tell Marie that her anonymous caller number one was now in hell or heaven or wherever else the dead went to? Would this put more fear into her?

"You are talking to yourself Wamathina. What's the matter? That can't be the receiver!" She interrupted my loud thoughts.

"I am aware ... I am just bothered." I accepted.

"Tell me what's bothering you. Maybe after that you'll feel different."

"No, Marie. Telling you would only have the two of us worried. After all, some of my worries are very personal. They concern my wife."

"Are you sure it is nothing to do with what you have just left behind? Did you use your gun? Please tell me the truth, Wamathina," Marie insisted.

"I did use my gun alright, but all it did was to send a man running away, holding the introduction letter."

"At least it did a nice job. You are safe, and I think that's why we need the gun."

"It wasn't a nice job, Marie. I did not do a complete job. I would have wanted to lay the killer's body next to his victim's. But let's not talk about it... there will be time for that later," I said, and went back to silence.

Here we are at last!"

Marie sighed with relief as she drove up to the gate. Before she cut off the engine, a guard and a lady came in sight. The guard, I was quick to note, was not a cop. However, there was no doubt about his having been trained, judging from the way he handled the rifle in his hands. He was almost six feet tall, but seemed not to have been keen on keeping fit. He was, or might have been approaching forty-five years. His face was not an inch friendly, which made it clear our arrival was being viewed suspiciously.

The lady was probably twenty years younger than the guard. She wore a dress that left you wondering whether or not she had shoes on, since it touched the ground. She had a fair complexion; you couldn't call her black, yet she was not as brown as Marie. Her hair was long and shiny black. She was a head shorter than the guard but unlike him, her physical build matched her height and, apparently, her age. The long free dress denied me much I'd have longed to see. I am the type that is able to study and judge a person or a person's likely behaviour or response from looking at his or her features. If I had seen the rest of her without the oversize dress, I wouldn't have dared step out of the vehicle wearing one of those phoney smiles of mine.

"What do you want? Stay right inside the vehicle!" It was the lady shouting at me. There was no indication at all that they were about to get any closer to the gate, leave alone open it.

"We've been sent by Mr. Aslam. Mohammed Aslam bin Aslam to get..."

"Where's the letter?" She barked at me again, even before I was finished. At this juncture Marie got out to try to assist me.

"Stay right there! Where's the letter of introduction?" She roared at us once more, this time facing Marie. I was already back in the car.

Marie didn't get back into the car but stood her ground, striking a pose that drew attention to her beauty and the smart dress. But this didn't impress the lioness.

"Get back into the vehicle and hold out the letter of introduction. Hurry up!" She shouted, drawing closer. Now I could see her, even her white teeth which were so lovely, though spitting fire. When Marie didn't move she grabbed the rifle from the guard, cocked it and aimed it at us. She approached Marie menacingly,

"If you do not have the letter, clear off immediately. I won't give you a second warning."

Probably to demonstrate her resolve she aimed at the vehicle and pulled the trigger.

"BOOM!"

Marie screamed and fell to the ground as the bullet tore off the driver's side mirror and blew it into smithereens.

I jumped out to assist Marie. I was aware she hadn't been hit but the shock must have done enough damage. The lioness instantly turned her attention to me.

"Easy madam, take it easy," I told the trigger-happy youngster as I hurried to help my colleague.

"Hurry up! The second shot might do more harm," the lioness threatened again and I believed her.

"Please don't," I begged as my mind worked on a gimmick. "That's enough damage. But I'd like you to know, just for the record, that this is bin Saiga's great granddaughter and that her father risked her life to come and collect..."

"Shut up!" She shouted at me a second before she pulled the trigger once again. The damage this time was just as she had warned – worse. We had to scamper from the scene on three wheels as the fourth was flat and damaged. Even as we cleared from the place with our limping Mercedes Benz, the Greener rifle, which was powerful enough to kill an elephant in one shot, was still trained on us. It was a relief when we turned a corner.

I parked the vehicle a few metres after the corner. I didn't have to park it off the road. I reasoned there weren't any more vehicles coming this way and if there were, I wouldn't have minded knowing who was going where. Who knew – perhaps in the process the killer might pass by with the introduction documents, an eventuality that I would turn to my advantage. He would have to be the better man to go beyond this point.

Marie had not recovered from the shock even by the time I replaced the deflated wheel with a spare one. She was still resting in the back seat where I had put her. When I was through, I drove back straight to Hotel Granado.

It was only after getting back to our respective rooms following supper that Marie was able to smile and utter some words with what one would call self-confidence. She joined me in my room where she found me lying on the bed facing the ceiling. I had a cigarette between my fingers which I puffed leisurely, releasing blue smoke that formed rings in the air. I was thinking of giving up smoking and had stopped buying cigarettes, even occasionally refusing to buy at all. But whenever I had something disturbing my mind, like now, I wouldn't help lighting up. I crushed the half-smoked cigarette when Marie talked to me.

"What next? I am finished, I do not know what to do from now on. If I had the guts to go home alone, I'd do so first thing tomorrow morning. That bitch almost killed me! That was her intention, wasn't it? I was just lucky she missed!"

I couldn't help laughing, even though this was not a laughing matter. The way Marie spoke told me she hadn't grasped the lady's intentions.

"She wouldn't have missed you, Marie, had that been her intention. She wanted to make a point with the side mirror and she didn't miss it. The second bullet got the wheel. Let me tell you, she is what they call a crack-shot or a sharpshooter... which is surprising considering her age."

"Whoop! At least that's encouraging if it is true she didn't mean to kill." Marie said and sounded relieved. "Now, what do we do next? Pack and go?"

"No. I won't leave here without that thing, Marie, no matter how long it will take me. I'll only give up when I am fully satisfied that it is not available. By then I'll have something to tell your father. Right now, I propose that you stay here. These two rooms will be our headquarters. Tomorrow morning I'll get back there to study the place. Like I had mentioned to you, if there's no option I'll have to try to get in over the wall."

"I am beginning to think that you are not a good man, Wamathina. How would you dare do a thing like that? Do you know what it'd mean if you were caught jumping over the wall or forcing any other way through to the villa apart from the gate?"

"I know that more than you do, Marie, I have done bad things in life and this one cannot be classified as such. I have never claimed to be good and that is why your father entrusted me with this kind of job. He is a very intelligent person, if you sought my opinion. In the first place he detects a person who can do a dirty job, which is what this one is, and secondly he detects honesty in the same bad guy. Do you get me? Do you know what a dirty job means?"

She nodded, but seemed not certain.

"Well, that is it – a job that could cost your life, his or mine. A job that is not clearly spelt out, but one that you cannot shake aside because it is well-paying. It is made sweet by money. Money, Marie, is the greatest enemy man has. It makes one blind and dumb. You don't see the risks involved and you refuse to listen to well wishers who tell you not to touch this or that because they know it is dangerous doing so. When your thoughts are on money, nothing else can stop you. That's what your father gave me – a dirty job and an advance of three hundred thousand Kenya shillings."

"I feel you are talking evil of my father, Wamathina. Why? You are portraying a bad picture of him!" Marie said after giving what I had said some thought.

"I beg to disagree with that, Marie. I am talking evil of money, not your dad. Don't you understand? All your father did was to give me a job which is best qualified by the adjective 'dirty'. A job he couldn't do because it needed a bad guy to do it. That's all there is to it. Your father is not a bad guy, so he cannot do the job personally. This is why we have bad guys all over he world. If you took time to read the Bible, you wouldn't be doubting what I am saying. Someone like Samson was a bad guy and that is why he was assigned to kill the Philistines, yet he was good in the eyes of God." I thought for a while then said, "I feel like going out and I wouldn't mind your company. I think we need to ease our minds so that we can think straight." This was designed to put her off the former topic which I felt would go on and on.

Together we left Hotel Granado and drove about two kilometres from the town to Makuti Club where hundreds of residents in the vicinity met for drinks, *nyama choma* and dancing.

The loud music played by a live band from Zaire caught our attention half a kilometre away. I noticed Marie was carried away by the music and was tapping her thigh with her right hand fingers and slightly following the rhythm with movements of her head.

"I love Lingala music ..." she was telling me.

"You don't have to tell me. I've already found that out. You started swaying half a kilometre away. Do you dance?" I was interested to know because I was a good dancer myself.

"It won't take long before you find that out!"

By now we were entering the main hall.

The place was lit by coloured fluorescent lights that made it look heavenly. There were bars surrounded by high stools at several points and they were almost full.

Those who didn't prefer high stools took sofa sets which were arranged in small circles, each catering for six to eight clients. There were also easy wooden chairs whose seats and back were cushioned.

The bars and open cubicles in which the majority of the patrons sat were facing the stage where the live band was performing. We entered just as the crowd was cheering some lady dancers and four gentlemen who were displaying wonderful rhythm.

Marie started clapping her hands immediately, swinging her hips as she did so. I let her go a step ahead so that I could watch her from behind. I like watching people without them watching me, and the way Marie was doing it was worth watching. I was pleased that she had forgotten, though temporarily, the worries she had had in mind before we left for here. It was funny to watch the other side of her. All I had known of her was that she was a highly-educated daughter of a multi-millionaire who would have made a good judge or an administrator. Now I was learning she was good at more than one thing.

I ordered a Bond 7 quarter-litre bottle, and a half-litre bottle of Ginger Ale. Marie ordered some Wood Pecker wine. In two minutes we were served. In the next hour those who loved dancing and those driven by drunkeness got onto the floor, each dancing the way they knew best to beats of Lingala music. We joined the floor and enjoyed ourselves. We left the club some minutes past midnight, our minds refreshed.

CHAPTER NINE

I woke up with my heartbeats so loud that I could hear them. It took me about thirty seconds to know where I was. I looked around my room and the first thing I noticed was that I had not put off the light which I normally made sure I did before going to bed. I hated waking up at night only to encounter plenty of light. It must have been a result of the long journey we had covered and our sleeping late after a little too much whisky.

Marie too had taken a good share of her Wood Peckers and couldn't tell black from white by the time we left there. She hadn't misbehaved in any way, but that hadn't stopped me from wondering whether that wasn't a bit too much for a lady of her age and status. The trouble is, I couldn't have told her that.

I jumped out of the bed and went to the window. The day was promising as the sun was already up. It didn't seem like it would get hot. I went back to the bed from where I picked my watch. It was after 8.00 a.m., a good time to have a shower, take breakfast and move into action.

Whenever I am in the bathroom with cold and hot water raining alternatingly on me, my mind takes a trip down memory lane, taking me from my bad days to the good ones. It always leaves me confused, not really knowing where to classify my life. It always makes me wonder whether fate treats other people differently. Do they need to struggle as much to make ends meet?

Right now my mind was on Mrs. Wicks. I was missing her and this came as a surprise. I flashed back to whatever had taken place between us. What would happen at long last? I was already married. I hadn't told her this, yet she had confidence that she would eventually win my heart. Should I tell her the truth?

Then my mind went to Eva. What was she doing? How was she coping with her parking-boy son? I had called her again and to my surprise, the phone had been picked by a young boy who wanted to know who I was and what I wanted to tell his mother. He hadn't sounded friendly and the manner in which he had answered my questions had displayed a lack of discipline. What worried me now was whether I would really cope with the boy, and to an extent Eva, because I was certain life wasn't going to be the same after this. The presence of Kimesh would be a constant reminder of the fact that Eva once belonged to or had been known by another man before me. Most men don't love that and I happen to be one of them. Had Kimesh not come on the scene, I guess it would have been possible to overlook that reality, since I loved Eva and wanted to believe that I was the only man who knew her. To make the situation worse, Mrs. Wicks who had been a virgin was now expecting my child. All the same it didn't mean I was for Janet yet ... I wasn't ready, for whatever reason, to part with Eva.

Out went Eva and in came Marie. The water was still raining on my head and back, making me feel some relief with each passing minute. What would happen to her when all this mad business was over, I wondered? Was it the love for her father that made her take this risky, non-paying business? Or was there something else? When I had hinted that she had better go home before worse became worst, she had insisted on going through with it.

When she was tipsy, I had noticed she had some extra courage to engage me in romantic debates that left me wondering whether she wasn't trying to project a different picture from the one I knew. It was like she was trying to tell me that I should stop treating her like we were both men and that she wouldn't mind sharing the same suite with me as I did with Janet. What a surprise! Would she remember this when she woke up sober, or would she cover it up with drunkeness? If she decided to do the latter I would gladly let it slip by because I wasn't ready for a third engagement.

Then my worst enemy took centre-stage – money! Oh! My mind almost blew up. Why was it that whenever money entered a relationship, even between great friends, things started going wrong? Why was it that I had allowed it to play chess with my person? Why? An answer was not forthcoming even as I left the bathroom.

I left the hotel premises at 9.30 a.m. My first stop was at point 'A' where I met the same guard manning the barrier. I wasn't driving I was surprised that he recognized me immediately.

"Hallo, sir. How was your trip to the sultan's place?"

"It was okay. You have a good memory."

I then remembered I had given him a tip of a thousand shillings. That must be what had made him memorize my face.

"Yeah... I don't need to see you twice to remember your face." He bragged with a knowing smile.

"Let me try that," I said, then produced another one thousand Tanzanian shillings note and extended it to him.

"Try me," he said, picking the 'bribe'. To me it wasn't a tip; he had to part with some information.

"How many faces have you seen this morning?"

He eyed me quizzically before answering.

"Five, in three different cars,"

"How many among the five have you seen before?"

"Two. In different vehicles, at different times."

"What about the police?" I asked after thinking for a minute.

"A Landrover with six police officers has just gone that way. What's going on there? Is there trouble?"

"I don't know. I thought you'd allow me do the questioning considering that I've just bought you some tea, okay?"

"Go ahead, sir. I was only curious."

"Now tell me, is there another way of entering the place apart from through this gate?"

"Yeah. There's a footpath through the forest. That would mean trekking over ten kilometres."

"I do not mind. Where is the path?"

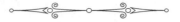

It turned out that I had got a chance for road work, which I had missed for two days. After being shown the foot track, I went back to the hotel and changed. I put on a dark track suit and a pair of track shoes, not forgetting to pack my gun as well. I picked a green cap Mrs. Wicks had given me as a present and put it on. I felt great.

"You look wonderful, Wamathina." Marie said as soon as she entered my room just as I was about to leave. "I've never seen such a nice cap, it matches the tracksuit wonderfully!"

Women are funny. This one was concerned with the matching of clothes instead of wishing me good luck. What good would it do me being smart if I stopped a bullet? However, I just smiled and thanked Marie for paying me the compliment.

I started off on what to an observer would have passed for a leisurely jog.

My first stop was after fifteen minutes at a place where I found two young boys playing near a stream where they had brought two heifers to drink. I stopped by, had a chat with them, after which I washed sweat from my face then got back to my tactical jog. In the next fifteen minutes I was there!

I didn't waste time but went round the wall. I noticed that the gate was to my right and that it could be over a hundred metres away. Trees and many kinds of shrubs grew thick against the wall making it completely impossible to locate where the gate was.

I decided to go round the wall from the left. The foot path was no more because it had started wearing out over a kilometre back. The only traces of foot-steps went to the right, towards the gate, indicating that there were times the residents of the villa thought of venturing outside the wall. My guess was they would occasionally go to the stream.

Just as Mrs. Wicks had warned me, the wall was around fifteen feet tall. On top was barbed wire that added about three more feet. Though I made little progress because of the shrubbery, I managed to cover a good stretch. It looked like the wall would go on and on. Even after an hour I hadn't come across any corner that would give an indication of the width or length of the compound.

Large trees that dotted the perimeter had caused parts of the wall to get cracks. I was still trying to figure their number when I came across one that must have escaped the sultan's security-minded staff. Its branches had extended beyond the wall and bent deep inside the compound, some through the barbed wire. This presented an opportunity to try my luck at getting into the compound. However, I was aware I wouldn't jump over the wall during the day as that would be risking being seen. First I needed to study the place thoroughly. I would then wait for the time to put into practice what I had planned.

I tried to climb up the tree with my shoes on, but each time I slipped and fell back. I decided to take them off and this helped me. I had to pull off my socks as well, which meant some pain as I held my feet fast against the rough bark for a proper grip.

I was able to climb over twenty feet high, partly because after ten feet the branches arranged themselves like steps in a staircase. From here I could see the villa clearly. The 'great wall' was close to three quarters of a kilometre from where the villa was erected. From this position the house looked very beautiful, with its single storey, built as it was in an area almost one acre square. The gate was also visible from this vantage point. It wasn't as hard to get to the back of the villa as it was outside the wall because there were no shrubs here. The apparent recent neglect had allowed weeds to creep into the flowerbeds surrounding the villa, which I surmised had probably come after the death of the sultan.

I was on the lookout for the existence of dogs. That kind of security would mar my plans, especially because I planned to break in at night. All was silent and when I sensed some movement, it turned out to be some monkeys playing with their young ones on nearby trees. Somehow the monkeys had made a path from this same point to the back of the villa, a path that seemed to go round to the kitchen which was proclaimed by its chimney.

The plan was already forming in my mind. If I went down on all fours, whoever would spot me by mistake at night would pass me for a monkey. All I needed now was to spot 'milestones' which would guide me during the night raid. I picked out a number of four to five feet tall plants that bordered the path which led to the kitchen. Those would be easy to locate at night.

I surveyed the compound without hurry; I was naturally patient and took time to digest what was crucial to my survival. By the time I turned my mind away from the villa, I had all its map in my system.

Now came the question of how I was to drop the twenty feet to the ground inside the villa. I had to have a twenty-foot-long rope. There was no alternative but to race back to the town to purchase one rope and a few other silent weapons which I thought I would require, a dagger or a simi for instance. I would then jog back in the evening. I gave the place another look and hoped all would be well when I came back. I faced the playing monkeys again. I wondered where they went to at night, and whether they would come in my way when I came back. Well, that remained to be seen, I concluded and immediately started to climb down.

The shoes and the pair of socks I had put inside the shoes were not there. I looked around and by reflex drew my gun and cocked it. I immediately hid behind the tree with my knees on the ground. How careless of me! Why hadn't the thought crossed me that there would be other WWMs with the same ideas as mine? I lay still, not knowing what to do next, thinking about the man who was shot the previous day, and ready to shoot if need arose.

"Wree!... Wree!"

The sound cut the silence mercilessly from up a tree, making me almost jump out of my skin. When I faced its source, I saw who had taken my shoes – a grey adult monkey. It eyed me from about twenty feet up a tree, six meters away from where I was. Realizing it was not a person who had picked my shoes, I stood up and went to the bottom of the tree. The monkey was showing me its teeth in a derisive grin. When I indicated I would climb up, it climbed higher. Then it decided to show me how good it was on top of trees. It held both shoes in one hand then jumped from the tree it was on to the one from which I had been surveying the villa.

I was getting anxious. An idea crossed my mind but I thought it risky. I would have shot the monkey and got done with it, but then the thought of what would follow in case the police I was told had come this way happened to hear the bullet shot checked me. I looked up at the monkey, hoping it would somehow let go my shoes. It continued in its crazy display of jumping skills. There was no way it would know it was offending me. Then came panic as the monkey indicated it was going to join the others inside the wall. If it did that with my shoes, I'd be sunk, because I could hardly move bare-foot in the midst of a forest that had all types of thorns and thistles.

I watched it as it climbed towards the heavy branch that led to the inside. It didn't even face me, all its mind on the other monkeys inside the villa compound. I aimed at it and pulled the trigger.

BOOM! I hated the sound because it echoed all over, but I liked my accuracy. The monkey fell over its back, crashing from one branch to the other and sending the others scampering up neighbouring trees, sometimes getting held by some branches. By then my shoes were already on the ground. Ten feet from the ground the body got held by stout branches. It lay there lifeless in a spread-eagled position. It was a fitting bye.

CHAPTER TEN

I got back in time to join Marie for lunch at the hotel's dining room. At the barrier I had talked to the guard who had informed me that the police had not yet returned, as well as two of the three vehicles. This only meant there was plenty of action taking place around this villa, my centre of interest since losing the briefcase containing vital documents at the Norfolk Hotel.

The information from the guard, coupled with the fact that I had fired a shot that had echoed all over the area surrounding the villa, had made me change my mind and postpone getting back until the following day.

I would leave at 4.00 o'clock or some minutes before, get to the place and resurvey the area, then hung around till time came for me to drop in.

Over lunch, I gave Marie an account of my findings and the reason why I wasn't going back there that night. Later I went to my room to get some sleep.

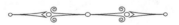

I called Mrs. Wicks the following day, just a few minutes before leaving for the villa. For some strange reason I was missing her. I had reviewed and considered her love for me and decided she deserved my attention, especially at this time when she was in the family way. She was surprised and overjoyed to hear from me.

"Addy, I am pleased that you could think of calling me. You Know I cannot help worrying about you. I know how bad and difficult that mission is ..."

"It's bad, Janet. A man I had met once died as I watched, shot dead by another familiar face. The dead man had the introduction documents on him. I'll give you the story when all this is over.

Right now I am on my way to storm that place." I tried to put triumph into my tone as I said this, but it made little impression.

"Please, Adams, don't do that. Please. For your child's sake..."

"Stop that!" She had stung me and I found myself almost shouting over the phone. "If you try to interrupt my plans again I'll not call you till I'm through – if at all. How do you expect me to go along with that kind of discouragement?"

"I am sorry, Addy, but please take care of yourself. I'll pray for you. I'll hold the devil, in Jesus' name, not to come near you. Will you call me again?"

"Sure, Janet, I will. All the best," I said and hung up.

I dialled another number. The phone was picked on second ring and the voice came very clearly, just like it was fifty metres away.

"Hello ... Wamathina's residence. May I help you?" What a lovely voice! Eva's!

"How is my beautiful woman?" I asked after identifying myself.

"I am alright, dear. And you?"

"Beautiful. How are my children, Kimesh and the one in you?"

She did not answer immediately; she burst into laughter. I let her have her amusement. Thirty seconds elapsed before she answered.

"They are both well. It's wonderful to hear your voice darling. It's like you are calling from our gate. Could you by any chance be calling from around?"

"No, I am right in the heart of TZ, in a town called Mgambo. But I'll soon be coming home, dear." This was added for the sake of it.

"Darling, Kimenyi is a bit. . ."

"Please don't tell me on the phone. In the next thirty six hours you'll be surprised by a knock on the door and when you open ... guess who will be there?"

"You, of course. But how long is thirty six hours ... mhh ... one and a half days. I'll look forward to it..."

That took care of that. In the next twenty minutes I was at what I called point 'B', the place I had found two boys looking after cattle. Somehow this point reminded me of Kareithi, my late grandmother's herdsboy, whom I hadn't had time to visit ever since I left Githagara where my grandpa and grandma were buried. I sometimes missed the boy and wondered how he was faring. But just like I did every other thing that required my attention in the recent past, I put him aside to the day my star would shine. Perhaps then I'd be in a position to think straight.

By 4.55 p.m., I was again on the tree tops overlooking the villa. The monkey's body wasn't there, to my surprise. It wasn't anywhere near and this made me wonder what might have happened. I looked around hoping to find a clue as to what might have happened. It couldn't have been removed by a person just as it couldn't have resurrected. I noticed a trail of blood from the bottom of the tree. Only now did I notice that the grass had been disturbed. I guessed that the other monkeys might have found the body of their colleague, taken it and buried it.

Getting through over the wall was not as easy as I had thought. I had to be very careful not to lose balance while at the same time aping monkeys and trying to move on tree tops. It was a hard balancing act but, spurred on by the survival instinct so sharp in me, I eventually made it.

I moved forward with plenty of caution, my heart beats louder than my footsteps. I avoided stepping on dry leaves which were visible since the moon was full and bright. Halfway to the villa, I encountered a number of monkeys. Fortunately they only made a little noise, perhaps to warn others of this intruder, and went their way. I saw some light from the corners of my eyes and I apprehensively swang round. It was someone in the villa who had put on a light in one of the rooms. I inched forward as cautiously as a cat stalking a mouse. Nothing but total silence. I reached the kitchen from the back.

The time was already 8.20 p.m. I hid behind a large dustbin right opposite the kitchen window and close to the wall. Dressed in dark clothes and a black leather jacket, one had to have very keen eyes to spot me. As a bonus, I was shielded from the bright moon by the villa's wall. My anxiety was rising.

Twenty five minutes of waiting and no sound. I stood up and to the window. It was partly open and the curtain drawn. I was about to strain my neck to peep when I heard a heavy, harsh once talk from somewhere in the room. I didn't hear clearly what was said but from the tone I knew right away there was some trouble. The man had sounded like he was demanding something. I held my gun ready and inched still closer. The window had been opened a fraction, and through the opening I saw and heard everything.

There was more trouble than I had guessed. There was a woman tied to a chair. On taking a second look I recognised her; she was the same lady who had scared the wits out of Marie, the granddaughter to the sultan. A man, the killer who had ran off with the introduction documents, was standing threateningly over her.

"Are you ready to hand over the compact to me or do I deal with you the way I did with your grandmother?" The voice itself was enough to send a chill down any spine.

I looked around when he said this. At another corner I saw an old woman, also tied to a chair. If she wasn't already dead, she was unconscious. Her head was limp and her chin rested on her left breast. The lioness seemed to have had her share also, because her voice sounded tired and weak.

"I told you it was stolen. I swear that. We do not know where it is. How could we hide it from you and yet it is you who has the right documents?"

All her pleas fell on deaf ears.

"How much money do you want?" The man was bellowing. "Tell me or I'll kill you. How much are you planning to sell it for? I am sure it is here as there's no way it could have been handed to anyone without this letter. That lie about it being stolen cannot work. Through where did the thief enter? This place has not been broken into. Do you suspect the guard? Tell me!"

"No, It cannot be the guard."

This answer prompted more wrath. The killer slapped her on the face so hard that she lost balance and went down with the chair.

'ACT YOU FOOL!' It was my psychological friend prompting me to action. Like a machine, I pulled the curtain aside, pushed the window without making any noise and found myself announcing' "Police, hands up!" I fired at the man and got him on the shoulder. Before I could fire again he ran off towards a door close to where the old woman was. I heaved myself up and held onto the window sill. I tried the latch and it gave way. In one move I had opened the window and dropped inside. I had hardly touched anything when I heard a vehicle start and drive away. The killer had made his escape and it would be foolhardy to imagine I could follow him. I turned my attention to the lioness first, because she was conscious.

I bent down to untie her. I had started to lift her when I saw the card, cut diagonally, which had been among the documents grabbed from, me at the Norfolk. The missing part was taped in place. The letter, too, was on the floor, but partly hidden by the lady's body. She turned a bit, and the pain she was experiencing was evident on her face.

"Easy, madam, I'll help you. Was he alone?" I asked.

"Yes. He had the letter of introduction, so we had to open the gate for him. He didn't appear harmful."

"That man is a killer, a dangerous person. He'd have killed both of you. Why did you take the risk?"

I had now freed her and we were both trying to assist the old woman.

"He does not understand ... he is so adamant. How can I deny him the compact yet he had the right documents? I would have given it right away were it in my possession. What would I do with it, anyway?"

My mouth almost flew open. What did this mean? That after all the killing, all the hatred and all the tiresome running after this so-called compact, we'd go back home empty-handed? I couldn't believe what I was hearing. Supposing it was the truth, that the compact had been stolen, what would be my fate when I gave the news to Aslam? Would he bang the door in my face and say he owed me nothing? After all I had gone through?

"What do you mean by that?" The lioness asked me to my surprise.

"By what?" I asked, in turn.

"Who will say he owes you nothing?" She asked, and faced me. "That's what you've just said."

The lioness was extremely beautiful. I'd never had such beautiful eyes trained on me. They were seemingly thanking me for saving her, and she was surprised that I was complaining about her owing nothing to me.

"Sorry, dear," I told her and touched her shoulder. "I have a disease of talking to myself, I keep speaking my thoughts aloud."

She faced me again and a smile broke around her lips. How beautiful! She had taken my explanation for a joke and I was glad about it. Somehow it thawed whatever tension had been there. The next thing I knew, I was doing something I hadn't had the courage to do before. I held the lady and turned her round. I pulled her close to me. Surprisingly, she didn't protest. When she was close enough I let her body lean against mine and her head to rest on my chest. I used my right hand to caress her hair while I muttered words of comfort.

"All will be well, dear. Just relax your body and try to forget what happened. It's all over," I said to her.

"What's your name?" I asked her. She was breathing gently and seemed comfortable with where she was. She didn't seem to want to let me go. I guessed she hadn't had someone hold her like this for some time. From my recent experience with rich ladies, specifically Janet and Marie, I had learnt that women liked to feel protected – to feel there was someone for them to turn to and probably lean on when they were depressed. This lioness would be no different.

"I am Catherine Malowe," she said, looking into my face with the pleading eyes of a lonely young girl. "What's yours, please?"

"I am Adams Wamathina, or Son of Fate. Haven't we met before?" I asked, to her surprise.

"No. You just look a little familiar. You are a cop, isn't it?"

"No. I just wanted that killer to think the place is infested with cops. And secondly I didn't know how many I was up against."

I kept silent for a while, debating within myself whether to remind her who I was or not.

"How did you get in here?" She asked, cutting my train of thought. "There is no way through to the back except through the rear exit which was locked."

"I jumped over the wall. I sensed the killer might be on his way here when I learned he had been spotted in town," I lied. "I wanted to take him by surprise. He's dangerous man."

"Oh, I don't know how to thank you. I owe you my life, Mr. Wamathina. Let me prepare some coffee for you. It must be cold."

I let her go. I wanted the coffee as badly as I wanted to sit and talk with this beauty. I couldn't help flashing back to two days ago when she had held a rifle and accurately blasted off parts of our car. I understood her perfectly. She had to be harsh . . . what with the kind of experience she had had since the death of her great grandfather.

The old woman was unconscious. I placed my gun under a saucepan and we picked her and took her to her bedroom where we laid her comfortably on her bed. Malowe seemed to know how to handle such a case and I let her do it. She wasn't wearing a gown by now, and the curves of her figure stood out clearly. She wasn't bad-looking and you wouldn't have imagined anything evil would come out of her. She didn't have to take an oath to convince me that the 'compact' had gone missing. She exuded honesty and faithfulness. The distant signs of hardness that an expert eye read in her were a result of overworking her mind and probably lack of adequate sleep. She was not cut out for the rough life of guns, conmen, and murderers. I was going to counsel her the best I could, and see to it that she got back to normal. If anyone would be a hindrance to my acquisition of the trophy, I was sure it would be her.

The compact was gone, that was for certain. Malowe explained what had happened.

"It was the kitchen radio we first noticed was missing. My grandmum wanted to hear the evening news. She told me to switch the radio on. When I opened the wall unit to pick it, I was met by an empty drawer. The compact has been in that drawer since my grandfather handed it to us, together with the instructions we were supposed to follow. I just then remembered that I had kept some food I intended to warm in there as well. It was not there. I wondered whether it was my grandmother who had gone hungry and taken the food, but she said no. Whoever stole the radio, the compact and a few other simple items must have been very hungry. He ate whatever was edible. We later discovered that even the bread, stale bread we were to throw, was missing." She paused a bit then continued, "That's why I was sure the killer you surprised, who had his introduction letter, was going to liquidate us because we couldn't produce the compact."

"Tell me Adams, what was there in that compact? You seem to be the only friendly person who knows about it." She paused for a while, then she added, "If it wasn't for my grandmother, I would have left this place forever. But my grandmother swears she'll die here and ... well, I cannot bring myself to leave her alone.

People have been coming here since my great grandfather died. All types of people and all seem wild. There were instructions given by grandfather, but they wouldn't listen. This house has been searched repeatedly. Fortunately no one ever entered that kitchen. Infact, all had been quiet for a while. Until a few days ago."

"That was when I went for the introduction letter and it was robbed from me," I now said. "It is good for you now, and I think for everybody else."

"Why do you think so?" She asked, her face flickering with renewed hopes.

"Everyone will be convinced now that the compact was stolen. No one will bother you again. I can assure you that within hours from now, a good number of those running after the compact will know that it is no longer here. I happen to know how news about it spreads. Now that the bearer of the introduction letter was here and went away without it, all the dogs of war will go back to their kennels, to wait until they are recalled for another job. Take that from me." "You haven't told me what the compact carries and why it was so important," she reminded me.

"I do not know. You are better off than I am, in fact. At least you have had a chance to see it. I can't even guess what it looks like. Actually, I was sent by the owner. All the others were thieves, killers, robbers, name it. What I would think is that the thing carried a top secret between your great grandfather and some other people we wouldn't know, perhaps a will of some kind, or a record of things that were here years before we were born. It is quite a puzzle, Miss Malowe," I said finally, not sure if I meant it. "Look, let's celebrate that it is all over. Personally I'll never want to hear anything more about it. I've lost plenty of weight thinking about it and I left behind all else to run after something I did not know. What will you do with yourself after this?"

Almost immediately, I wondered why I had asked this. What did I expect? Where else would she go?

"It's you I should ask that question. I'll hate to see you leave. Listen Adams, I'll repeat again that I owe you my life. I had only a few more seconds and then I'd have been shot or strangled, believe me. May I ask for a favour, please?" I looked at her, not having the slightest notion of what she had in mind. Her pleading young eyes that potrayed her youth and beauty did me in.

"Ask," I said, and immediately my heart beats went berserk.

"Thank you. Stay with me here for at least a week ... just one week."

I looked at her and dropped my gaze. "No, that wouldn't do."

She seemed to realise I had a problem judging. A cold sweat broke out on my forehead. As usual I had talked my thoughts aloud. She came to me and took my right hand in both of hers.

"You are my only hope right now, Mr. Wamathina," she pleaded. "Look at the situation my grandmother is in. The guard is in hospital recovering from wounds from another attack. One househelp went to bury her father and the other one is right here, in bed and very sick. I was planning to take her to the hospital first thing tomorrow morning, in fact. Just quote your fee for staying and I'll have it arranged right away. Anything, any amount, Mr. Wamathina. Will you stay with me?"

I found myself bemused as I thought about the kind of women fate brought my way. They were all lovely and loving, mostly very rich or coming from very rich families. But what I found amusing was that they all wanted to give me funny jobs, telling me to quote the payment I required. Where on earth did an employer tell the employee to name his fee?

"Will you? Please, Mr. Wamathina," she pleaded. Funny that they all seemed to know my weakness.

I was beaten, defeated. What else would I tell her but hold her tight as before, promising her everything within my reach and ability?

"Thank you so much, Mr. Wamathina. You are such a nice .. ."

She did not finish. In a flash the door was banged open and

uniformed police officers stormed in, guns at the ready. In the next two minutes I was placed under arrest.

No pleas from Malowe could stop them from arresting me, not even the cash bond she insisted I be given.

"You are dealing with a triple killer, you stupid lady," the leader of the group said. " You think he'd have left you alive? Just keep off. You'll see him in the station tomorrow, if you wish."

I was handcuffed, searched, then thrown to the ground. Fortunately, I had put my gun under the saucepan. As I was shoved into the back of the Landrover, Malowe was wailing madly. That comforted me somewhat. I was very sure that no one could convince her otherwise, especially that I was a triple murderer.

The police cell was cold. There wasn't a single blanket, not a piece of anything I could cover myself with. They had taken my jacket, shoes, socks and belt. I was down to my shirt which could do nothing against the cold. Just like in other police stations I had got locked up, other convicts peeped to see who the new fish could be. Most did that just to find out whether the new-comer might, by coincidence, be their friend or a bearer of important news. Convicts from different cells prayed that you be mixed with them so they could get latest news. In my case, unfortunately, the cops had other things in mind. Instead of giving me the privilege of mixing with fellow inmates, they opened an empty cell where I was thrown by myself and the door locked.

I knew how to live in such places so I didn't waste time standing at the door. I went to the right hand corner and sat huddled, deliberately diverting my mind from the semi-darkness and the staleness that hang in the air. I closed my eyes and reflected on my life. That was always my lullaby and it always worked wonders.

Soon I was lulled into sleep.

I was awoken at midnight by several senior officers. I wasn't even given time to rub my eyes. I was marched into an office nearby and questioned over an assortment of things. Some I had never heard of and was at a loss what to tell my interrogators. At one point I was even accused of being a spy from Zambia! It took long, and when they were through with what I believed was intimidation they came to the point.

"Where's your gun?" I was asked.

'I don't have one. They searched me before locking me up. Just ask these two officers here," I pointed them out.

"Shut up!" The head of interrogation bellowed as I was slapped. I almost hit back but held my anger, very well knowing the consequences.

"We have it here. If you had one on you, we'd probably have thought otherwise. But you left it at the forest beside the man you killed. Then you used his gun to kill another."

The following morning the interrogation went on for three hours, and then I was dumped back into my cell. At around 11.30 a.m., I was called. I was put on the back of a grey police Landrover, registration number CCM756T. I was sandwiched between two officers behind the driver's seat. I was being led back towards the villa, where according to the officers with me at the back, we were going for evidence to help in preferring murder charges against me. After a few kilometres, the vehicle stopped and I was ordered to get out. At the roadside I saw about five people looking at a body that lay on the ground, covered by a black sheet. One of the officers I was with bent down and lifted the sheet to reveal the face of the body.

"Come closer!" He barked at me.

I went closer. Surprisingly, I felt as calm as if I was watching all this in a film. I wasn't going to allow them to intimidate me into giving the answers they wanted to be able to frame me.

"Do you know this man?" The cop asked and stared at me, I was surprised more by the face than by the question. I had seen the man once, but I never saw him again. On the ground was the body of the man who had impersonated me in hospital, the very person who had slipped between my fingers when I bumped into him searching Aslam's hospital room. Saying I knew him would be a lie – and I wasn't going to give them the account of what had happened between us.

"I do not know him," I answered, while shaking my head. But the officer didn't believe me. He had read my face when I first glanced at the body and signs of recognition hit my face.

"Well, that's good for the time being. Your face tells me all I need to know, but let's wait till we get back to the station. We have a way of reminding people what they know but unfortunately tend to forget." He grinned at me, displaying long front teeth that reminded me of the monkey I had shot dead. He closed his wide mouth as fast as he had opened it, then gestured to his subordinates to throw me back into the vehicle. The body was then dumped right at my feet and the vehicle took off. The two Adams Wamathinas, the real one alive and the phoney one dead, were driven down the rough road towards the station.

At least I now knew two of the people I had allegedly killed. Who was the third one? Did I know him? How many others had died pursuing this compact that would never be found?

I had deduced the state of things after seeing that body. The killer of Marie's anonymous caller must have waited till I left. He had then came out and went to the body of his victim and taken the deadman's gun, which I had not touched. He had used it to kill the phoney Adams Wamathina, to make it look like there were two killers. When I met him at the villa he had known it was me inspite of my attempts to impersonate a cop. When he got to the town, he had called the police and probably tipped them that the killer they were looking for was at the villa. That explained why the police had stormed the place and arrested me.

I didn't want to exhaust my mind thinking about this because I was sure time was soon coming when I would need all my brains. But I found it difficult to block from my mind the fact that all the troubles I was getting were in vain, since I was certain the compact had been stolen.

I was thrown back into my lonely cell to await further developments. In the afternoon, I was called to the O.B. desk where I found Malowe talking to a cop who seemed very friendly. She jumped out of the seat and came to me. The cop allowed her to hug me but I was in a bad mood and no hugging would console me. Maybe only Eva's hug, when I arrived home from here. That would be different because it would be an assurance of total freedom.

"I am sorry, Adams. I am so sorry. This is all my fault..." Malowe muttered as she released me.

"What do you mean it's your fault? You didn't bring me ..."

"No. Not that. If I hadn't insisted that you stay with me ..."

"I still wouldn't have left by the time they came. There was a lot I would have wanted to discuss with you and it'd probably have taken the whole night. After all, Malowe, I was aware I was dealing with trouble all along. Don't feel guilty."

I patted her on the shoulder to comfort her. She responded with that smile I have told you about, a smile that would ease any pain just observing it.

"Adams, I'll get you out of here. I swear, I will! I am not without influence in this territory if not country. I am sure you are not a killer; anyone can see that from miles away. I know who the killer is and if you were one you wouldn't have let him go. You had him in your hands last night. I have never seen a system like this that allows the guilty to vanish in thin air and punishes the innocent." She sounded harsh, despite the presence of the friendly cop.

Surprisingly, I noticed that the police officers had high respect for her. What had she meant by the statement she wasn't without influence? The respect being accorded her right now seemed to lend weight to that remark and it made me feel better. When one is in such a fix, one needs a strong and influential person behind him, and it appeared I had one right here. Infact I decided there and then to tell her about my partner, Marie, and to send her with a message of my whereabouts.

Before five o'clock, I was summoned again. This time I was ushered different office where I found two gentlemen seated opposite each other. The one whose back was facing the door turned to look at me as I was ushered in. He nodded to his companion and said,

"Yes, this is the man." He followed me with his eyes until I took the seat I was shown and which faced the two officers. I recognized the other fellow.

"Hello, Adams Wamathina. It's a pleasure to see you again. Remember me?" He asked. He didn't look like he was pleased to meet me again – the expression on his face was sending a message of never wanting to set his eyes on me ever again.

"Yeah, I recognize you alright. It's just under two weeks. You are Chief Inspector Immanuel Kibwana," I said .

"Well, that's it ..." he said, and looked at his counterpart right opposite him. I felt there was some message passed between the two. The Tanzanian excused himself and left me with the Kenyan.

"I am Immanuel," he introduced himself gruffly. "Not yet a chief inspector, but a superintendent of police. Do you see what has come of your withholding information and lying to the police? If you had told me the truth, I'd have been in a position to help you out of this. Now I understand you have a list of charges facing you, ranging from assault to first degree murder. I wouldn't like you to be charged with things you might not know, especially when we come from the same country. That is why I am volunteering this information. You might be innocent, I do not deny, but on the other hand I might be defending a guilty person. There are chances that you have committed one of the crimes. Why? Because you chose to do things your way, in a case involving criminal activity. You have all the makings of a bad man and I would be a fool to try to protect you. Unless you are willing to tell me something helpful..." He paused hopefully and looked me in the face.

"About what?" I asked like a fool. I was confused. Why was he here? For the same trophy? How had he known I was already arrested? Or had he followed me ever since that day I was in his office ... hoping that in doing so he would arrest the robber?

"Okay, let me not bother," he continued. "I know your type. When they say they don't know, they don't change it to the end. Let me tell you what I came for. The Commissioner of Police back in Kenya has revoked your licence as a private investigator, as well as the licence to carry a gun. Your firm has also been closed. I have been sent to get the gun, the licences and all that. What happens to you after this is not any business of ours ..."

A series of questions bombarded my mind. How come that this had to happen? How possible was it that the C.P. would revoke my license and send someone to come for the documents in a foreign country, instead of waiting for me to get back? How could he have known I was here and that I had them on me? Might he have known that I was running after some kind of treasure on a client's orders? And what was wrong with it? Wasn't it the work of private investigation agencies? Who could have put the C.P. into this? Mrs. Wicks? This so-called S. P. Kibwana? Coming to that, how could I know whether this Kibwana wasn't taking me for a ride so as get what I had found out so far? Was he after the same trophy?

The S.P. seemed to detect what was going on in my mind. To break the silence he produced a letter to cast away any doubts.

"The letter introduces me to you and informs you of the fate of Wicks and Wayne Detective Agency. It requires you to hand over the license to carry a gun to me. I have been detailed to repossess the gun and make sure that the office is not operational until further orders are issued. You understand, don't you?"

I did not give an answer immediately but instead asked to see the letter. It had the rubber stamp of the Commissioner of Police alright, and even his signature, but I still felt suspicious. I took out my job card and firearms certificate both of which had the Commissioner's signature and stamp and tried to do a comparison. If there was any difference at all, I could not tell. Mr. Kibwana was eyeing me silently and rather confidently, which told me there wasn't any point of trying to compare the signatures. Whether they were by the same hand or not, the man knew what he was doing.

"Satisfied, Wamathina?" There was a frown on his face.

"Well, I think it doesn't matter whether or not I am satisfied. You must know what you are doing and I believe that is indeed the position, the Commissioner acted on your advice. The unfortunate thing is that I do not have the gun and I never travelled with it. As for these documents, I do not think they are of any help to me in my present circumstances, and I think even after this I do not need them, so you may have them ..." I pushed them to him and stood as I did so,

"I guess that brings us to the end of the meeting. As for helping me out of this, I do not think I need your help or anybody else's for that matter. I am innocent and, anyway, I couldn't have shot anybody with my bare fingers. After all, I have a very tight alibi which would cause the whole world to cry foul if I were convicted for that crime ... So unless on top of coming for the documents, which I doubt, you had the mandate to assassinate me, I think I have nothing to worry about. The time they'll hold me behind bars does not matter to me. I am used to it for your information, and where facing hardships is concerned, I may claim to have a special degree, Mister Kibwana. So let's call it a day." I turned to get to the door. As I touched the handle he called me.

"Mister Wamathina..." I noticed he had now added the mister. It had occurred to me that Kibwana was more interested in knowing how far I had gone in this case than in getting the documents which, as I had told him, were presently useless to me. Up to this moment I had gone 'nowhere' and I did not want to tell him this. Every other person in the chase knew it was lost. What else did he expect me to have found out? I turned to look at him. This time it was I who had the confidence.

"Make it snappy. Mister Superintendent. I want to go back to the cooler to rest. I have plenty to think about while I rest."

Kibwana smiled, a smile that I thought would be envied only by a gorilla, but a smile all the same. "You surely don't seem to worry about the poor situation you are in. That's very interesting. Don't you think ..."

"Don't speculate, sir. I told you it is just a matter of facing hardships the way I've done since I was a kid. Not that I do not mind being held here incommunicado — who doesn't love his freedom? But there's a class of people that has to maintain their freedom the hard way, because their fate is controlled by the likes of you who intimidate others so as to be told what they want to hear. Take yourself for instance. You take so much trouble to make that my license to operate freely is revoked. You want me to go down on my knees to beg you to let me operate, and since I am not the type that licks your boots, I automatically get into trouble. Since you wouldn't want to see me succeed, you remain on my heels and when a nice chance avails itself, you put me in."

"How then do you expect me not to get used to hardships? There are even times when I love it because it's through troubles that I get a morsel of bread to keep my family going."

"One day, Mister Superintendent, one day – it doesn't matter after how many years – you'll pay for the evil you do to mankind. Make no mistake about that – in one way or another you will pay. You might not know when or how you will do it. Maybe you"ll go home and find that your wife is seriously ill and you have to take her to an expensive hospital where you pay hundreds of thousands of shillings. You think that is normal, but you are actually partly repaying your evil to mankind. Eventually you might just drop dead, it's the reality, but let's forget that. Now tell me, what do you want from me? For God's sake do not promise me freedom in exchange of even a single word from me because you won't get it. I am very certain that if there's anything you'd want to do for me it is to put me out of your way completely, to immobilize me. You paved my way into this prison, let me find my way out."

The SP seemed to realize the bitterness that was in me. He gave out a long sigh of relief and said, "Well, what else is there for me to say? I thought we could work together for our government and ..."

"Our government? Work together with you for a government that has just revoked my license so that I may become a beggar, a government that does not want me to earn a living? Then you must have been lying when you told me that the person acting on behalf of our government had cancelled my license. If not, he was not acting for our government, which makes it criminal. Do me a favour, Mister Superintendent, and let me go back to the cooler to rest."

I shrugged my shoulders to show that it was over. He wasn't going to get anything from me because I was certain he wasn't here to rescue me, but to put me out of the way. So far I had not committed any crime against 'our government' and there wasn't a single thing I could justifiably be prosecuted for. If I managed to get out of here and landed back in Kenya, I would walk freely. The only problem right now was to get out of this Tanzanian police station. Somehow I was convinced I could do it by whatever means, including breaking out if there was no other way.

The second day in the cells wasn't a bad one for me. Early in the morning both Miss Malowe and Marie Aslam visited me. Apparently she had gone straight there after her first visit. Marie looked badly shaken, especially on learning that I was in for several murders, but Malowe had plenty of self-confidence. They had brought me some food which I hadn't had since my arrest. With a full stomach, the days and nights in the cell wouldn't be so cold and time would pass more easily. We didn't have much to talk about. What was there, anyway, but to wait till the authorities charged me or for Malowe's connections to pull the trick?

But even as these considerations occurred to me I knew the person I should trust more was myself. If only I managed to convince someone to get me a gun, I would make good my escape from the place. If that proved difficult to execute alone, I would seek Mrs. Wicks' assistance. Perhaps she could oblige to send Stranger and his trigger-happy boys to assist me escape. This possibility was however reserved for the final minute, when I was certain the trumped-up charges of murder would be preferred against me.

Anyway, the ladies had brought me plenty of food. It was like they wanted me to fill up my stomach with enough for two days, as if telling me they wouldn't be coming to see me the following day. Well, it didn't matter since they hadn't told me that, and secondly a visit without news didn't mean much to me. I was however glad that they had met and become good friends.

When they left, I felt like I had been left in a desert while they were airlifted by a chopper and that from now on it was for me to find my way out of the desert. I picked the food – roasted meat, bread and some *chapati* – and went back to the compound at the back, which carried about six cells. I placed the food on a form that was outside and moved from cell to cell peeping in. All those who had been arrested earlier had been taken to the Law Courts and charged. It was only one cell that I found still occupied. A young boy was huddled up in a corner. He was still on the floor with his knees held up where he laid his head and covered it with his hands. That was how you beat cold in the cells.

He didn't look up, which told me that he must have been having a nap or that he thought it was a cop on patrol and was deliberately ignoring him. The latter was most likely. What could this minor be in for, I wondered? He couldn't have been more than sixteen years old.

I knocked at the door and called, "Hi there." He looked up immediately on realising it was not a cop. They weren't that friendly. "Come up and share some food with me."

It was like he had heard I was offering him freedom. Though I could tell that the boy was weak, this time he managed to gather enough strength to leap to the door. I could guess why – like me, he hadn't taken anything since he was locked in. And he could have been arrested before me.

I couldn't open the door for him and the cop at the O.B. desk didn't bother following me to the cells, so it wasn't that easy to give him the food. The only space through which I could smuggle in some for him was ten feet from the ground. I had to spring up and hold onto the bars with one hand while the other dropped a loaf of bread inside. I dropped to the ground to pick up some roast meat and I struggled up again so as to drop it. Twice I missed and fell down. The third time I held but the meat slipped. I had to let go of the bars to collect the pieces, now on the dirty ground. As I tried to jump a fourth time, I heard a voice from behind.

"What are you trying to do and why are you out?" The voice Wasn't friendly. I turned and faced the sergeant.

"I am trying to assist my fellow prisoner with some food, and I am out because I've just had visitors. I think the officer at the desk can explain better."

Cops are not used to that kind of language that doesn't 'sir' them and which is devoid of fear. When you are that bold' they either became very harsh or comply with you. Luckily for us, I mean the youngster and me, the sergeant opted for the latter.

"I see you are a good Samaritan. Why don't you ask the corporal to open for you?"

"Simple ... because I am not an officer like you."

To my surprise the sergeant laughed.

"I like that. It makes sense. We don't like being told what to do." He then called out to the officer who had the keys to the cells. I picked my food and joined the young boy. When you are two or more in a cell, you don't feel as lonely as in solitary confinement because at least you can pick a subject to talk about. You can pry into each other's lives and console one another.

The youngster turned out to be a stranger here, just as I was. He was a refugee from Rwanda who had found life very difficult in a refugee camp and chosen the hazards of trying an independent subsistence.

"My fellow countrymen are dying in tens each day that passes. We are usually brought food which isn't enough for all in the camp. Most are wounded, yet medical facilities are almost nil. You spend days and nights listening to cries of horror from the injured and the sick till you feel like your head could blow up. Yet there's nothing you can do to help even your own brother or sister, because the circumstances there have made you impotent. It is like a camp of the physically disabled where each expects assistance from an equally incapacitated colleague.

"I travelled for days and nights without food. This food you've given me is the first meal I've taken in six days. You are the kindest person I have met in my life. I have watched people eating in this same cell and none has ever invited me to take even a morsel of bread. They'd even pick what dropped down and eat instead of letting me do the cleaning. I cannot really imagine you almost fell, trying to give me some food. Thank you, Adams."

There was no doubt he was highly educated. My judgement of his age was not very wrong because he was about to celebrate his seventeenth birthday right here if he was not released within two months. The way the police were handling his case, I decided, it was highly unlikely that he would be released.

I was called to record my statement in the evening. The very officer who had, a day earlier, introduced me to the Kenyan superintendent was the one I found in the office. To me he didn't seem to seriously consider that I was the murderer. Perhaps he was aware of what was going on ... perhaps even aware his own Government was interested in the compact and that the chase had started long ago. He also was aware, it seemed, that I had been sent by the sultan's grandson, implying that he must have been briefed on this by his Kenyan counterpart. What he was doing now was routine questioning which he hoped would lead him to the killer. I knew by now that they'd only release me if they found the killer or killers, and that if they failed, I stood every chance of being framed. Unlike him, I already knew that the killer had learnt that the compact could not be found and that he must have fled the town and probably the country. This put me in an even more awkward position.

"This dirty thing has left us littered with dead bodies. Six corpses in six months, in the same area. Someone has to go in for this. I cannot lose my job on account of stupid bastards who cannot keep their distance from killing for something that does not exist. Get back to your cell, I'll come for you in the morning."

He sounded quite annoyed. It was as if he hated my story, which I had rehearsed almost to perfection. He buzzed the outer office and an officer came for me.

'BACK INTO THE COOLER, SONNY BOY. IF THIS IS HOW YOUR STAR WILL SHINE, THEN YOU'VE GOT IT COMING — TROUBLE!' It was the same old voice in me - my companion.

My fourth day here was different. Mrs. Wicks, looking her best, turned up early in the morning to pay me a visit. This prompted the officer, who by coincidence had twice opened the cell to take me to see my visitors, to comment as he led me out of the cell.

"You don't seem to have men friends. Only good-looking, rich who do not drive anything less than Mercs."

"What does that tell you?" I asked with a sense of elation.

"That you are, or might be, a well-placed person. It makes us wonder how you'd get involved in something this dirty."

He appeared convinced about my VIP status, for which I pitied him. He had no way of knowing that I was a hired hand who had started by being a cart pusher and graduated to a watchman, a houseboy, a chauffeur and, lately, a private investigator who had nothing to show for it.

Mrs. Wicks wept uncontrollably on seeing me. I think she was touched by my hair which had not met water or comb for a couple of days. Perhaps too by my being without shoes, socks or belt, which as a result made the trousers go down a few inches below where they were supposed to be anchored. I had grown thin and was dirty, quite the opposite of the man she knew and had obviously expected to meet,

"I am so sorry, Addy, I'll do anything to get you out," she said between sobs.

"How's Stranger? I guess he could bond me out of this place." I winked and she understood, I liked her for being intelligent.

"When do you think it's best for him to come? I'll have to get back home and bring him here. He knows the place well enough but I'd like to ..."I was afraid she'd reveal much out of excitement so I had to interrupt her.

"Friday evening is best. By then I'll have received the final report from the authorities and will be in a position to advise him on whom to see and what to do," I said.

Again, I could see she understood me perfectly. I had allowed myself three more days for Malowe to either succeed or give up. Then I'd embark on my own plans. Mrs. Wicks hugged me goodbye and reluctantly turned and left.

How she had known I was already inside is something I never found out because she didn't want to talk about it. What I was certain about was she hadn't learnt it from Marie whom, I had come to realize, she didn't like for her own reasons.

I picked the package of assorted foods and went back to my cell which I now shared with Mtumukiza, the refugee young man. We shared the food as usual and chatted. We didn't have much to talk about ourselves as we had exhausted all we had, but there was a whole range of other issues to be talked about. His pet topic appeared to be the political situation in our countries, to which I had very little to contribute. He soon gave it up, wondering why I had little interest in such an important topic. Like the officers in this station, he too wondered what I was made of.

On Wednesday night I had terrible dreams. Twice my friend Mtumukiza shook me to wake me up after I had screamed. I didn't know what to say because the dreams were not clear. In most of them I would see Kimesh holding a sharp dagger, approaching his mother's bedroom which was wide open. Eva would be heavily asleep with my son, hardly a toddler, lying beside her, facing the ceiling with eyes closed. Kimesh wanted to kill my son, claiming that the mother loved my son more than she did him. I would scream when he raised the dagger to kill my son. When the same dream appeared for the fourth time, I decided not to go back to sleep. I stood up and went to the door. For three hours I peeped into the night, dark save for the little light afforded by a single dilapidated bulb somewhere along the veranda outside. I was relieved when finally Thursday morning arrived. I didn't know what to make of the dream, but it kept me worried.

When Marie came to visit me later in the day, at precisely 1.30 p.m., the first thing I told her was not to make the mistake of telling Eva that I was in police custody. What I saw on her face told me she already had committed that mistake, which almost made my heart stop.

"Tell me frankly, have you called Eva?" I asked with a trembling voice. Such information could easily kill her in her pregnant state.

"I am sorry, Wamathina. You didn't tell me not to. I am sorry," she begged. I could see she really was sorry but I was beyond thinking straight.

"I warned you not to mess things up. I told you to keep your mouth shut. What prompted you to tell her? Why? When did you call her?"

I was raving mad. The officer in charge was watching us, apparently stunned.

"Last night. I am sorry."

"What was her response? Tell me!" Before she could answer, I gave her a slap that sent her sprawling on the floor. I wanted to jump over the desk and get to her but the officer intervened. More officers rushed in and I was thrown back into my cell. It was fortunate that I didn't do anything as foolhardy as hitting out at the three cops who held me. I was locked up.

"I now know why I had such a terrible dream, Mtumukiza!" I told my friend minutes before I dropped into heavy sleep.

I was called again in the evening. The sergeant came and peeped through the tiny spy hole and told me to say goodbye to my friend because he had heard I might be freed. He didn't add details.

"I was just passing close to the senior superintendent's office when I heard him discussing it with the station commander," was the much he would divulge, "It is an order from above. You may not know it, but the lady who comes to see you here is very influential. Young, but very influential. I cannot give you the details now. I could meet you in a bar in town after your release. Where can I find you?"

"Hotel Granando. Ask at the reception, they'll direct you to me," told him. I knew he wanted a beer and I didn't mind buying him one.

When the officer left I turned my attention to my cellmate. "What assistance do you think I could give you, my friend? That is assuming there is truth in what we've just heard."

"I don't know. I think I'll finally be taken back to the camp ..."

Suddenly my name was called from a distance. Before I answered, I looked at my friend. "I'll see what best I can do for you, Mtumukiza. Just leave it to me. The lady who has helped me might help you too," I told him as he rose from where he sat to shake my hand.

As my name was called a second time, Mtumukiza seemed to remember something.

"Adams ..." he called.

"Yes, please ..." I answered.

"I want to give you something to remember me for. It's not so important to you I think, but I would be happy if you kept it." For some strange reason, I listened keenly, though I didn't think whatever it was would mean anything to me. All I wanted now was to get as far away from this place as possible. Get back to Kenya and know my wife's fate. All my mind and attention was on her.

"I jumped over a wall of a house in the forest and stole a radio and a camera. I was looking for food but decided to take the two items so that I could sell them and get some money. Unfortunately, there happened to be forest rangers patrolling the area that day. When I saw them I hid the two items in the bush. Just before they arrested me and brought me here ..."

I was struck dumb. A camera and a radio from a house in the forest! My God! That had to be the trophy, the compact! Could be it looked like a camera. I remembered the story I had been given by Miss Malowe about the loss of a kitchen radio, food and the compact.

The officer was now heading for my cell, holding the key.

"Where in particular are they hidden?" I asked in a hurry.

It turned out to be on the side of the wall opposite where I had gained access to the villa. Just as I got the picture, the door was opened and I was asked to get out. In the next twenty minutes I was a free man. Free and happy!

I found Marie in her room, in a very downcast mood. I was touched, but I didn't regret having slapped her. She couldn't believe her eyes because she hadn't imagined I would be freed this day. As usual we discussed what had transpired between us at the police station and agreed to bury the hatchet. All my mind was focused on the villa. I had no doubt I would find the compact lying hidden in the very shrubs that surrounded it. I wanted to get there before anything else, both to hunt for the compact and to thank Malowe for doing whatever she had done to secure my freedom.

After taking a bath, shaving and changing into fine clothes, I took the Benz and drove to the villa. I parked about twenty metres from the gate. I didn't want to enter because my destination was not within but outside the wall. As I pressed the remote button to set the alarm the guard appeared. He looked at the vehicle, recognized it by the missing side mirror and smiled. He saluted and proceeded to open the gate. This gesture told me that he had received fresh regulations, among them that I was most welcome to this place any time of the day.

"Welcome, sir. Madam called to say she's on her way home and that you should wait. Drive in, please."

"Well," I thought, *"if my star doesn't shine this time, it never will."*

"I want to look around. I'll be back in ten minutes. Just relax!" I told him.

"Quite alright, sir. Please yourself," he said as I declined to enter the gate. Instead I turned right and went round a corner.

There was a footpath alongside the outside perimeter of the wall, but the shrubs were thick and grew close to the wall. I however made quick progress, partly because of the eagerness I had to find out whether anyone had beaten me to the hidden treasure.

I looked behind me every three or four steps, to be sure I wasn't being followed on this final leg. If someone appeared and stood between me and this compact, which I was so certain was only a few minutes from where I was, I would this time go in never to come out, because I'd just shoot to kill. I had a feeling fate was with me for once.

"Count trees from the dried-up cinder and stop at the fourth. About three to four metres towards the wall, there is a trunk of keiapple sprouting some branches. You won't find it if you are not observant. That's where

I dropped them. There are a few other items but ..." I remembered Mtumukiza telling me. He wouldn't know how helpful he had been. I found the keiapple. How could I miss it anyway? If I found the thing intact I'd owe him a good turn. After pushing shrubs aside and clawing the leaves away, I found the treasure.

I saw the radio first, then a tiny carton in which were six drinking glasses. Below this was the 'camera'. It looked like a camera alright, with even something that looked like an internal flash, but it wasn't. It would have passed for a pocket camera because of its size, but it felt heavy in my hands, and I agreed with those who had referred to it as a compact. It made no sense to me; I couldn't even guess what it contained. But even as I put it inside my pocket from where I swore it would not leave until I got back home, I knew I had pocketed an explosive. For the first time since I embarked on this assignment, I found myself wondering whether Aslam would really keep his part of the bargain now that I had the compact with me. If he did, all the struggles I had had in my life would be compensated for, and I would not need to complain about fate anymore.

I looked down at the expensive radio and wondered what to do with it. If I picked it and gave it to the owners, they'd automatically and rightly deduce that I had found the compact as well. They'd get fishy about it and there was no telling the direction this thing would take. No, the radio was safer not discovered. I pushed it deeper into the thickets, then turned and left.

I found Malowe's vehicle parked right behind mine. It was quite clear that she wanted me to know that she was around and that she didn 't want me to leave before I saw her. How could I leave without seeing her anyway? The gate was opened by the guard who saluted me as I entered. This reminded me of my earlier days in Mrs. Wicks' residence, where the guard always made a point of saluting.

I hadn't seen the villa clearly the last time I was here. I had entered through the kitchen window and at night. Secondly, the cops who had arrested me on suspicion that I was a killer would not have given me the chance to stroll around and appreciate its beauty.

Now as I entered the compound, I got the right picture of the place and a taste of how those with wealth live. It was the cleanest place I had ever set my foot in. From the gate the vehicles turned left and drove about fifty metres to where there was an expansive parking that would take over thirty cars. To the right of this, one passed a round-about which was plastered and painted white. At one side there were four stairs that were used by the gardener who tended the beautiful flower garden enclosed by the round-about. Twenty metres from this round-about was another parking which could take some fifteen or so more vehicles.

The footpath was carpeted, from the gate area to the main entrance to the vast visitor's sitting room which to me looked like a red carpeted hall. The back of the villa might have been neglected, but the front was magnificent.

Malowe met me at the entrance with her arms wide open to take me. I did the same and we embraced each other happily.

"You are a wonderful lady, Malowe. You are great," I told her and meant it.

"Thank you Adams. You too are wonderful. You brought peace to this place, and that is something everyone feels and appreciates. Everyone here wants to thank you for this. Where is Marie?"

I didn't answer immediately. I was thinking about what she had just told me. What did she mean by that I brought peace here? Was it because of scaring the killer who had almost killed them?

"Is she alright?" Malowe pushed me, regarding Marie's condition.

"Oh yeah, she is. Well, let me say I didn't invite her to come with me. I wanted to be alone for the time being. We could pick her from the hotel if there's a party," I said with a touch of humour.

"I'll throw one for you. I cannot imagine it is you I am holding. Adams, I have come to like you very much. You are so good."

Her words surprised me. She was being brutally frank, and I liked it. She was the type that never beat about the bush, just like me, but there were times when words failed me, like now. What would I tell her? That I liked her too? If I did so, where would it take us? All it would do would be to invite confusion. She looked up at me, waiting for my response which wasn't coming.

I decided I wasn't going to play deaf. I lifted her and balanced her in my arms. This way I carried her to the sitting room where I placed her on a day-bed and gave her a light kiss on the lips.

"You are a wonderful lady, Malowe." I repeated, then asked, "Would it surprise you to learn that I am married?" The question just came to my mouth and I immediately regretted it. But she made it easier for me.

"I wouldn't be surprised, Adams. That's expected, but it doesn't stop me from liking you, Should it?'

"No, it shouldn't. But still, it doesn't mean you want me to marry you, does it?

"No. It doesn't. You know, you are the first man I have liked this much. Believe it.

"I do, thank you ..." I said, "... I am not surprised ..."

"You are not? Why, if I may ask?" She seemed surprised I had said that.

"I didn't mean to upset you. I was only thinking that this wall might have held you a bit, blocking your eyes from encountering many wonderful, more appealing men. Some are so good... I mean, Malowe, I wouldn't know why you think I am good while all I have given you is trouble. If I have helped, it's just like any other person would have ..."

"Adams my great grandfather taught me a lot when he was alive. I know what to touch with my hands and what not to touch, even with a one metre-long stick. Beauty is in the eyes of the beholder. Another thing you do not know, Adams, is that I am widely travelled. I went through my higher education in Britain, for six years. I know Nairobi and Mombasa as well as I know this town. I came to this place when my great grandpapa was ailing, hardly a year ago. So the wall hasn't blocked me as much as you think. You don't seem to like me, Adams, Why?"

This surprised me. *'What a wrong observation,'* I thought.

"Your great grandpa might have taught you a lot, but he doesn't seem to have taught you good judgement skills. He should have taught you to pick on more worthwhile fellows. Your beauty would keep a rattle snake from biting you and every human being in this world loves beauty. I am no exception. Can you imagine what it means to me to have you liking me?"

"I guess I can, but I..."

"Don't speculate, Miss Malowe. I feel so proud of you, I'll miss you always."

"Me too, Adams. It will be too much for me." Her eyes looked at mine, which made me feel weak as her young eyes pleaded for more. And that did it.

I lifted her again and carried her to her room and she seemed to enjoy it. I locked the door behind us and what followed I wouldn't have liked Eva or Mrs. Wicks to know. It was quite an experience. What surprised me most was that I did not feel the least guilt after the love session with Catherine Malowe.

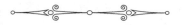

I called Mrs. Wicks from the villa. When she answered, I went straight into the point I had called about. "I don't need Stranger," I said. "I am free."

"When are you coming? It's great to hear your voice, dear."

"Tomorrow I might get there in the evening."

"No, dear. Please come by air; I'll pay for it. There's an airfield in a town fifty kilometres from where you are. I'll make connections and all you'll need to do is present yourself there. Trust me." I knew she meant every word of it. Flying was not odd to her. Money! It was the first time I learnt that arrangements for a flight could be made from miles, away in a different country.

"Janet, I am not alone. I have a vehicle and Marie is with me." I told her, not liking the idea of leaving unprepared.

"The vehicle can be driven across by a hired driver. Don't complicate things, Addy. I cannot wait to see you."

"What about Marie? Why are you ignoring her?"

"I am not, Addy, for God's sake. How could I do that? Give me her full names and I'll book her as well. Will you?"

"Yeah, and thanks. I'll come straight to you."

I put the mouthpiece down gently. There was a mirror right opposite me and I looked at myself. A smile had formed around my lips. It wasn't beautiful, but it was a smile all the same. I guess it was my best because what had caused it was good to think about – the fact that travelling by air would save me risks of losing my hard-earned compact. The knowledge that I had beaten all the others and that the compact was in my pocket made me widen the smile. 'I don't look much different from a happy gorilla,' I thought and smiled even more. Who cared what I looked like provided I got loved wherever I landed? At least fate never denied me love.

My second call was to the Garden of Eden. The phone rang repeatedly, but no one picked it. This instantly dampened my good mood. Where could my wife be at this time of the day? And Kimesh? I wished I hadn't called and unconsciously banged the mouthpiece onto its handle.

I hadn't wanted to think much about Eva since I learnt Marie had committed the crime of telling her I was in jail. To make matters worse, she might have been told I was being held for murder! If there had been someone there to console her, I would have felt more at ease. But I didn't know of anyone. *My God! I'll blow up.*

I was rescued by Malowe telling me supper was ready. After supper, I got the pleasure of sitting in conversation with others in the villa, a jolly group that looked at me as their gallant saviour.

When I recalled my first meeting with Miss Malowe and how she had scared us out of our wits with the rifle, everyone, including her grandmother, laughed themselves dry. They all knew how harsh Malowe had been whenever dealing with anyone who showed up at the villa to demand the compact,

At 10.30 p.m. I excused myself. I was given a driver to drive the Mercedes back to the hotel, from where he'd pick a taxi to get back. No one at any single time bothered to mention the compact which was now safely in my pocket. *'Bye bye villa,'* I thought as the driver slowed to take the second bump from the gate. I had what I had come for.

The airline took off from a Tanzanian internal airfield in Morogoro at precisely 10.45 a.m. I was seated next to Marie who was in such a jolly mood that part of it rubbed off onto me. I had had to apologize to her for the slapping incident at the police station after I realised that it wasn't her wish to spoil anything.

At the field, just after the flight had been announced, we had said goodbye to Malowe who had struggled to keep from crying. She liked Marie quite well. For me she showed undisguised love. She was so open she had even discussed this with Marie and promised to follow us into Kenya in a month's time.

My appearance at the villa seemed to have closed a file that had remained open for a long time. The chase was over and everyone seemed to agree. Malowe's work at the villa was over. She had seen the messenger from the rightful owner of the compact and she had explained the situation. That had been her prime responsibility. She would now be visiting the villa from her home, just like the other members of the large family. As we left, we had agreed that we would talk more when she came to visit us. For now it was good bye and good wishes.

We arrived in Nairobi shortly after 1.00 p.m. We spent some time getting cleared, after which we got into our vehicle and left the airport. By 2.00 p.m. we were on our way to the Garden of

Eden. Janet's plan was that after our arrival we would travel to Mombasa where we would have some ten day's rest before we moved onto whatever else that would follow. But as far as I was concerned, the first thing I'd do was drive straight home to find out why Eva had not picked the phone.

"You seem worried about something, Wamathina. We are back home and safe. What is it?" Marie asked me.

"Eva didn't pick the telephone last night when I called from Malowe's place. I had a terrible dream the previous night and I've been worried ever since."

"I am sorry. I didn't know you had called her. You didn't tell me. I pray all is well with her. She'll be alright, Wamathina."

"Thank you. She worries so much about me. She forgets that I am a survivor."

We drove in silence until we came to the road leading to the Garden of Eden. Marie reminded me of her father and the story he was about to listen to, which she guessed would give him peace of mind.

"The fact that the thing is nowhere to be found will remove his mind from it. What would have bothered him would be its being in the hands of enemies. But a good thief wouldn't even know what ..." she stopped when she noticed I wasn't attentive. "It looks like I am boring you."

I smiled.

"You are not, because I am not listening." I said making her laugh at the thought that she was talking to a deaf mute.

There was no sign of life at the Garden of Eden. The Pajero was parked right where we had left it. I hooted twice, hoping someone would come out, but no one did. As I got out, our neighbour's wife, whom we had taken to hospital at night weeks back, came to her gate. We learnt that Eva had been taken ill and admitted at the Nairobi Hospital. On hearing this, I didn't even want to know when. I reversed the car and took off. *'God, let her not be in any danger,'* I prayed almost loudly.

We arrived at the hospital in a few minutes. As I parked the car, I turned to Marie. "Here we are, Marie. Now get ready for good or bad news." As I said this, I saw the lady whom Eva had introduced me to. "If Eva is here," I told Marie, "this lady will know. She was her classmate and she's a doctor here."

"How good. I didn't know she had such great friends. She doesn't seem to be keen on communicating with friends."

She was right about that. It was again a mark of her intelligence that she had observed this within such a short time of knowing Eva.

"You are right. Well, life hasn't been very kind to her ever since she was a kid. She's had no ups but plenty of downs in her life. It's such a pity. Hello, Dr. Wambui."

Eva's friend was a few metres away. She heard me call and turned. She recognized me immediately. I didn't like the expression that etched on her face. Fear gripped me.

"I am sorry, Mister Adams ..." she said, and started weeping. I had to hold her.

"Take it easy. Have some courage. How is she?" I asked.

She didn't answer. She seemed not willing to tell us anything. After some consideration, she decided to break the news. Eva had had a miscarriage and hadn't carried through. *She was dead!*

"We did our best to save her life, Adams, but it was terrible. .."

If she said more, I didn't hear it. Had I not been leaning against the vehicle I would have hit the floor. I held myself up with great effort and managed to open the vehicle's door to sit down. When I had recovered I looked around. I found Marie seated in the back, crying uncontrollably.

We were not allowed to see the body and I decided we should leave the premises immediately. I asked Eva's friend to organize for the body to be taken to the Lee Funeral Home, after which we left.

I called Mrs. Wicks from home. After exchanging a few pleasantries as usual, I let her know the bad news. "Janet, Eva is dead. She died a few hours ago at the Nairobi Hospital." Then I quickly added everything, every truth about our love and marriage.

"Jesus Christ! May God rest her soul in eternal peace. Where are you, Addy? May I come to assist you?"

"Yes. I feel like I might blow up."

"Please, take it easy until I come. Where are you?"

"It's not easy to locate this place on instructions given over phone. Get to the office and tell the secretary to bring you here. She's the one who found this house for us."

"Which of the two is that?"

"I don't know their names. The tall black one ..."

"That should be Evelyn. I'll see her," Janet said, and hung up. Marie was still weeping. She insinuated that she might have been responsible for what had happened, but I washed the idea out of her mind. That eased her somewhat and she too was able to hold herself together. As for me, this was the most loathsome blow fate had ever dealt me. With Eva dead, I didn't see any future at all. Why Eva of all people? I lay on the bed, next to Marie, and fell asleep.

When I woke up it was already night. My mind was fresh and I remembered everything. Marie was still heavily asleep beside me. I was aware somebody had covered us with sheets collected from a different room, removed my shoes and belt and emptied my pockets. It could only be Mrs. Wicks because she was the only person I had called to assist me.

I stepped out of the bed and stretched myself. The realisation that my pockets had been emptied made me get wide awake. The compact – where was it? After a moment's panic I checked in the bedside locker. It was there, and I remembered it was me who had put it there. Whatever else had been emptied from my pockets was on top of the locker including my watch, a gas lighter and a packet of cigarettes. I covered Marie properly and left the room.

I went downstairs without making the slightest noise. It was already 8.05 p.m. I was surprised to find the sitting room fully packed with over ten new faces. I recognised my immediate neighbour and his wife, two others who lived right opposite us and, top of the list, Mrs. Wicks. Silence hang heavy in the air. The only slight noise that came was from the kitchen. I went straight and shook hands with each one of them. My immediate neighbour, whose name I didn't know even up to now, introduced me to three other neighbours with their wives, then Mrs. Wicks introduced me to two lady friends she had come with.

In the kitchen was the secretary from Wicks and Wayne and two other ladies making tea for the visitors. Mrs. Wicks had taken over my house and was organising everything.

On the coffee table I noticed Bibles. A good number of the visitors had brought theirs. I didn't need to be told that a prayer session was in the offing. I moved to where there was a vacant seat and sat down.

If there was anything I was uncomfortable with, it was this kind of gathering. I had never been in any before and it was a pity that it had to be here in my house. If by some mistake someone asked me to address them I would feel embarrassed since I wouldn't have known what to say. Secondly, the hangover of the inferiority that has dogged me in life hadn't wholly disappeared. As I sat with them, I was hoping they would spare me the agony of being in the spot.

I decided to have some fresh air before the pot started boiling. I gave my immediate neighbour a wink and he followed me out. I could feel all eyes on me as I closed the door. What the hell were they thinking about me and why, in the first place, were they here when I hadn't called any of them?

"*Pole sana, Bwana Wamathina.*" The Luo neighbour told me.

"*Nimepoa.* Thanks for your concern," I replied. "The news was such a shock. Would you by any chance know what was going on here? There was a kid called Kimenyi or Kimesh, do you know anything about. . ."

"Yes, a little of it. Your wife was discussing the boy with my wife ... I don't think they were pushing on well. The kid was, allow me to say, naughty. Your wife couldn't contain him in the house. I can guess you haven't had a look at your Pajero here..." I didn't let him finish the sentence. As if stung by a bee, I rushed to the vehicle, Marie's father's Pajero. I noticed that the driver's side mirror was missing, that it had been broken into and the radio cassette player had been plucked off, leaving an ugly hole staring from the dashboard. I didn't comment. I walked back to where we were leaning against Marie's other vehicle.

"Two days before your wife got sick the boy had vanished. When he slept out, your wife accompanied by mine went looking for him. I think that is what brought this bad luck. That evening she got sick. She had just learnt that the boy, together with several others, had been arrested after stoning and seriously injuring a motorist who had hit a pedestrian. That must be the reason why she was taken ill..."

That was the neighbour's speculation, but I knew better. Anyone would have gone mad with the two closest people in one's life arrested the same day, especially when one had no way of assisting them. It was worse still when the one you depended on to cater for you and your family went in for no less than a murder charge. To think that the husband she so loved was a murderer must have been too much for Eva.

We remained in silence for some minutes. From the house the gathering started singing, *"Shetani Akiniona Anatetemeka."* It was a chorus I had not heard before, but it sounded sweet. My neighbour excused himself to go back inside just as Mrs. Wicks appeared.

What advice did she have this time, I wondered? I watched her take short slow steps towards me. She was approaching cautiously, like she thought I would explode if mishandled. For the first time in my life, I found myself thinking about death and hating it. "Death is the greatest enemy man has ever made," I told myself inwardly.

"You are right, Addy." Mrs. Wicks told me. She was standing right next to me and I hadn't even noticed it.

"Right about what? You startled me."

"Right about death being the worst enemy. Still, we have a very easy way of beating death."

I knew what was coming and didn't in the least like it.

"Okay, go ahead and beat this one. I am not in a mood to joke, Janet."

"I am sorry, Addy but I am serious. Jesus will. I hate to see you looking defeated. Join us inside and you will feel different."

"I do not understand what the hell is going on here. Who called all these people? I wanted to be all alone, with you and Marie. You are the only people who can really understand me. What am I supposed to do now? I have never been in such a state, Janet. I've lived a lonely life, a life confined within myself. You know that."

"Addy, these people have come to assist you. Eva's life must have been different from yours. She must have made good friends without your knowledge. This is an indication that they loved her. Among the things you should assist us in, is telling us where you'd prefer Eva to be buried. These friends are here to make that possible. I want you to be good, Addy. Show them your appreciation and solidarity. Will you take my advice for once, Addy?"

"You know I have always done that Janet. Especially at such times. I need all the advice you can offer."

"The first thing I would suggest is that we bury the body the soonest possible."

I nodded in agreement.

"Secondly, let's not go to great expense. Not monetary, I mean. That should not bother you with me around. Let's get a place in one of the cemeteries and bury her there ..."

"No, Janet dear, no," I said firmly. "I have a place for her to be buried in, a large place. At least I owe her that. I want to lay her beside my grandmother."

Nothing was going to change what I had decided the moment I tied the knot with Eva.

If my mind hadn't been so heavily loaded, I'd have noticed Mrs. Wicks' reaction to what I had said. I had a feeling she had been severely pained to learn that all along I had been staying with Eva as husband and wife. And I also felt she was certain to stop hiding behind being born again very soon. If there's a good bush in which to hide oneself, Jesus Christ the saviour is one.

Janet agreed that it was okay to do what I felt was best for Eva. Her advice was that I make arrangements to go to my late grandmother's place and organize with those at home, especially the authorities concerned, and propose the best date for burial. She offered to accompany me while her friends and Marie took care of the duties in my Buru Buru residence.

"Thank you so much, Janet dear," that was all I could say, she held my hand and led me inside where I enjoyed listening to their tunes, prayers and the 'Living Word.'

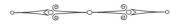

It wasn't bad to see Kareithi again. I realised I had missed him. It was sometime since I had visited this place last, the place where my inheritance lay. It was at this place I had been assured of a guiding star and a traditional talisman had been put on me, like a gold medal, by my grandmother. She had assigned me to look after the herdsboy Kareithi, who had assisted her greatly during her last days. She had also asked me to look after the talisman. So far I hadn't done my best about one of the two because I had not remembered Kareithi until now. Could it be that this happened so that I could remember my grandmother's last wishes?

I spotted Kareithi coming towards the shop where we had made a stop to greet my aunt Njeri. The boy had grown a lot. When I stopped the vehicle and called out his name he seemed confused, perhaps wondering how strange people would know him by name. Then he recognized me and came running. He was on his way to collect some animal feed he had ordered for his two cows, he said. We drove to my grandmother's place with him, having put the bag of the cows' dairy meal at the back of Janet's four-wheel drive pick-up. That same car would ferry Eva's body from Nairobi when the time came.

Kareithi, working on his own initiative on the eight-acre piece of land, had done a great deal to improve the place. He had followed my earlier advice that he had built a better house for himself with the money he raised from the farm. I had given him authority to sell anything which grew there and that is what he had done. He had sold a number of trees to woodcutters and had made good money. And from the look of things around, he had made good use of this money.

He had also matured a lot. He was so familiar with the requirements of funerals that we felt we could leave it all to him and work according to his advice. He had made tens of good friends who came to greet us and who were willing to assist. This situation made me feel a bit awkward. It was sad that I could not reach this young boy's level of understanding in some matters, yet I was supposed to be his caretaker.

All was over in the following five days and I laid my beloved Eva to rest beside my grandparents' graves. It was not an easy experience to overcome, but I felt some great relief when finally I laid her body to rest. I was the last person to leave her grave. I touched my talisman with an absent mind and felt restored. By the time I left the graveside, all was over. I knew I would never see her again -never. No preacher could convince me otherwise. And as with most of my other experiences in a turbulent life, I felt I would never want anybody or anything to remind me of Eva's death. As far as I was concerned, that went into my 'Buried Memories' file. After all, when you have the 'World' as your teacher and 'fate' to control you, you acquire an exceptionally strong heart, and hardness that doesn't give way to anything that doesn't seem to favour you.

CHAPTER ELEVEN

The telephone rang repeatedly, jerking me wide awake. I turned and stretched myself to flex my muscles, enjoying the crackling noise the bones made. I picked up the phone.

"Hello, good morning."

"Good afternoon, Adams. It's past mid-day." I recognized Janet's voice instantly.

"That's surprising." I said as I reached for my watch to confirm. It was getting to twenty five minutes after twelve. "You are right. It's twenty five past. That makes me a hungry man."

"Why don't you come over? Lunch is ready."

I didn't want to go to her place just then, or let me say not that soon. It would appear, I argued to myself, that I had turned to Janet after my wife died. I wanted to go to the nearest hotel and order some lunch, or as I had been used to since I buried my wife, go for some *nyama choma,* after which I would take some soft drinks.

The house had become too big for me and an idea of shifting to a smaller one had started beckoning. Three bedrooms were too many for a single man who was not intending to marry again. I was uncomfortable with the idea of another woman becoming my wife. I felt that Eva was the only woman who had understood me. She was the only woman I had given my whole story to willingly, and truthfully. She had accepted me just the way I was – whole-heartedly.

We had met and fallen in love when we had nothing we could call our own. By then we had been employed by a rich woman we called Mrs. Wicks and whose mouth only opened when spitting fire. I was the tigress's driver and Eva her housemaid. We had agreed between ourselves to save whatever little we earned from the spit-fire princess and opened a joint account. The tigress had then sacked Eva and had her sent to jail on trumped-up charges. Somehow I had managed to rescue her and married her immediately. She had moved from the law courts straight to her own home – our Garden of Eden. Her love for me had been immeasurable and had ultimately led her to the grave.

Since her death her best friends, among them the gynaecologist and the magistrate, had become close and kept in constant touch. They'd call often, in person or on phone. Mrs. Ndungu had become freer and had in fact gone as far as confronting me with the issue of marrying again. I had hinted to her earlier that I had no intention of marrying again but she had insisted that I should.

"If you had children, I would have advised you not to. But now that you don't, I do not see why you should lead the life of a bachelor. I don't want you to be lonely, Adams."

"Find me a woman as good and as beautiful as Eva," I had challenged her, "and I'll marry her. You wont find one, I assure you, and I wouldn't take anything less."

"I'll get you my best friend, just as Eva was to me," she had told me rather teasingly. But I hadn't pushed any further. I was just too sure that Eva could never be replaced.

I turned down Mrs. Wicks' invitation for lunch. Each time I had done that she'd driven up to my place. This time I was surprised that she arrived at the gate five minutes after I had put down the phone. I was to learn later that she had a mobile phone and had been already on her way to my place when she called.

"Janet, dear..." I told her after lunch, which she had prepared in my house, "... I am intending to leave this place. This house is too big for me,"

She came over and sat on my thighs. She then held me around the neck and planted a light kiss on my left cheek. "You know I love you, Adams, don't you?"

I nodded in agreement but said nothing.

"Thank you ..." she continued then looked me straight in the face,"... are you telling me you have not made up your mind? Have you had it on your mind that I am expecting your child? Have you?"

"I do," I said and again resumed silence.

"SOF, have you ever thought what a woman feels when she's in hospital giving birth to a child whose father is not available? That the child must be given a name, and that in the same form where the name is filled, there's a space for mother's name and father's name? Do you know that?"

"I do."

"That's great then. What do you want me to enter as the father's name? N-A, meaning Not Available? Me of all people, to state that my child has no father." You cannot be that inhuman, Adams! You surely are not that heartless. Do you remember what you promised me before you went to Tanzania?"

"I do."

"Well, now that the whole thing is over, isn't it high time you made up your mind? You should have come up with an answer."

"It's not over, Janet. I haven't met Aslam as yet. I am intending to do so next week."

"I would like to accompany you, Adams. I want to tell him a few things he doesn't know about the whole thing. That will help him understand that you are telling the truth."

"You will, Janet. You will have to be with me when I see him."

"Thanks so much, dear," she said as she kissed my left cheek again. "You are such a wonderful man. I love you. I do not want to push you further during this time of sorrow. I know how you feel."

"Thank you. It's good to be loved and it's just great to love, Janet," I said.

Two hours later she left. She called me at 8.30 p.m. to tell me that she had arrived home.

It was exactly one week after Eva had been laid to rest. I had mostly stayed indoors, only going out when it was very necessary or when entertaining a friend. I realized that together with the sorrow of losing my wife, I had in the recent past overworked myself, mostly mentally, and that my mind needed plenty of rest. My few friends stayed in touch, which helped me to go through this period with ease.

This particular day Marie, who had not gone back to Mombasa, came for me in the evening and took me out for supper. Just like Mrs. Wicks, Marie was as concerned about me as she was about her father. She wouldn't go to see him without me and we agreed to do this that Friday. We had however called and been informed that the old man would leave hospital a day earlier. By coincidence my parking boy friends, Chali and Mchacho, were to be taken to court the same day to be officially handed over to a probation officer. The magistrate handling their case had somehow decided that a probation officer could rehabilitate them. I highly doubted the wisdom behind this decision. All the same I would be there to meet them possibly after seeing Aslam.

Mrs. Wicks and Marie had over this sorrowful period struck some incredible closeness. Nobody would have suspected that there had once been bad blood between them. They took turns rendering whatever help was needed in my residence. Janet's driver would sometimes be instructed to drop Marie at her hotel room whenever they left my place late.

Marie had everything figured for the weekend. She had two tickets for Safari Park where Kofi Olomide, a popular Lingala artist, was performing. I wasn't surprised – I had already learnt Marie was a great fan of Lingala musicians, especially the one performing this night.

There was plenty of fun. We were at the venue at 6 p.m., just when the show was starting. We took our drinks slowly, but by 10 p.m. we were intoxicated enough to get onto the floor. Marie not only loved Lingala music, she was also a good dancer. She did it so well that she caught the attention of the maestro who left the stage and came to dance with us. The whole place clapped for us. By the time we left, at 2.30 a.m., we had had enough fun.

I realized I was in Marie's grip, or to put it as she had said it once, in her purse. I ended up spending the night in her room at the Panafric Hotel. Why and how this happened I'll never know, but I certainly didn't regret it, She put her heart into whatever she did.

I called Miss Malowe the following day She wasn't home, but I was advised to call her later, which I did that evening.

"Hello," came the voice of the lady who had picked the phone, "this is bin Saiga's residence. Can I help you?"

"May I talk to Miss Malowe, please," I said.

"Just a moment. Could that be Mr. Wamathina?"

"Yes. I am calling for the third time."

"Hold on please. She's very eager to talk to you."

"Thank you," I said and waited. In two minutes, Malowe's lovely voice came through.

"Hello, this is Malowe. How are you, Wamathina? I am overjoyed to hear from you."

"Thanks, Malowe. I love you," I said. It was true. I did.

"Me too. It's unfortunate you are telling me this on phone. How was your journey home?"

"Fine, but something went wrong somewhere. I will give you details later. Malowe ..., is it possible for you to come to Mombasa on Friday this week?"

"If you insist."

"Please do. I have good news for you. There is something I want to do and I cannot do it in your absence."

"What is that?" She asked in a voice that seemed worried.

"I wonna commit suicide," I joked. "I want to see your face before I do it."

It appeared like she took it seriously.

"Please, Adams. Please don't do that. I'll come. I'll start packing right away. Please .. ."

"If you do I might change my mind. You don't want me to die, do you?"

"No please. Are you serious, Adams?"

"May be I am. I'll meet you at Moi International Airport, Friday."

"Thank you. I'll leave here at 2.00 p.m. The journey takes just about an hour."

"Thank you. I will be there."

Chapter Twelve

I had just stepped out of the bathroom when the telephone rang. I let it ring the fourth time before I picked it.

"Hello, this is 765891," I said and smiled. I knew it could only be Mrs. Wicks whom I had requested to wake me up at 6.00 a.m. so that I could go out for road work. We had parted late the previous night, and instead of going straight home I had visited the Makuti Club where I had stayed two more hours. I had crawled into bed a few minutes after three.

"Good morning, Addy. You sound like you are already wide awake," she said. She also sounded like she wasn't calling from bed.

"Good morning. I've done about five kilometres and taken a bath already," I lied.

"I am glad to hear that. It tells me quite a lot." I knew what she meant by that. She had realized I had gone back to my normal self and that whatever had taken place was now behind me and a new life had began. If that was so, she was right.

This particular day I had much to do. Fortunately I was feeling fit for anything that would come my way. I had first to visit the law courts where Chali and Mchacho would be handed over to the Probation Officer.

I wanted to meet the PO so as to make things easy for the two. I had a feeling that their poor conduct would make the officer change his mind and, if this happened, it would mean they would be given a custodial sentence. I wanted them to be free, to be good on their own without the force of law. I had always felt that the best rehabilitation was self-chosen. I had organised with my three friends, the social workers from Undugu Society, and they were to meet me at the law courts where I'd introduce them to the notorious pair. This, I hoped, would also influence the Probation Officer to decide in their favour.

After this I would have to travel to Mombasa. All arrangements had been made. Both Janet and Miss Aslam had adviced me to take a good holiday before embarking on my next job. I was meeting the two later in the day. We would together go to the hospital and pick Mohammed Aslam and welcome him home. We wouldn't discuss the compact until the following day to avoid, according to Marie and Janet, "making Aslam get a shock from the loss of the trophy." Up to this moment, two weeks since Marie and I arrived from Tanzania, no one had talked about the Sinister Trophy and no one seemed eager to. I couldn't tell them anything at this stage. I couldn't trust anybody but the owner. When he had touched it and held it in his hands, in front of three witnesses, then I would cease to care about whatever happened from then on.

"I expected you to tell me something now that you've had your workout," Janet's voice said, jerking me back to the present.

"What are your plans, Janet? I'll be at the law courts by 8.00 a.m."

"I could meet you there. From there I'll go to make arrangements for the trip. I'll pay for the air tickets."

"Thanks, Janet. You are so good to me. God bless you for this," I said, knowing she'd be surprised to hear me talk about God's blessings.

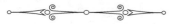

I shifted a bit for comfort, then I fastened the belt across my waist when we were instructed to do so. As I took off my cap, dusted it and put it back, I wondered whether I was looking out of place.

Mrs. Wicks, or if you like it Miss Janet Wanjiru, had made sure she sat next to me. Marie was in the seat in front, but close enough to communicate with us. I didn't have to blame fate always; sometimes he took me to places I would have never gone to, and availed experiences I would never have had. Right now I was about to take off in a plane to Mombasa.

I could detect Janet stealing sideways glances at me every now and then, making me wonder what was going on in her mind about me. Was she preoccupied with the fact that she was the one who had facilitated this luxurious flight to Mombasa? Was she trying to recall how I looked like when I presented myself at her residence to ask for a job? Was I misbehaving, not knowing what I was supposed to do or how to behave on a plane? Or was I still allowing the usual termites of inferiority complex to consume me inwardly?

"Am I... eh ... what is it? You have had your eyes on me since...?

I felt embarrassed. My old disease of speaking up my mind aloud had struck again.

"Please, Addy, don't start finding fault with me. I am only happy that you are back home and safe. You cannot guess my feelings. You know, I am aware of what you went through in Tanzania. I wish you knew the number of people who died there. Some did not even see the villa with their eyes, yet they are buried deep in the dust back there. I am so happy, Adams."

I believed her. She had displayed a love that sometimes made me pity her. It was the kind of love that had killed Eva.

We didn't talk much because I fell asleep a few minutes after take off. Being airborne, and assured of a bodyguard whose eyes were on me each second, I had nothing to get cautious about.

Within one hour we were in Mombasa. We took a taxi to Aslam's residence where we left our luggage and proceeded to the hospital.

Aslam walked out of the hospital with plenty of confidence. We watched him from a distance as he shook hands with some of the nurses who had been attending to him. With the kind of money he had, there was no doubting he had been given V.I.P. treatment. The nurses escorted him to where we had parked the vehicle, and it was at this juncture that he saw his visitors. Marie rushed forward and embraced her father. He was still strong, despite having been on a hospital bed for such a long time. As I watched father and daughter hug, I found myself flashing back to the day he was swallowed halfway by a python and was just a few minutes away from death. This had neccessitated a long stint in hospital. Then, just when he was about to recover, someone had shot him and forced him into another long period in hospital. I found myself wondering why fate had been that unfair to the old man. Had he trodden on sensitive toes in the process of enriching himself? Would whoever had shot him try it again, or would things cool down with the circulating information about the lost compact?

My thoughts were interrupted by Aslam. "My dear son, Adams, how are you?" He embraced me as well and hugged me. I felt like a kid in his strong grip.

"I am alright, Mr. Aslam. *Pole sana kwa yale yote yaliyokupata,*" I said not knowing what else there was to say.

"Nishapoa, mwanangu. Ahsante sana," he answered.

Marie then introduced his father to Janet, calling her a very close friend she had met during the period he was hospitalized. They shook hands. It was a joyous moment which left everyone with a smile. I soon realized Aslam was eager to leave the hospital premises and I suggested that we do so. Aslam sat beside me in the front seat. I drove straight home. A chauffeur would always be a chauffeur, I thought. Why should they pick on me?

We didn't talk much on our way home because we realised Aslam had started mumbling a silent prayer. He had an Islamic rosary with a number of beads which he seemed to be counting, muttering words only he understood. When we reached his residence he stepped out of the vehicle with an 'Allahu Akbar!' I guessed he was thanking God for getting him home at long last. A good number of friends were there to welcome him and there was a general cheer when we entered.

There was feasting and more guests kept arriving. Two hours later, after Aslam had assured all in attendance that he was now fully recovered and thanked them for their assistance during that period, he begged them leave to have a nap.

I beckoned Marie who was seated alone close to the wall unit. When she came I asked her for some drink. I felt I wanted to strengthen my nerves because I couldn't smoke in the presence of visitors, most of whom were ladies.

"What drink do you want? Hot or soft?" She asked sotto voce.

"You know my taste. Make a good choice. I just want to shake off the fatigue in me."

"And you?" Marie turned to ask Mrs. Wicks, seated next to me.

"What about me, please?" Janet asked. Apparently her attention had wandered.

"Wamathina wants some whisky. Tell me what drink to get you," Marie replied with a smile. Janet turned to face me as if to ask me why I wanted to get drunk. She didn't ask but seemed to admire my guts.

"I'll take cold water, some Ribena if possible."

Marie didn't bother asking the rest because they were preparing to leave. As she reached the wine cabinet, the telephone rang and she picked it.

"Hello. Aslam's residence. May I help you," I heard her say. She talked on for a few more seconds then turned to face us with a broad smile. She beckoned to indicate the call was mine. I went and picked the phone.

"Is that you, Adams?" I didn't get who the female caller was and it surprised me that she knew me. However, I recognized the voice when she talked again. It was Malowe and she was calling from the Moi International Airport in Mombasa where she had just arrived. It was a surprise because we expected her the following morning.

I felt some strange excitement which Marie seemed to note. This made it even more difficult for me because I did not want her to find out the hold Malowe had on me. Something was happening in me which I found hard to believe. Malowe was stirring my feelings more than I'd have loved. I tried to suppress them with little success.

"Malowe," I called after getting some breath, "I'll come for you right away. Just stay put," I said and put the phone down. I sighed and remained silent, hating Marie's eyes which seemed to challenge me to deny that I hadn't fallen in love with Miss Malowe.

"I am going to the airport. May I borrow your car?" I asked and forced a smile. Up to this moment I had avoided Janet's eyes which I felt on my back.

"You are not going alone. Do you get that?" Marie barked suddenly to my surprise.

"Easy, dear. You are most welcome – let's get going!" I said, then to leave. I would have preferred to go alone, but these rich ladies wouldn't allow it. It didn't matter much, however. What was there to be gained or lost anyway?

"We have a visitor at the airport, Janet," I said to Mrs Wicks, "Do you mind joining us?" It was just to conceal my unwillingness to have her company. I knew she'd jump at the idea because, in the first place, there was nothing for her to do if left behind in this home. Secondly, it was because of me that she was here.

As we entered the waiting lounge, I was holding Janet's arm after a freak fall at the airport's entrance. I always felt proud of Janet but, surprisingly, a bit uneasy in her presence. I didn't know what to make of this contradiction in feelings. I would have wanted to love her without forcing my heart, but it was taking too long to develop the trust, even though I had wholly forgiven her past crimes against my person. I had promised myself to adopt a positive attitude towards her, hoping this would help cement our relationship.

Miss Malowe spotted us even before we had had a chance to sit down. She came over, pulling a travelling bag behind her. She let go of it when she got near and came for me. I received her with open arms and hugged her passionately.

She hugged Marie then shook hands with Janet whom I assumed she hadn't met. However, the looks on their faces told more. They must have met before, but no doubt the previous meeting had not been friendly. Anyone who knew about the compact wouldn't need to be told why and how and under what circumstances they had met. All I prayed and hoped for was that they would let whatever had taken place between them pass. I was aware Janet had questions concerning my relationship with Malowe but whether she liked or hated it, there was nothing on her face to show it.

We left for Aslam's place ten minutes later. My mind was already made up. I was going to hand over the compact to Aslam today and get done with it once and for all.

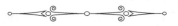

THURSDAY - 7.30 p.m.

We were all in the sitting room. I had a bottle of Bond 7 on the coffee table before me and had taken a good portion of it. Marie had also taken a few tots, but the rest were engrossed in a movie on the video screen.

Aslam came downstairs and joined us. He looked refreshed after three hour's rest. He greeted us with the respect expected of a father to his children. Soon he had dropped his sombre demeanor and cracked joke after joke to cheer us up. Then after a while he begged our attention. Marie switched off the video and we all turned to him.

This was the time I had been eagerly waiting for. Before he said anything, Aslam stared at Malowe for a long time, evidently trying to make up his mind whether he had seen her before. He gave up and asked. When she was introduced to him by Marie, his face lit up with a kind of excitement not common in aged people. He looked up, muttered some inaudible words in a strange language, then went to Malowe with open arms. He embraced her passionately. This meeting had a sweet surprise for Aslam in the form of the young girl. It was only later, that he explained to us the relationship between him and Malowe's grandmother.

Bin Saiga, he told us, had had eight wives. Malowe's maternal grandmother was Marie's maternal grandmother's sister. After some five passionate minutes, Aslam let Malowe take her seat. He took his and turned his attention on me.

"My child," he addressed me, "I gave you some work a few Weeks ago. Did you get the time to attend to it?"

All eyes turned to me. I could see they were eager to hear how I would handle it so as not to give the old man a shock. There was only one way to do it as far as I was concerned.

I applied it.

"Yes, Mister Aslam. I did the job." The three pairs of eyes in the room shifted to Aslam.

"Thank you my child. Did you succeed? Did you get the case?"

Again the eyes shifted back to me. This was the question they had feared most. All of them assumed that the compact had been lost, and they knew the news could easily break the old man's heart. They were in for a surprise.

"I succeeded after a lot of struggle, Mr. Aslam. I eventually got the compact."

I took it out of my pocket and stood up. I took two steps forward and handed it over to him. The three ladies watched in utter surprise, not quite absorbing the fact that what I was handing over was the compact. Aslam took it in both hands. Before anything else he thanked God for making this possible. He then came to me and almost crashed breath out of me as he embraced and hugged me.

It was after this that I told them the story they were eager to hear. I told them everything, save for the Mtumukiza bit. Somehow I felt it was not right to expose the person who had led me to the trophy as a burglar. I concluded by thanking the ladies.

". . . Let me say that the three ladies you see here, Mr. Aslam, contributed to the retrieval of this compact in one way or another.

As for Miss Malowe, I owe her plenty although she seems to think that if it wasn't for me she'd be dead. The rest is up to you. As far as I am concerned, I don't want to have anything to do with this thing from now on. What I can assure you is that everybody who was after this same compact believes it is lost."

Silence fell when I was through. No one seemed to know what to say next, but it was obvious there were many unanswered questions. Top among them, I knew without being told, was why I had kept this a secret to even those most close to me. But that didn't worry me. If they insisted I would have to refer them to my grandfather. I would tell them what he thought about sharing a secret with women.

I remained silent, watching Aslam as he admired the compact which had caused the deaths of a number of people, including my wife. He didn't seem to care about the lives lost. He didn't even seem to think about me and the problems I had encountered in the process of retrieving it for him. All he seemed to care about was the compact, with a smile of joy and contentment hovering about his ageing face. Like most of the other multi-millionaires, he had the poor and desperate to make his ends meet while disintegrated even further. He had added millions on the heap of other millions using me, at the expense of my wife. What good would the money do me if Eva was not there to spend it with me?

I suddenly felt annoyed. I hated myself for leaving Eva alone to go for something that had only clouded my future. I hated seeing Aslam smiling and engrossed in the compact. I felt like I was getting sick each second that passed.

I had only one thing in mind – I wanted to go home. This was not the way my star would shine. No! Not when I had caused the death of my wife! I didn't want Aslam's money or anything to do with him. Somewhere, somehow, lay my luck. I stood up, my eyes still on Aslam who was lost in his own world that revolved around the compact.

"May I beg your attention, please," I said. When I reached him the ladies in the room were all watching me, wondering what had got into my mind. After giving them a few seconds to speculate, I spoke.

"I want to begin with thanking you three ladies. As I said a while ago, your contribution to the success of this mission was immense. You are the most wonderful people I've met in my life, and I am sure I'll miss you all very much when we part."

"I have taken time to deliberate on what I am about to tell you. This compact Mr. Aslam is caressing here has caused many deaths, including my wife's, and I have reason to believe that most of those who died were innocent. As a result of this I feel my conscience wouldn't be clear if I accepted any kind of payment. Just as I do not want anything to do with the compact, I am also not owed anything by Mr. Aslam. It has been a long dark night since I accepted the assignment. I have achieved what I did. I feel that the best thing to do is to leave things at that point and try my best to forget them. When I leave this room I'll not turn round to face you, that is as long as you'll be in here. Nothing is going to change my mind because this is the only way to gain personal freedom. Freedom from within, freedom that cannot be questioned by anybody because it is self-made – that is what I'll work towards from now on.

"I owe you two vehicles, Mr. Aslam. I'll organize to get them back to you. As for me, I have entirely nothing to thank you for. If you had told me the whole truth about this mission, chances are my wife would still be alive because I wouldn't have touched the crazy job. I am now ready and willing to put all that behind myself and, as I leave, my conscience will be clear. Turning down payment from you is the only way I can feel I have appeased my wife . . . for leaving her. After all, I have realised that there is a class of people who cannot afford a rich life and I unfortunately happen to be in that class."

I was through and I felt the better for it. After a moment's pause to regain my breath, I turned to Malowe and continued, "Could I have a word with you?"

She stood and followed me out. I did not have time for Janet, Aslam or Marie. If there was anybody who could console me right now it was Catherine Malowe. As for Mrs. Wicks, alias Janet Wanjiru, as I had told her earlier, I wanted time. Enough time to think because, as they say, only time can tell.

The End

Printed in the United States
By Bookmasters